FALCON
MOON

Lakota

Cassie Edwards

A SIGNET BOOK

SIGNET
Published by New American Library, a division of
Penguin Group (USA) Inc., 375 Hudson Street,
New York, New York 10014, USA
Penguin Group (Canada), 90 Eglinton Avenue East, Suite 700, Toronto,
Ontario M4P 2Y3, Canada (a division of Pearson Penguin Canada Inc.)
Penguin Books Ltd., 80 Strand, London WC2R 0RL, England
Penguin Ireland, 25 St. Stephen's Green, Dublin 2,
Ireland (a division of Penguin Books Ltd.)
Penguin Group (Australia), 250 Camberwell Road, Camberwell, Victoria 3124,
Australia (a division of Pearson Australia Group Pty. Ltd.)
Penguin Books India Pvt. Ltd., 11 Community Centre, Panchsheel Park,
New Delhi - 110 017, India
Penguin Group (NZ), 67 Apollo Drive, Rosedale, North Shore 0632,
New Zealand (a division of Pearson New Zealand Ltd.)
Penguin Books (South Africa) (Pty.) Ltd., 24 Sturdee Avenue,
Rosebank, Johannesburg 2196, South Africa

Penguin Books Ltd., Registered Offices:
80 Strand, London WC2R 0RL, England

First published by Signet, an imprint of New American Library,
a division of Penguin Group (USA) Inc.

First Printing, January 2008
10 9 8 7 6 5 4 3 2 1

I lovingly dedicate *Falcon Moon* in memory of a fan who became a dear friend . . . Mary Doss.

Also included in this dedication are Mary's daughter, Trenda Kennedy, and the rest of Mary's family.

Love,
Cassie Edwards

FALCON MOON

Oh, Falcon Moon,
As I sit underneath thee,
I feel the presence of your bird of prey,
So quiet, so quick, mighty as the glorious falcon.

Oh, Falcon Moon,
Your mighty glow, so impressive, so mysterious,
A moon with eyes so sharp, so swift,
As the mighty falcon glides within your glow.

Oh, Falcon Moon,
As I look beyond your light tonight,
Fill me with the might of your talons,
As I look into the Falcon Moon this night.

—Mordestia M. York,
poet, fan, friend

Chapter 1

Complete my joy—let not my first wish fail
—John Keats

The Arizona Territory
1840

The moon splashed its white beams through the two windows of the expansive study. The beautiful light shone into a room lined on one side with shelves of books, mostly of a religious nature.

On the far wall opposite the bookshelves stood a stone fireplace, where a great fire wrapped its flames around logs stacked on an iron grate.

Three rocking chairs creaked on this cool late evening as Wylena Schrock sat with her twin brothers before the fire, taking in the warmth not only of the fire, but also of one another's company.

Wylena was eighteen years of age. She had long black hair, dark eyes, and pale skin. Petite and pretty, she was attired in a lovely lace-trimmed yellow silk dress. Wylena had recently traveled from her home near Harrisburg, Illinois, to live with her brothers on a mission in the Arizona Territory, near the Mexican border. Her brother Joshua, a priest, had established the mission.

When Wylena had arrived there yesterday, she discovered that her other brother, Jeb, lived at the mission now, too. He had come to help and protect his identical twin, since Jeb was more skilled with firearms and would not hesitate to use his pistol if the need arose.

As they sat contentedly in silence—a family together again after being apart for so long—Wylena felt comfortable in her environment, but still found it hard to accept how her parents had died.

It had been on a hot summer day not all that long ago in Illinois when one could scarcely get his breath, the humidity was so staggering and oppressive. Wylena had been outside watering the flowers in her mother's garden when she had seen the clouds collect quickly overhead in strange, blackish green colors.

What happened next had been so quick, so violent, that she still couldn't believe she had escaped the viciousness of the tornado with only a few scratches, while her parents, and so many neighbors, had not lived through the storm.

Those scratches on Wylena's skin had healed, but she doubted that the wounds to her heart from the loss of her parents would ever totally mend.

But it was good to be with her brothers after not having seen either of them for many years. For so long Joshua and Jeb had gone their separate ways and had not seen each other, either.

Now, as fate would have it, the brothers and sister had come together as a family again.

Wylena smiled as she looked from one brother to the other.

While gazing upon their faces, she still found it difficult to tell which brother was which. They were so identical in looks.

When they were small, their mother had to tie different-colored ribbons on their wrists in order to tell them apart.

As they grew into young men, most times their personalities could reveal who was who.

One brother was gentle in every respect, while the other was always in trouble.

Eventually Joshua had sought out the religious side of life.

And Jeb?

Wylena still had no idea what Jeb had been doing before joining Joshua at the mission, and when she had asked him, he had not volunteered any answers.

She had just accepted that Jeb was Jeb and so be it.

"Joshua, are you truly comfortable living here so close to the Mexican border now that the fort that was supposed to be built near your mission has been established elsewhere?" Wylena suddenly asked, breaking the silence.

While she waited for him to answer, she looked from one brother to the other.

Since her arrival at the mission, she had seen Joshua only in his black robe with its white collar, while Jeb wore his own usual outfit of black, but nothing akin to a priest's robe. His pants and shirt were both black, and when he was away from the mission, he sported a lone pistol holstered at the right side of his waist, and boots with a design sewn into the leather on the side of each that resembled orange flashes of lightning.

"It's a hard decision to make," Joshua said in his smooth, soft voice. "It took me a long time to get the mission established after I found the building abandoned by other priests who fled for one reason or another. After making this my home for several years now, I would find it hard to leave."

He looked slowly around the room, stopping at his vast collection of books, then smiled at Wylena. "I feel God everywhere in my mission," he said softly. "God was with me as I made it livable, and my own. I am not ready to give up on it this quickly. Perhaps I can eventually do some good to some lost soul, even where no homes are established for miles upon miles."

"Joshua, you are so very close to the Mexican border," Wylena again reminded him. "Aren't you afraid that the soldiers under General Zamora's command might be somewhat threatening? You told me yourself that General Zamora does not approve of having this mission so close to his fortress. He said that he believes your mission will draw more white people too close to where he has had free run of the land on both sides of the river, in Mexico and Arizona, for way too long. Don't you believe that it was he who was responsible for the other priests abandoning this mission?"

"General Zamora talks big, but as far as I'm concerned, his words truly carry no threat," Joshua said, shrugging nonchalantly. He looked over at Jeb, who had sat there soaking up the conversation while not giving his own opinion about anything. "Jeb here makes me feel safe enough."

Jeb smiled sardonically. "My reputation follows me," he said, chuckling as he glanced over at his pistol lying in its holster on a table beside a long leather sofa.

"Jeb, that's nothing to joke about," Wylena said sharply. "What reputation? What did you do in order to get such, as you call it, a reputation? Of course, you must be only jesting with us, but I would feel more comfortable if you would tell me what you were up to before joining Joshua here."

"Sis, you worry too much," Jeb said, rising and going to the fireplace to lift another heavy log onto those that had burned low.

He returned to his chair and began rocking again, obviously not wanting to delve into his past. Instead he just silently stared into the flames of the fire.

Seeing that she could still not get any answers from her hardheaded brother, Wylena sighed heavily. Then she tried again to appeal to her more genteel, sweet brother.

"Joshua, not only do you have the danger of General Zamora and his soldiers to concern yourself with, but you also have Indians living in close proximity to your mission," Wylena said, hoping to one day break through Jeb's wall of silence. "Can you tell me more about the Indian chief you have befriended? Can you really trust this friendship, or might it be a ploy of his to get something from you? And I don't mean godly things. You have brought many valuables with you to this mission. Surely the Indians saw you bringing them here in your wagon."

"My Indian friend's name is Chief Falcon Moon," Joshua said smoothly. "I have no cause to believe that he has made friends with me for any reason other than just being a friend. He is a fair man who rules his people with peace in his heart. He is a young, unmarried chief."

He glanced over at Jeb. "Jeb hasn't met Falcon Moon yet, but the chief knows of him," he said, then looked back toward Wylena again. "Falcon Moon is Chiricahua of the Apache tribe."

"Apache?" Wylena said with a low gasp. "Joshua, I have heard that all Apache are heartless, murdering savages, who even . . . even . . . take scalps from those they murder."

Jeb gave her a scowl at the mention of scalps and the Apache in the same breath. "There are some renegade Apache who kill, but rarely do any Apache, good or bad, scalp people for the fun of it," Joshua gently explained to his sister. "As far as I am concerned, the Apache, those who are not renegades, only fight and kill if they are pushed into doing it in order to protect their loved ones. If they must, given no other choice, they do fight for their people's survival."

"Joshua, isn't it unique, even rare, for an Apache chief to befriend a white man as this chief has befriended you?" Wylena murmured. "I have heard that the Apache call white people 'pale invaders.'"

"Yes, some do call white people such a name. As for Chief Falcon Moon, it is true that he does not make friends with white people all that easily," Joshua said, nodding. "In fact, the chief has led his people high up on Mount Torrance, where he has established a safe and protected stronghold away from white people and Mexicans."

He paused, then again smiled over at Wylena. "Because Falcon Moon has more or less cut himself and his people off from the white world, accepting a white man as a friend, which Falcon Moon has done with me, is a tribute to the one he befriended. No greater praise could be given me than to say that I am Chief Falcon Moon's friend."

"After hearing all that you just told me about Falcon Moon, it seems that he has truly, sincerely befriended you. I would like to meet him myself one day," she murmured. "Joshua, how did this friendship come about? And does he also see Jeb as a friend?"

"As you know, Jeb has not been here at the mission for very long, so he has not yet had an opportunity to meet Chief Falcon Moon, for it is very rare for the young chief to come for a visit at my mission," Joshua said, then gave Jeb a look that Wylena could not comprehend, one that drew Jeb's attention. She did not understand what that particular look might imply.

Wylena was reminded of how the two brothers had never had anything in common and it had surprised her to know that Jeb had joined his brother at the mission.

Their personalities had always clashed, even as younger men, when they both were growing in separate directions in so many ways.

Joshua was always so sweet and gentle, whereas Jeb was oftentimes rough talking and brusque. Jeb had not taken what their father had dished out. He ran away from home when he was old enough to be on his own.

There was one main thing that made the twins no longer identical in appearance, although it was not always plainly visible.

There were lasting scars on Joshua's back from the time his father had brutally whipped him with his belt for not getting as much work done in the garden as was expected of him.

That day, after seeing his soft-spoken brother beaten so unmercifully, Jeb had fled to parts unknown. Shortly after that, Joshua had fled their home, as well, but had chosen to live a peaceful life as a man of God.

Wylena loved her brothers equally, no matter the difference in their demeanor.

"Tell me how you met Falcon Moon," Wylena blurted out. She wanted to interrupt the strange sort of silence that had fallen in the room.

"At first, I saw Falcon Moon more than once riding close to my mission on his white stallion," Joshua replied softly. "He was watching. I believe he was intrigued by my long black robe, although he must have seen the other priests when they lived here. I was not aware at that time that he was a powerful Apache chief. Then one day, as I was out searching for special herbs for my cook pot, I ran across a pretty young Indian maiden who had fallen from her horse and injured her ankle. I carried her inside my mission, where Jeb offered to see to her injury. You know he learned skills from our father about caring for injuries, since we needed those skills with our farm so isolated and far from a doctor."

Wylena was very aware of how her brothers exchanged quick glances when Joshua paused for a moment. When he continued his story, he was looking into Wylena's dark eyes.

"I was very surprised that the pretty young thing knew English quite well. She said she had learned from other white holy men who came and went in the area, and told me and Jeb that her name was Bright Star, and that her brother was Chief Falcon Moon of the Apache tribe," Joshua said.

"And?" Wylena prodded. She looked over at Jeb. "Jeb, did you take care of her ankle?"

Jeb gave her another strange sort of glance, but it was Joshua who explained the situation to her. "Sis, your brother Jeb, as intrigued as he was by this Apache beauty, took care of her ankle by binding it, but it was I who dared return her to the stronghold," Joshua said. "I felt that the chief might trust me more than Jeb because he had observed me enough times and knew that I was a man of peace—especially since he'd never seen me with any firearms on my person—whereas he, as far as I know, had never seen Jeb. After all, Jeb had not been here for very long."

"And were you accepted into the stronghold?" Wylena asked, her eyes wide with wonder to even envision her priestly brother riding on a horse up the steep mountain pass. "Joshua, it was such a dangerous thing to do—to confront the Apache firsthand, and to travel so high on Mount Torrance. You never had much to do with horses when we lived at home together. Mainly Jeb and I went horseback riding. So how did you get the courage to do that?"

"God was with me, that's how," Joshua said matter-of-factly. "I felt his presence every inch of the way."

"And once you were there, how were you treated?" Wylena continued. "Surely you were at least a little bit uneasy over finding yourself alone with a full village of Apache people. Did they meet your arrival armed with bows and arrows?"

"I never felt threatened, although I was met, face-to-face, by heavily armed warriors as I approached the entrance to the stronghold, but Bright Star, the chief's sister, spoke quickly on my behalf and took me on to meet with her brother," Joshua continued in his soft, smooth voice.

"And?" Wylena asked, growing more in awe of her brother Joshua by the minute. He was strong in so many ways that she had never been aware of before. She should have realized how strong he was to have gone off on his own at

such a young age. He had even established himself near both Mexican soldiers and the Apache!

"A fast friendship was formed between myself
and Falcon Moon, and the least expected happened from that one meeting between Jeb and
Falcon Moon's sister," Joshua said thickly as he
gave his brother another quick glance.

"What was that?" Wylena asked, leaning forward just as Joshua looked at her again.

"Bright Star and I met secretly after that first
meeting and fell in love," Jeb suddenly said,
drawing a quiet gasp from Wylena.

"You . . . and . . . Bright Star are in love?"
Wylena said, looking into the dark eyes of her
brother Jeb. "How on earth? And . . . how did
you act on that love? Surely her brother would
not approve."

"Like I said, we met secretly, but Falcon Moon
found out somehow and forbade his sister from
ever seeing me again," Jeb said sourly. "He saw
me in a much different light than he saw Joshua.
He saw me with my pistol belted at my waist
and knew, somehow, that I was not the saintly
man that my brother was, although I would
never harm Bright Star. But he didn't know that,
so Bright Star and I found it hard to be together
after that, yet we did find a way sometimes, and
are still very much in love."

"I rarely see Falcon Moon, either, since he
found out about Jeb and Bright Star," Joshua
said solemnly. "I haven't met with him since I

first knew about you coming to live with me here at the mission, so he has no idea that you are here, Wylena, especially since you arrived at night under the safe escort of six soldiers from Fort Hood after you traveled there by stage-coach."

"And the worst of all of this is that word spread about my secret meetings with Bright Star. Not only did the Indians hear about this, but also the Mexican general became aware of it," Jeb said tightly.

"Why would he care?" Wylena asked, search-ing Jeb's eyes. "It's none of his affair what either you or Bright Star does."

"He made it his affair," Jeb said bitterly.

"How?" Wylena asked, her eyes widening. "What did he do?"

"Jeb, tell her about what the Mexicans are ac-cusing you of doing," Joshua said, his voice strained.

"I am being falsely accused of being a scalp hunter who is active in this area and inside the Mexican territory," Jeb said, flinching when Wylena stiffened and gasped again. "But, of course, they are wrong. It is mistaken identity."

"And that is why Jeb makes his residence in the underground room beneath the mission that was dug by someone who lived here before me. It must have been built to protect them from an attack from either Indian renegades or the Mexi-cans," Joshua softly explained. "I'm certain you wondered about him living there instead of up here with us, where the rooms are much nicer."

"Yes, but Jeb being Jeb, who has always done things differently, I didn't openly question it," Wylena said. "Are you in true danger, Jeb? Why can't you make them believe that you aren't the one guilty of such crimes?"

"Like I said, it's a case of mistaken identity, and until the guilty party is found, I must be very cautious," Jeb replied. "I always flee to my underground room when we hear someone approaching the mission, until it is safe again for me to come from it. And I only leave the mission at night."

"But to be accused of being a scalp hunter?" Wylena said, and shuddered visibly. "You must find a way to prove that you aren't, or I just know that you will eventually be found and . . ."

"Sis, that still isn't the worst of what has happened," Jeb said, standing and going over to her. He took her by a hand and eased her up to stand before him, then held both her hands.

"What more could there be?" she asked, again searching his eyes. "I've heard enough to give me many sleepless nights."

He held tightly to her hands as he told her something that made the color drain from her face. "Bright Star has been abducted by the Mexicans." Seeing how Wylena suddenly looked so disbelievingly at him, he continued, "She was abducted as a way to lure me to the fortress to try and save her. That is the only reason she would have been abducted. Everyone in the area now knows of our love for each other. The Mexican commander truly expects me to come and try to save her, and then he'll nab me and place me under arrest or kill me on the spot."

"No," Wylena said, stepping away from him. "Oh, Jeb, no!"

"Don't worry," he said, releasing her hands. "I'm not going to go to their fortress. I wouldn't dare try. I wouldn't last a minute. I would probably die instantly."

"I am so glad, yet . . . yet . . . what of Bright Star?" Wylena asked softly. "If . . . if . . . the Mexicans did this to draw you to them and you don't come, won't they go ahead and kill her?"

"That won't be allowed to happen," Jeb said reassuringly. "You see, Chief Falcon Moon has to know where she is. Once he realized that she was missing, he surely sent out a search party to find her. When they discover where she is, the chief will rescue her. So you see, Sis? I don't have to place myself in danger."

"Jeb has to stay well hidden now, Wylena," Joshua quickly said in defense of his brother. He knew Jeb must appear cowardly to her for leaving Bright Star to her doom unless Falcon Moon would save her. "I have received word that even Falcon Moon believes that Jeb is the scalp hunter. Falcon Moon has no idea that Jeb is still here."

"All of this is so terrible," Wylena said, her voice

breaking. "I was so looking forward to a peaceful existence here at the mission, and what do I find? One of my brothers is in terrible danger!"

"Only for the time being," Joshua softly reassured her. "After all of this is straightened out and Jeb's cleared of the crime, life will be good again for our family."

"I still can't see why anyone would place blame on you, Jeb," Wylena said softly.

"Like I said, it is a mistaken accusation, one that will clear up in time," Jeb said thickly. "Until the true culprit is caught, I must be very, very careful. As far as anyone but us knows, I have left the mission and am making my home elsewhere."

Although Wylena was glad that Jeb wasn't placing himself in any more danger than he already was in, she couldn't help but see him as somewhat of a coward for allowing the woman he loved to remain in the hands of the ruthless, bloodthirsty Mexican leader, General Zamora.

"Enough has been said for the night," Joshua said as he slowly pushed himself up out of his chair. "I don't know about the two of you, but a bed would feel mighty good right now for these tired bones."

Jeb went to Wylena and kissed her on the cheek. He held her hands for a moment as they looked into each other's eyes. Then he left the room and went down to his underground hideout.

Joshua embraced Wylena, then framed her

delicate face between his hands and smiled into her eyes. "My dear sister, don't worry yourself over any of this that you just heard," he said softly. "God will make all things right. My prayers will assure that things will be all right for us, even Bright Star."

"I'm sure he will," Wylena murmured, taking his hands from her face and squeezing them fondly. "Go and get some sleep, big brother. So shall I."

He winked at her and left her to make her way to her room, as he went to his.

Wylena closed the bedroom door behind her and stared out the window into the moon-splashed darkness.

She knew that even if she did go to bed, she wouldn't fall asleep. Too much had been said tonight for her to be able to forget it all so quickly.

She recalled many a night back in Illinois when she couldn't sleep. An evening walk outside, where the stars were twinkling like diamonds in the sky and the moon was bright, always gave her peace, and that was what she needed now.

She grabbed a shawl and slipped it around her shoulders, then tiptoed through the mission until she was finally outside.

As she began walking beneath the beautiful stars and moon in the shadow of the mission's tall steeple, everything seemed all right.

But suddenly everything changed from beautiful to ugly.

Her shawl fell from her shoulders as she was grabbed, gagged, and blindfolded, then taken to a horse hidden in the nearby trees.

She was lifted onto the steed. Then she felt a hard body mount behind her.

An arm quickly slid around her waist to secure her against her captor before the horse took off in a hard gallop.

Wylena was so terrified, she felt faint, but forced herself to stay alert, for she needed to know where she was being taken.

She thought of her brothers back at the mission.

Surely they were asleep. They knew nothing of what had just happened to their sister.

She wondered what they could even do about it when they did know.

Joshua would surely pray.

And Jeb?

Would he think along the same lines as he felt about Bright Star, knowing that if he came out of hiding to help his sister, he would only be putting himself in danger?

Would he feel that way when his very own sister's life was in jeopardy?

Chapter 2

Thou hast sought in starry eyes
Beams that were never meant for thine.
—Percy Bysshe Shelley

The early-morning mountain fog was just lifting from around the tepees of the Apache village, where the morning lodge fires swept their spirals of smoke through the smoke holes, breaking through the moisture in the air like tiny gray whirlpools moving heavenward.

At this early hour, the women and children were just now awakening and moving about. The long day lay ahead of them, and the women were planning their day's activities while the children eagerly awaited leaving their homes for a full day of play.

The girls most generally played house with

one another, sharing their pretend babies made from corn husks, while the boys found many ways to entertain themselves, like hunting with small bows and arrows, made by their own hands, for tiny animals. They fashioned the weapons and were taught to use them by their fathers.

Or the young warriors might play a game of tag or stickball, or just very mischievously tease the girls until the boys ran away under threats of the girls interfering in their own games once they resumed them.

It was a peaceful existence up high on Mount Torrance, where a stronghold had been purposely built to keep all white and Mexican soldiers from entering the domain of the Bear Band of Apache!

On the far end of the village, warriors sat in their large council house, having awakened at dawn for this council with their chief, Falcon Moon.

They were discussing a sad event as a fire leaped high amid the fire pit in the center of the lodge, the smoke escaping through a smoke hole far overhead.

The news had been brought to Falcon Moon late last evening. One of his trusted scouts had finally discovered where Falcon Moon's sister was being held prisoner after having been abducted two nights ago by a party unknown to the Apache.

But now Falcon Moon knew the identity of his sister's captor, and his blood ran hot inside his veins for vengeance. He vowed to get it after he rescued his sister from the evil Mexican leader, General Zamora.

When Falcon Moon first discovered the absence of his sister, he had thought of only one person who might be responsible.

That man was white, and he had only recently come to this land of the Apache.

That man, Jeb Schrock, had lured Falcon Moon's sister into his arms and had stolen her heart away.

At first Falcon Moon had thought that the reason his sweet and beautiful sister had become awed by this white man was because the man had seen to her injured ankle after she had fallen from her horse. She seemed to mistake these feelings for love.

After having discovered their secret trysts, Falcon Moon had suppressed the rage he felt at knowing that a white man could trick his sister into believing he truly cared for an Indian maiden.

He had taken his anger, successfully holding it at bay, to his close friend Father Joshua, who was Jeb Schrock's brother.

Falcon Moon had explained to the white holy man what would happen to Jeb if he did not stop luring his sister away from her home, to meet with him under the guise of his loving her.

Father Joshua had at first been shocked at hearing what Jeb was doing, and then had been understanding about how Falcon Moon could be so upset over it. He had told the young chief, who was known to be a man of much compassion, that he would make certain that Jeb would stay away from Bright Star.

But soon after, Falcon Moon and Father Joshua both suspected that had not happened. Whenever Falcon Moon's sister left the village for any reason, even for a harmless reason such as going to dig herbs for her cook pots, Falcon Moon had not rested easy until she had returned home, for he could not help but think that she was still secretly meeting with Jeb.

Usually she did have herbs in her basket when she returned, but he knew that for the length of time she had been gone, she had surely done more than search for them alone.

Falcon Moon had refrained from following her, for that would show a total mistrust of his sister.

Now he wished that he had!

Bright Star would be safely in her lodge, which sat close to his own.

She would even now be rising from her bed of pelts for a beautiful day amid her people.

Instead she was being held captive and it made his heart ache to guess how she was being treated!

"I no longer need to go to the mission to speak

with Father Joshua about the possibilities of his brother being responsible for my sister's disappearance," Falcon Moon said to his warriors. "As you know, Brown Horse brought news to me that is both good and bad. The good news is that Bright Star is still alive. The bad is . . ."

He paused, for he found it so hard to say that his sister was a prisoner!

At least he had the knowledge that, thus far, Bright Star was still alive!

"The bad news is where she has been taken, and by whom," Falcon Moon then said, his hands doubling into tight fists at his sides. "She is being held hostage at the Mexican fortress. It is said that she is being held there as a ploy to lure the one we now suspect as being the scalp hunter, who was my sister's lover, there to rescue her. In that way, the Mexicans will finally get their hands on the scalp hunter . . . to kill him."

"My chief, what are we to do to rescue Bright Star?" Red Fox, one of his most trusted warriors, asked. Red Fox hated to see his usually gentle and caring chief embittered so much that his eyes were filled with a rage that he struggled to hold inside him.

The chief, a tall Apache with broad shoulders, his muscled body apparent today in only a breechclout and moccasins, was accustomed to commanding the tribe and expected instant and implicit obedience.

When people looked upon the face of this

proud chief for the first time, they saw a face that was perfectly impassive, yet noble, with bold, large, black eyes, and a firm mouth.

As all Apache gloried in their long, luxuriant hair, the chief's sleek black hair was worn long, to his waist, and held back from his face with a beaded headband.

The chief's eyes always held courage, but today there was so much more.

It was apparent that he ached to hold his sister in his arms and protect her.

Yet there was a look rarely seen there as Falcon Moon was surely thinking of the one who was responsible for his sister's abduction.

Falcon Moon was the epitome of a good man, a proud leader. Everyone respected and loved him, and would therefore do anything within their power to save his beloved sister.

For the moment Falcon Moon did not give his warrior an answer, but instead mulled over inside his head what he knew he must do. Enraged, all that he could think about was attacking the fortress and taking his sister back by force.

But he knew that it was not in his people's best interest that he use that tactic for her rescue. He knew that if he openly went against the Mexican army in order to save Bright Star, it would only bring much death to his own people when the Mexicans retaliated. A different plan must be used.

He reached a hand to the necklace he always wore around his neck, and clutched the lone bear tooth that hung from it.

The bear was his power.

The bear was his medicine!

It had gotten him out of many scrapes, but this was the worst he had ever faced.

"Her rescue must be done quietly without confrontation with the Mexicans," Falcon Moon said, still holding the bear's tooth within his fingers. "We do not want to antagonize the Mexicans into warring with us. To do so would cause an all-out war with the evil commander, General Zamora. We must avoid war at all costs because of our wives and children, who depend on us for their safety."

One of his warriors, who was always more outspoken than the others, stepped forth from the group. He stood stiffly in his breechclout, with a hand resting on the sheathed knife at his right side, as he looked directly into the eyes of his chief.

"How can we rescue Bright Star without the Mexicans realizing that we are there doing so?" Blue Lance asked, his dark eyes battling with his chief's. "You must know that it is all but impossible to save Bright Star from right beneath the noses of the clever, cunning Mexican soldiers."

"Do you have such little trust in my ability to plan well enough not to cause warring to begin between our two peoples?" Falcon Moon grumbled as he glared at Blue Lance. "You do show such lack of faith today, my warrior. Listen further to what I have to say. Then see whether you still have so little faith in my ability to lead our people."

He waited until Blue Lance sat back down amid his brethren; then he spoke to them all again as he started revealing his rescue plan to them.

Falcon Moon once again was made to stop when another warrior spoke his mind so quickly, it made some of the warriors gasp as they turned to look at the one among them who showed so little respect to their chief.

They were not all that surprised to see who it was, since this youngest warrior among them all was prone to speak up at inappropriate times. He seemed to believe that he had the right to do this, since he received special treatment from his chief.

"My chief, I will single-handedly rescue Bright Star," Bull Nose said, squaring his shoulders. "Please allow it."

Bull Nose held his chin high as he gazed directly into his chief's dark, now much angrier eyes.

Falcon Moon gave Bull Nose a silent glare. The young warrior, whose nose was so broad it covered half his face, was being trained by Falcon Moon to be his successor, but had let Falcon Moon down more than once.

Falcon Moon now saw Bull Nose as not worthy of the position he had been training him for. He was absolutely not worthy of saving Falcon Moon's sister alone.

Falcon Moon now recognized this young man as weak and sneaky—and the wrong man to have chosen to step into Falcon Moon's moccasins as chief one day.

But this was not the time to discuss anything with Bull Nose.

There would be a time and place for that.

"Bull Nose, we will all work together to release my sister," Falcon Moon said flatly. "To work in numbers is much better than to work alone."

He most certainly did not praise Bull Nose for offering his services in such a way, for to do so would be to play into the hands of a young warrior who deserved no praise at all, especially for a plan that would have ended in Falcon Moon's sister's death, for he knew that Bull Nose did not have the skills to rescue anyone, much less the beloved sister of this band's chief!

When Bull Nose did not seem to apprehend what Falcon Moon had said, and stood waiting for his chief to approve of his plan, Falcon Moon took a slow step toward him. "Sit, Bull Nose," he growled. "Sit."

Bull Nose very openly and disobediently glowered into Falcon Moon's face, then slowly sat down with the others.

Falcon Moon glared back at him. This young man's days as a part of Falcon Moon's Bear Band were numbered!

With Bull Nose now finally seated, with everyone completely ignoring him, especially Falcon Moon, the warriors brought their heads together to make a plan that would be successful at returning Bright Star safely home.

"There should be no signs left that it was we Apache who sneaked into the Mexican fortress and stole Bright Star away from them," Falcon Moon said tightly. "I believe they will suspect the scalp hunter more than anyone else, for did they not even consider the wrath of we Apache when they took my sister from her people? No. It seems they did not. Their plan included the scalp hunter only. And when they find Bright Star gone, their anger toward that man will be twofold. We must make certain no tracks lead to our mountain, but instead away from it!"

Falcon Moon paused and slowly smiled. "Any way you look at it, the Mexicans will feel foolish for allowing the captured Apache maiden to be taken with none of them being the wiser until they find her gone," he said, his eyes gleaming.

Then he grew serious again. "Prepare your families for what you will be doing as the sun starts setting in the west tonight, for that will be when we start our trek down the mountainside," he said thickly. "When the Mexican fortress is shrouded by darkness, and they all are escaping this world of theirs by sleeping, that is when we will move among them, as quiet as a panther moves through the night, and take my sister from their midst!"

Everyone let out a war whoop, loud and clear. The sound echoed through the overhead smoke hole, and reached each and every tepee and the wives awaiting their men. The war whooping made the wives aware of the conclusion to the plan for Bright Star's rescue.

They knew, without being told, that their husbands and sons were going to do something very risky very soon, risky enough to end with the loss of lives!

Chapter 3

Having lived alone for so long, and being accustomed to preparing breakfast for just himself, Joshua hummed contentedly as he stirred a pot of oatmeal. He had not realized just how much he missed his twin brother and his sister until they had joined him at his mission.

Now, with them there, all safe and sound under one roof, he felt as though he was finally a complete man.

He glanced over his shoulder toward the bedroom where his sister was surely already up and getting herself ready for the day ahead of her, which would likely be a day of exploring, although Joshua would warn her about not going too far from the mission.

But as she was an adventurous person, who

loved riding horses—she even had her own pony back in Illinois—he expected his sister to put up quite a fuss at being told not to travel far.

Yet he had seen how afraid she was. Afraid, not only of the Mexican fortress so close across the river from the mission, but also of the Apache, who made their homes almost as close as the Mexicans. He thought that a word of warning from her priest brother would surely be heeded and not scoffed at.

He loved Wylena so much, and now could not understand how he had managed to live away from her for so long. He would do everything within his power to keep her under his wing until she met a man she would want to marry.

But Joshua knew that was all but impossible here, because there were no settlers living anywhere close. Their fear of the Mexican army and the Apache kept them from claiming land and settling close to those two peoples, whom hardly any white people trusted.

Joshua was an exception, of course, for he had God in his corner.

Prayer and God were all Joshua needed to know that he was safe in everything that he did.

"And I'm going to make certain my sister is as safe," he whispered to himself as he took the pan of oatmeal from the top of the potbelly stove, which he had brought to the mission on his wagon clear from Kansas.

He set the pan on a pad on the wooden table,

then continued humming as he took three bowls from his small store of dishware in a cabinet on the wall opposite the stove.

After placing silverware beside each bowl and setting a bowl of sugar in the center of the table, alongside milk that he had milked at the break of dawn from his cow in the barn, he stopped and gazed at the closed door where his sister should soon come out to greet him.

He glanced then toward a tapestry that hung from the ceiling to the floor and hid steps behind it that led down to the room where Jeb made his residence. He, too, should be ready to come and spend the morning with his brother and sister.

"Yes, it is so good to have them with me again," Joshua said smilingly.

He brushed some lint from his black gown; then with the hem fluttering around his ankles, he went and gently tapped on Wylena's bedroom door.

"Wylena, honey," he said, smiling at the knowledge that he would soon have his arms filled with sweetness as she gave him a good-morning hug. "The oatmeal is ready and we have fresh milk. Come on, Sis. Surely you are up, aren't you?"

When he didn't get a response, his eyebrows arched.

His sister was never known to be a sound sleeper.

In fact, as he recalled, she had sometimes even

beaten their farmer father out of bed at the crack of dawn, to go out and gather eggs for their breakfast.

After waiting what he realized was long enough for Wylena to rise and answer him, if in fact she was still in bed, Joshua had a strange feeling inside his gut that things were not as they should be.

But he could not figure out why.

"She had to have gotten up even before me and is probably now out there on a horse seeing the loveliness of dawn here in Arizona land," he whispered to himself, then slowly turned the doorknob.

When he got it open, his eyes widened, for there was no sign of his sister anywhere, and there were no signs of her having slept in the bed.

He knew her well enough to know that she would never take the time to make a bed if she was eager to go out riding before anyone else was awake.

He shrugged.

Yes, surely she had changed in many ways since they had lived in the same house.

Perhaps she was more tidy now than she had been as a child and teenager.

She had probably not wanted him to make her bed if he found it unmade while she was out taking a ride.

"Yep, she's a changed young lady," he said,

then went and held the tapestry back and whistled to Jeb, the sort of whistle their father had taught them when they were tiny tots on their farm.

It was done by placing his fingers in his mouth in a certain way, and the noise it conjured was a way to get their mother all riled up and shouting at them from the front porch to stop!

"How I miss my mother," he said, tears sparkling in his eyes.

He just could not envision her being gone, the sweet thing that she was.

It had taken someone as sweet and kind as she had been to live with such a tyrant of a husband who barked at her from morning till night, and who took delight in whipping his kids for no set reason.

He reached a hand toward his back, the scars there a reminder, always, of the sort of man his father had been.

Joshua had sworn early on that he would never raise a hand to any of his children when he got married; then he had found God and needed no wife, nor children.

God gave him all that he needed for his happy survival.

Suddenly in wonder of both a brother and a sister not being there eager for their morning meal together, especially since they had spent so many years apart, Joshua could not help but be disappointed in them both.

"Jeb, you can come out of hiding," Joshua shouted down the steps. "You're safe."

And he still got no response.

He lifted the tail end of his robe into his arms and moved lightly down the steps to where a kerosene lamp burned dimly on a table beside an empty bed.

"Even he is gone?" Joshua asked. Frustrated, he ran his fingers through his thick crop of black hair, which hung to his shoulders.

He frowned at seeing Jeb's empty bed, for that meant that he was out there where someone might see him. Jeb did leave some nights, to get fresh air, but he had always returned before dawn in order to get safely back into hiding.

"Surely he didn't go with Wylena," Joshua mumbled to himself as he made his way back up the steps.

Frowning, he hurried on outside toward the barn. He wanted to check which horses were missing. When he got there, he saw that only one horse was gone—Jeb's.

He imagined that Jeb had gotten so involved in his own investigative work in hopes of finding the scalp hunter to clear his name, he had forgotten the time of day.

Yet . . . that didn't explain where Wylena might be. She was certainly not horseback riding, with only one horse missing from the barn. She had never liked riding on the same horse with someone else.

He left the barn and placed his fists on his hips as he scanned the horizon slowly. There was enough daylight now to see for many miles, but there were no signs of either his brother or his sister anywhere.

And then something grabbed his attention.

He looked more intensely down at footprints in the dirt.

There was more than one set. There were those made by a smaller pair of shoes, and then those made by boots.

He knelt quickly to the ground and studied the prints more carefully. They were on separate paths, and then they came together all in a jumble.

It was as though someone had wrestled with someone there. What he didn't like thinking was that if his sister's shoe prints were there with someone else's, and there was a scuffle, who could that other person have been?

She and Jeb were too old to play around, wrestling, or anything like that.

So who had been there with his sister?

Feeling many emotions, but primarily fear for the safety of his sister, Joshua stood tall again and followed the prints until they got lost in the thickness of the small aspen forest that stood not far from his mission.

There he lost the tracks because of the thick cushion of fallen leaves that were spread out and decomposing along the ground.

He rushed back toward his mission, his heart pounding. Surely what he was thinking was wrong. No one would have any reason to abduct his sister!

But once back inside he still could not relax.

He paced back and forth, the skirt of his long gown flipping around his ankles as he turned and paced one way and then another.

He stopped at the door and peered toward Mount Torrance. Chief Falcon Moon had told him more than once that if he ever needed help of any sort, he should never doubt that Falcon Moon was there to help him.

"Should I go there now?" Joshua mumbled to himself. "Or should I wait?"

He just did not want to believe that any harm might have come to his sister or his brother.

Yet he shouldn't ignore the fact that only one horse was gone from the barn.

"Surely Wylena has gone for a long walk and will be returning soon," Joshua said, sighing heavily.

He waited and waited and still neither his brother nor his sister arrived home.

Again he went to the door and gazed up at Mount Torrance.

Now should he go and seek the Apache chief's help?

"No, I'd best stay at the mission and wait a while longer," he whispered. "Both Jeb and Wylena will be home soon."

Surely Jeb had gone farther than usual and had suddenly realized that he could not reach the mission before dawn and was now out there somewhere, hiding and waiting.

"But where is Wylena?" Joshua said, his pulse racing at the thought that something terrible might have happened to her.

He hurried to the chapel, knelt, and began praying.

Chapter 4

The foul smell of the small cell in which Wylena was imprisoned was so horrible that she could hardly stand taking another breath. It reminded her of the time she smelled a dead rat in her family fruit cellar back in Illinois. It had been partly decomposed, with maggots crawling in and out of the holes that once were eyes.

But there was something more than that here. The cell reeked of dried urine and feces and she wondered who might have been there before her.

Her wrists were bleeding where they were held high above her head by irons that secured her in place against the cold stone wall behind her. Thankfully, her feet touched the floor where she was shackled to the wall. She was a true prisoner of the man she now knew was General Zamora.

Tears filled her eyes as the morning sun crept through a long barred window at her left side, giving her a full view of Bright Star, who was stretched out on the ground in the center of the courtyard of the Mexican fortress.

Flies were buzzing around the lovely maiden's bloody mouth.

She was not conscious.

Wylena was afraid that Bright Star might be dead, or dying.

Thus far, Bright Star was the only other woman Wylena had seen at this fortress.

Mainly Mexican soldiers came and went with pack mules.

Wylena had seen them unload large bags and heard them speak of gold in clear enough English.

That had to mean that they were mining for gold somewhere close to this fortress, but she didn't know where.

She was glad that the Mexicans' main interest seemed to be the gold, which meant they would perhaps forget she was even there and not treat her as Bright Star had been treated.

General Zamora had beaten Bright Star with a whip and slapped her across the mouth before taking her outside and throwing her on the ground in the morning sun.

The lovely copper-skinned maiden had not moved since!

"Oh, what am I to do?" Wylena whispered as

the saltiness of her tears rolled across her lips. "Why am I here?"

She already knew why Bright Star was there— to lure the scalp hunter, who so many thought was Jeb, to the fortress, to chance saving her.

Wylena was trembling from both her fear and the coldness of the cell, although she knew that the morning sun was already warming the air outside.

Her heart ached over her concern about Bright Star. After Wylena arrived at the fortress with her captor, she had been shackled to the wall beside Bright Star.

They were left alone long enough to be able to get acquainted.

Wylena had recognized the name Bright Star as soon as it was spoken to her. She was Chief Falcon Moon's sister . . . and Wylena's very own brother's lover!

How could Wylena ever forget the name Bright Star and all that she had heard about her?

Jeb had doctored her after she had fallen from her horse. In those brief few moments of being together, they had felt a connection, which led to them meeting each other whenever they could.

Even after Bright Star was forbidden from seeing Jeb again, she had sneaked away to be with him. Bright Star had admitted to Wylena that she had been on her way home after being with Jeb when she had been abducted by one of General Zamora's soldiers.

From that moment on, when the women had had a brief moment of acquaintance, things had changed, and not for the better.

Just as dawn had broken along the horizon in splashes of pink, General Zamora had entered the small, stinking cell.

He loosened the irons at Bright Star's wrists.

He grabbed her and shoved her outside.

When Bright Star had tried to run from him, he ordered one of his men to catch her.

He ordered another soldier to throw him a whip.

Shortly after that, Bright Star had collapsed onto the ground, unconscious, the back of her doeskin dress torn by the whip.

"Surely she's dead," Wylena sobbed. She tried to will Bright Star awake as she watched her. "Bright Star, please move. Please show me that you are alive."

But still Bright Star just lay there, the sun on her, the gnats and flies thickening around the blood not only on and around her mouth but also on her back, which was exposed through the tears in her dress!

Wylena's insides tightened and she scarcely breathed as the door to her cell crept slowly open.

She winced when it was finally all of the way open and she saw the short and stocky Mexican general standing there, a hand resting on a sheathed saber at his right side.

She trembled with fear as his dark eyes looked intensely into her own. A tiny sliver of a mustache over his thin lips quivered into a slow, cynical smile as he stepped farther into the room.

He wore a red suit, where gold buttons, looking as though they had been freshly polished, shone in the sunlight that wafted through the opened door.

The man's hair was coal black and reached his shirt collar. His face was grooved with wrinkles—proving that he was much older than most of the men who worked under his command.

He was particularly many years older than Wylena.

Her heart raced as he took another step closer to her, then clasped his hands behind him as he slowly rocked back and forth from heel to toe, his black shoes now also reflecting the shine of the sun on their polished leather.

Wylena's heart pounded hard inside her chest as she continued staring back at the general, almost in a dare, whereas she truly feared him. He had already shown his ruthless heartlessness by how he had treated the sweet Bright Star.

She knew that he spoke English well enough to tell her why he had chosen to abduct her.

Thus far he had ignored her queries.

So had everyone else who came and went, bringing food and water. They all ignored her pleas for help.

"Why am I here?" Wylena pleaded again. "And why did you treat Bright Star so unjustly? She might be dying. Please bring her in out of the sun, or at least try and awaken her and give her a drink of water."

"You had best worry about your own self," General Zamora said matter-of-factly in a deep and gruff voice. "Why should you care about a savage? Don't you know that they hate all white people? Even that woman you seem so concerned about would surely kill you if given the chance."

"That tiny, sweet woman is not a savage," Wylena softly argued, lifting her chin proudly. She knew the general might turn on her at any moment as he had assaulted Bright Star, but it was not in Wylena's nature not to argue her point when she was being done wrong!

General Zamora stepped aside as one of his men came into the small cell carrying a pot of food and two bowls and spoons on a tray.

The smell of the food made Wylena's stomach growl and she eyed it hungrily as the man handed the tray to the general.

"Release her," General Zamora snapped at his soldier. "Now."

The soldier removed the irons from her wrists and Wylena felt the blood returning to her fingers as her arms fell down to her sides.

She gazed at the blood where the irons had cut into her flesh, only now aware of the pain. While her arms were held over her head, she had felt nothing in them, or her hands.

"One of these bowls is for you. The other is for the Indian woman," General Zamora said, nodding toward the tray. "Take the tray. Eat, then take a bowl of the soup out to the Indian squaw, but . . . do not feed her. Just think of yourself now. Do you understand?"

"Why can't I feed her, if I can get her awake to eat?" Wylena asked as she took the tray. She realized just how weak she was when she almost dropped it. The weight was too much for her.

"You waste your time thinking of someone else," General Zamora said, slowly twisting and untwisting the tip of his mustache as he talked. "I want you to remain strong."

"And . . . why do you want me . . . to remain strong?" Wylena dared to ask, not sure she would want to hear the answer. "And why can't I awaken and feed Bright Star?"

"She does not deserve to eat," General Zamora said, idly shrugging. "And I want you to take a good look at the Indian squaw. She was too feisty and had to be silenced, and so shall you, should you try and run away from me or my men. Now set the tray on the floor and eat."

Knowing it was in her best interest to eat and build up her strength, Wylena placed the tray down on the floor in front of her, then ladled out some of the creamy soup into a bowl.

She was too hungry not to eat, so plucked up

a spoon and dived into the soup. It was absolutely delicious, whereas she had expected it to taste like dishwater.

She ate one spoonful after another as the general stood there playing with his mustache and watching her.

After eating several spoonfuls, Wylena looked up at the general. "Why did you bring me here?" she asked between bites, although she had asked him the same question many times, only to be ignored.

But this time he might answer her!

She paused eating to listen.

"I brought you here for the same reason the squaw is here . . . to lure your scalp-hunter brother here with the intention of saving you," General Zamora said, smiling sardonically. "The squaw? She is in love with the scalp hunter, even though he takes scalps from her own Apache people and sells them."

Upset by the answer, Wylena was rendered speechless for the moment.

"Having both the scalp hunter's sister and lover here, how can the man not come to rescue you?" General Zamora said. He knelt down and looked Wylena square in the eye. "I wonder which one he'll decide to save, for he has to know that he can't save you both."

He pushed himself up and stood over Wylena again. "Your brother won't save either one of you, because he won't be given the chance, but should he have to choose, he would choose the one who gives him the love of a woman for a man. I am not talking about the love of a sister," he said.

He threw his head back in a fit of boisterous laughter, then sobered and glared down at Wylena again. "You are now free to come and go from the cell, but do not go farther than the distance of this building's shadow on the ground. The more you are seen outside, the better the chance is that your brother will see you. It's important that he sees both you and the squaw. Seeing the squaw lying there lifeless will anger him into doing something crazy, which will end in his death, and then it will be over. I might even be tempted to let you go. But as for the squaw? I might keep her all to myself. She's not dead, you know. Only unconscious. After getting cleaned up, she'll be a good bed partner."

"You are insane if you think you can get away with any of this," Wylena said, no longer having any appetite.

She threw the spoon at the general, but succeeded only in getting a sardonic laugh out of him as he kicked the spoon away. It landed on the floor next to his feet.

"You are becoming much too feisty for your own good," General Zamora growled as he reached for her hair and grabbed it between his fingers.

He yanked on her hair, causing Wylena to cry

out with pain as she scrambled to her feet, glad when he released his hold on it.

"Please reconsider what you are doing," Wylena said as tears spilled from her eyes. "You are so wrong about my brother. He hasn't killed or scalped anyone. Both of my brothers are loving and caring. You have the wrong man in mind."

He laughed into her face, then again grew somber. "You can go into the courtyard, but remember what your boundaries are," he said tightly. "You'll be shot if you try to run farther than that. And remember not to feed the squaw or even speak to her. Put a bowl of that food beside her, then get away from her."

With that, he turned on a heel and left.

Trembling, feeling so many emotions, Wylena stepped up to the door and gazed through it at Bright Star.

The maiden still hadn't moved.

Oh, but she did look more dead than alive!

Then Wylena's thoughts went to Jeb.

She remembered him saying that he wasn't going to try to save Bright Star. Would he feel the same about his very own sister?

But Wylena also didn't want him to come and try.

He would be walking right into a trap! He would be killed!

"Oh, Lord, no matter what he does, someone is going to die," she murmured.

Then remembering what the general had said and knowing that she had better do as he had ordered her, she ladled some soup into a bowl and turned toward the door with it.

When she got outside the sun bore down onto her with its heat, although it was not yet noon. She went to Bright Star and purposely shadowed the maiden's face by standing so the sun could no longer reach it.

Wylena badly wanted to try to awaken Bright Star, but she knew that the general must be watching her every move, so she did as she had been told.

She placed the bowl of soup a short distance from Bright Star's mouth.

"Please, Bright Star, wake up," Wylena whispered. "Please . . . ?"

But knowing that she had perhaps stayed there too long already, Wylena stood up and backed slowly away from Bright Star.

She flinched when she saw General Zamora come from the main building of the fortress. He wore a frown and sent Wylena a contemptuous look that seemed to cut right through her.

She swallowed hard and hurried away from Bright Star, then stopped and stood in the shadows of the building where she had been shackled to the wall.

From there she could smell the unpleasant odors wafting through the door. She shuddered, then looked slowly into the distance, where she thought she could see a light flash high on a bluff that overlooked the Mexican fortress just across the border.

And then her breath caught in her throat when she thought she actually saw movement there!

Chapter 5

In what distant deeps or skies
Burnt the fire of thine eyes?
                    —William Blake

Falcon Moon lay prone on a bluff overlooking the Mexican fortress. From there he had a good view of what was happening down below him, and what he saw made his blood boil.

He could hardly believe his eyes, yet there she was. His sister lay on the ground, apparently lifeless, with no one paying any attention to her.

At first he had thought she was dead, but when a white woman came from the building carrying a bowl of food for his sister, it had given him hope that Bright Star was still alive. But what confused him was that the white woman had not attempted to awaken Bright Star, to tell her that food was within reach.

Instead of attempting to awaken Bright Star, the woman now stood at the door, watching Bright Star, even though it was obvious she was too weak to move even if she was awake, much less feed herself.

As his sister continued to lie on the ground in the sun, a soldier came to stand over her.

What happened next made Falcon Moon so angry, it was hard not to stand and aim an arrow straight at that soldier's heart, for as the soldier stood there laughing, he kicked the bowl, spilling the food closer to his sister's mouth.

Falcon Moon's eyes went quickly to the white woman, who still stood at the door. He waited to see if she might intervene in this madness and go to his sister's rescue.

But she stood there, only watching.

It was hard for Falcon Moon to understand how one woman could stand by and watch another woman being treated so inhumanely and make no attempt to help her. This white woman must have a heart of stone, and Falcon Moon could not help but feel the need for vengeance against her!

But he quickly put that thought from his mind as he saw the soldier walk away.

His spine grew stiff and his jaw tightened with a despair he had felt too often in his life as he watched Bright Star begin to awaken and then slowly scoot closer to the food now spread all over the ground around the bowl.

His heart pumped blood quickly through his veins and he could not refrain from whimpering to himself over what he could now see.

The back of his sister's dress was ripped in shreds. He could see the dried blood on her back. Someone had whipped her!

His beloved sister had gotten close enough to the spilled food to scoop it into her mouth with her fingers. Flies scattered, only to again settle around the food. Bright Star ate what she could.

He could hardly endure the pain of waiting. He wanted to move now and start the planned rescue before anything else could happen to his sister. Yet he knew that he could do nothing until the fortress was covered with the shroud of night.

As it was, there was a lot of constant activity at the fortress. Soldiers were coming and going with pack mules.

Falcon Moon knew that the soldiers would take the mules into a canyon not far from the fortress, where they groveled in the earth for the forbidden ore—gold—that they took from Mother Earth and that was sacred to Ussen, the Creator of Life.

Falcon Moon knew that Ussen would one day make these men pay for the wrong they were doing to Mother Earth.

He had sometimes felt slight tremors of the

earth, even as far up the mountain as where he made his home, and knew that it was Ussen who caused the tremors. Falcon Moon expected a much larger earthquake one day.

He prayed to Ussen, his Great Spirit above, that his Bright Star would last until the rescue. If not, he would set the fortress aflame and then kill all the soldiers who remained alive, especially the evil General Zamora.

He would reserve the worst for that man.

Yes, General Zamora would be taken away and dealt with by a means that would make him beg, over and over again, for mercy.

But actually, at this moment, Falcon Moon could not hate anyone as much as he hated Jeb Schrock, for it was because of him that his sister had been taken hostage.

Falcon Moon's trusted scout had cleverly been the one to discover why his sister was a hostage at the Mexican fortress.

She wrongly loved a white man who was said to be the scalp hunter.

The Mexicans had not caused Falcon Moon any problems. Until now.

But to avoid starting an all-out war with General Zamora—knowing war brought too many deaths—Falcon Moon had decided that he would rescue his sister and take her home without confrontation.

The warriors under his command were skilled in all ways of rescuing their people from harm,

sometimes stealing back those who had been
taken from beneath the noses of the abductors.

The Mexicans would not know who stole
Bright Star away.

They would believe it was the man she loved
who had done it.

If by chance General Zamora discovered
where she was, and who had truly rescued her,
and attempted to capture her again, Falcon
Moon would have no choice but to make him
pay. If that was the case, then General Zamora
would suffer first, and then he would die!

Falcon Moon saw Bright Star reach a hand out
toward the white woman, who remained by the
door of the small building. It looked like his sister was attempting to say something to her. With
the white woman unresponsive, Falcon Moon
decided there and then that he would take this
heartless woman with him as he rescued his sister from the fortress.

This white woman was the only woman besides his sister that Falcon Moon had seen inside
the fortress walls. She must belong to the general
and she would be the one to pay for General
Zamora's crime. Perhaps her capture would
cause hurt to the general's dark heart, for to lose
one's woman was to lose one's soul!

"Tonight," Falcon Moon growled to himself.

Yes, he would get both women tonight!

He said a soft prayer to the heavens, where
Ussen saw and heard everything, praying deeply

from his heart that his sister would survive until her rescue, and for many years to follow.

He wanted to grow old with her.

She was not meant to die young!

If she died because of how the general had treated her, Falcon Moon would ensure that the ground ran red with the blood of those who had caused her death!

He gazed at the slant of the sun—it had moved past the midpoint in the sky, sinking lower and lower toward the horizon—and then at his sister, who seemed to have fallen asleep again.

He ached terribly inside his heart for his beloved sister. He wanted to go now and sweep her up into his arms and carry her to safety!

The hours were passing by too slowly.

His jaw tightened as he looked back to where he had seen the white woman.

She was gone!

His eyes slowly scanned the courtyard for any sign of her, but he saw nothing. He was determined to find her tonight. He would not leave the fortress without her!

She had a role to play in the evil general's comeuppance!

He frowned, for although he planned to use this white woman as a way to achieve vengeance against the general, he could not deny her beauty, or how innocent and tiny she had appeared from this distance.

What if she was a captive, too?

He could see from her attire that she was obviously not Mexican!

Either way, taking her would anger the Mexican general's heart.

Falcon Moon studied the lay of the land and thought through the escape route he had planned.

A stream flowed through the fortress walls.

His sister was imprisoned close to where the stream entered the fortress, near a large two-story building.

One of his warriors had one time been taken prisoner, but had escaped the fortress.

He learned by his time there with the Mexicans that the larger building held the forbidden ore until it was taken away for trade.

An irregular row of small adobe huts sat behind the larger building. This was where the soldiers made their homes, homes shared only between men, no families with them.

He knew that all activity at the fortress stopped by the time the moon was high in the sky. The soldiers retired to their huts, as the general retired to his own home, which sat in the center of the courtyard.

When all the lamps were out and there was only one sentry to deal with, he and his men would enter the fortress as quietly as panthers, take the two women, and leave.

No one would be the wiser until the next day.

Then it would be too late. The general would have no way of knowing who had taken the women, for all tracks made by the Apache and the departing women would have been wiped clean!

His sister would be safe and the white woman would be an Apache captive! She would be Falcon Moon's prisoner!

That thought made a slow smile quiver across his perfectly shaped lips.

Chapter 6

The moonlight of a perfect peace
Floods heart and brain.
                    —William Sharp

Wylena could hardly believe that a second person had abducted her. She was being carried in strong arms, but she had no idea to where, or by whom.

All she knew was that as she had lain on the cold floor of her cell, without even a blanket, powerful hands had grabbed her up from the floor and held her, while at the same time someone else had quickly covered her mouth with a gag before she had the chance to scream.

In the dark she had seen neither person ahead of time. Only moments later someone had tied something around her eyes.

After her wrists were bound together, someone carried her from the cell as she tried to com-
municate through the gag about the Indian
maiden, for Wylena thought that any place
would be better than this imprisonment that had
been forced upon both herself and Bright Star.

She wasn't certain whether Bright Star had
been taken, too, for Wylena had not been able to
see anything since the cloth was tied around her
eyes.

She did know, though, that General Zamora
had ordered that the petite Indian maiden be
brought into Wylena's same cell when darkness
fell around the Mexican fortress.

At first, Wylena had not been able to see much
of what was going on because the moon had at
that time been hidden behind clouds.

But as soon as moonlight wafted through the
bars of the one window, and Wylena saw Bright
Star on the floor, so weak and helpless, Wylena
had fallen to her knees beside her to see what she
could do to help her.

Bright Star had awakened for a few moments.
Each knew who the other was now, and why
they had been abducted by the cruel general, but
Wylena was the only strong one. She had sat
there on the cold, damp floor and held Bright
Star on her lap when the tiny thing had fallen
into her strange sleep again.

She had rocked Bright Star as Wylena's
mother had rocked her as a child; she hoped that

somehow that might give the pretty thing some solace as she slept.

But Wylena had been able to do that for only a short while because the trauma of the day had worn her out so much that she, too, needed to sleep.

She needed rest in order to have the strength to find an escape from the hell of captivity in the fortress. She knew that Bright Star was too weak to go with her. But if Wylena managed to escape, hopefully if the sentries fell asleep while on duty, she would make certain that someone from her brother's ministry returned for Bright Star as soon as possible.

Wylena would make certain that word was taken to Bright Star's chieftain brother about her imprisonment. Falcon Moon would save her!

Wylena had moved Bright Star off her lap, then nestled as close to Bright Star as she could, so they could feel each other's body warmth.

It felt like she had been asleep for only minutes before the hands grabbed her and blindfolded her.

She was now being carried by someone who was running, yet she could hear no footsteps. That might mean that the one who carried her wore moccasins! Her hopes soared, for surely Falcon Moon had found a way to save, not only his sister, but also Wylena!

She prayed over and over again to herself that this was true, for she knew that if it was the

Apache chief, there was hope for both herself and Bright Star.

Finally the person carrying her stopped running.

She heard the soft neighing of a horse, and then felt herself placed roughly on it.

Only moments later, someone sat behind her on the horse, his muscled arm holding her in place as the steed rode off in a hard gallop.

She was keenly aware of many other horses; their hoofbeats sounded like thunder beneath the dark heavens.

She hoped that whoever was taking her away from what would have been certain death should she not have found a way to escape was not someone taking her to another imprisonment that might be even worse than what she had experienced at the fortress. She prayed that whoever held her on his horse was not a renegade Apache but instead one who had a good heart.

She prayed over and over again that this was one of Chief Falcon Moon's warriors who held her, and that Bright Star was on another horse, hopefully in her very own brother's arms!

Wylena wished they would remove the gag and the blindfold, as it was getting harder and harder to breathe through the spit-dampened cloth.

Suddenly everything grew quiet as the horses stopped. Wylena became aware that the person who had been on the horse with her was no longer there. Then she gasped with pain as strong hands yanked her roughly from the steed and threw her to the ground.

Her pulse raced as fear crept into her heart, for if her rescuer was being so rough with her, surely that meant that this person was not a friend.

And what of Bright Star? Was she still there? And was she being treated as roughly?

Wylena knew that the petite maiden could not take much more abuse, or she might die.

Suddenly her gag was yanked off along with the blindfold.

She breathed deeply and found herself looking into the fierce, dark eyes of an Indian warrior. The light that the moon gave off was enough for her to see the hate in his eyes.

And when he spoke, it was in plain English. His voice was deep and masculine, a voice of authority. He turned away from her and began handing out orders to those warriors who stood around him holding their horse's reins.

It was then that Wylena saw Bright Star lying on a thick cushion of pelts and blankets on the ground beside a softly meandering stream. The moon's glow was like a caress on her lovely copper skin.

It was such a relief for Wylena to see Bright Star being treated so wonderfully, for if these were Bright Star's enemies, they would not have bothered placing her on such a comfortable pallet.

Wylena looked quickly at the man who seemed

to be in charge, as the warriors nodded to his commands and began leaving to take their places as sentries who would keep watch through the night.

The tall, muscled, authoritative Indian, who was dressed only in a breechclout and moccasins, was the only one giving out orders, and his orders were obeyed without question. Her gaze went to a necklace he wore, a long, thin strip of buckskin. On it was some sort of tooth.

She looked at his face again. She knew that this could be Bright Star's chieftain brother. But if it was Chief Falcon Moon, why was he treating her so unkindly when she was not guilty of any wrongdoing?

The way he looked into her eyes with so much contempt had made her blood run cold through her veins.

For some reason, he saw her as his enemy!

She thought perhaps his hatred of her was because her skin was white. Yet her priest brother's skin was white, and Falcon Moon had befriended him.

But suddenly it came to her—the reason why he was treating her so miserably.

It was because of Bright Star.

Wylena's brother had found Bright Star injured and had taken her to his mission, where Jeb could treat her injuries!

She knew that things had since changed. Chief

Falcon Moon saw Jeb as his enemy because of how Jeb had secretly courted Bright Star.

Suddenly the warrior with the icy stare and rough hands turned to her, grabbed her by the arm, and shoved her down on the ground beside Bright Star.

A desperation that Wylena had never felt before filled her veins when she saw that Bright Star was again in a deep sleep. Bright Star would not be able to speak in Wylena's behalf, to tell this man that she was not at fault for any of this!

"Please untie my wrists," Wylena found the courage to say. "I have done nothing wrong to warrant your anger at me. Just like your sister, I am innocent of any crime. So is my brother Jeb, who is accused of being a scalp hunter. Please, Falcon Moon, please take me to my brother Joshua's mission, for that is where I now make my home."

At first Falcon Moon was stunned to hear that this woman knew who he was. But of course the Mexican general had to have explained everything to her after he brought Bright Star to the fortress.

"You are a smart woman to have thought up such clever lies," Falcon Moon hissed at her. "You are the general's woman. And I am a friend to Father Joshua and he has talked of having a sister who lived far from him, not with him."

"Our parents recently died in a tornado," Wylena said, a sob escaping from the depths of her throat. "I was left all alone in Illinois. That is why I came to live with my brothers. I have been at the mission for only one day. That's why you don't know about me being with my brothers. And I was in that horrible cell with your sister. If I were General Zamora's woman, as you accuse me, do you think he would make me stay in such an ungodly place as that?"

"I have no idea why the general would enclose you with my sister in the cell, unless it was a clever ploy to make her think you were a friend, to get answers from her, which could be used in one way or another," Falcon Moon said tightly. "All I know is that I saw you earlier this afternoon. You took my sister food but did not attempt to help her eat it. You even watched as a soldier kicked the bowl over. You saw how she crawled to the spilled food and scooped it up into her mouth from the filthy ground."

"The Mexican general warned . . . ordered . . . me not to help her," Wylena sobbed. "I was taken prisoner for the same reason your sister was . . . to draw my brother Jeb there, for him to rescue us so that he would, in turn, be killed by the Mexican soldiers."

"Your brother? Ha! And why would the general allow you to be free and unharmed, while he was being so cruel to my sister?" Falcon Moon said. He reached for Wylena's wrist and yanked her back to her feet. "Say all you want to say, but I see you as, not only my sister's enemy, but also of all my people."

He gave her a rough shove. "Come with me," he growled. "I do not want you near my sister ever again. You will not have the chance to tell her lies, or pretend to be her friend. You will sleep far away from her. You will be guarded at all times, so do not attempt to flee."

"I wish you would listen to me," Wylena sobbed as she stumbled along beside him. "My brother Joshua will be stunned to hear how you treated me after he was so kind to your sister. I was, too, after she was brought back into the cell. I even . . . held her and rocked her after she went into her strange sleep again."

"Your lies are wasted on me," Falcon Moon growled as he forced her farther away from where Bright Star lay very quietly.

Suddenly they both walked into a thick mass of cobwebs that hung among the tree branches.

Wylena became entangled in them. She screamed hysterically and flung her free hand in the air in an attempt to dislodge the cobwebs. When Falcon Moon quickly led her out of the cobwebs and dropped his hand from her wrist, Wylena turned to him and flung herself into his arms.

Sobbing, she clung to him and thanked him over and over again for saving her from the spiders that were surely somewhere in those cobwebs.

Falcon Moon felt how hard she was trembling as she clung to him. He could not help but see her as a fragile, beautiful woman as she stood there in the sheen of the moonlight, helpless and afraid.

His gazed moved slowly over the wonders of her face. It was delicately boned and her lips were sensually shaped. In her eyes he saw much more than he had seen moments ago. They were wide and bright, and shone with tears.

He did not force her away from him, but instead allowed her to stay in his arms as she finally composed herself enough to stop crying.

"I am terribly afraid of spiderwebs," she said softly as she gazed at him. "You see, there were times back in Illinois when my cruel father would put me in the fruit cellar, alone, in the dark, for punishment. There were spiders there that crawled over my flesh as I waited to be released. Then one day one of them bit me. I was ill for several days after I was taken from the cellar. Now . . . I . . . I . . . have a total fear of all spiders, large and small."

Falcon Moon listened intently as she continued to tell him about a father who was so cruel to her. He found it incredible to believe that any father could do what this woman said her father had done to her. Yet he saw such sincerity in her words and behavior.

"My father punished my brothers in a different way," Wylena murmured as she slowly eased out of his strong, comforting arms. "They were beaten. My brother Jeb left before Joshua, to get away from the beatings. Joshua left soon after that and became a priest. My brother Jeb seemed to be a lost soul until he came to live with Joshua, who is such a good, godly man."

Falcon Moon was truly confused now. This woman did seem very knowledgeable of Father Joshua and his brother, Jeb. Perhaps she was really their sister and not the Mexican general's woman.

But she also might have heard the Mexican soldiers talking about the brothers.

Or the general might have discussed them in order to give her knowledge to get on Bright Star's better side.

He gazed into Wylena's eyes. "This is where you will spend the night," he said, gesturing with a hand toward thick green grass beneath an aspen tree. "I shall bring you blankets. But as I said before, I warn you not to try and run. I have sentries posted in many places. You will be seen and caught."

"Please tell me how Bright Star is doing," she asked softly. "She sleeps too much. The Mexican general was so cruel to her. He beat her with a whip and slapped her in the mouth for no reason. That's why there is blood on both her mouth and back."

"There is no longer any blood on my sister's body, anywhere," Falcon Moon said, puzzled as to why this woman seemed genuinely interested in his sister's welfare.

If she was working with the general, she

should know there would be no need to continue pretending to care for Bright Star. She would never see the general again to report back to him!

"We will arrive at my stronghold tomorrow," he said. "My people's shaman will make my sister well."

"I hope that she awakens soon so that she can speak on my behalf," Wylena murmured as she settled down on the grass. "She knows the truth about why I was at the fortress. I only wish that you would believe me, too."

"My sister was wrong to listen to anything you said," Falcon Moon said flatly.

He gave her another lingering look as he tried to see truths or lies in her eyes beneath the shine of the moon, but he could not read her well enough. He turned and walked away from her.

Bull Nose had observed the exchange between his chief and the white woman. He was standing only a few feet away, in the shadows.

He stiffened when Falcon Moon looked quickly over at him, as usual appearing as though he could read Bull Nose's every thought!

Bull Nose walked briskly away into the dark shadows of night, while Falcon Moon walked onward to get blankets to take back to the white woman.

He had seen Bull Nose's interest in the woman and knew that he must be watched closely. Falcon Moon didn't know what to expect from this warrior anymore.

Falcon Moon stopped and knelt beside his sister before bringing blankets to the white woman.

His heart skipped a beat when her eyes slowly opened, enough for her to see who he was, and to know that she was safe. Then she smiled and fell asleep again.

Ah, he was so relieved that his sister had woken long enough to see where she was. Falcon Moon had hope now that his sister would be all right. With this heavy weight lessened on his shoulders, he took two blankets to the white woman.

"Thank you," Wylena murmured as she spread one out on the ground, then settled down on it and pulled the other one over her, up to her chin.

Falcon Moon suddenly reached down to smooth out a corner of the blanket, then rose and walked quickly away from her.

In that one gesture she saw the possibility that perhaps he was beginning to believe she was who she said she was! Maybe tomorrow he would finally realize the truth when Bright Star awakened and told him.

She gazed heavenward and pleaded with God that there would be a tomorrow for Bright Star, for if not, Wylena was not certain what would happen to her.

Chapter 7

How sweet it were, hearing the downward stream,
With half-shut eyes ever to seem
Falling asleep in a half-dream!
—Alfred, Lord Tennyson

Before dawn broke, Wylena had been awakened and she was soon on the horse with a warrior again, but this time neither gagged nor blindfolded. Nor were her wrists tied.

As the morning sun crept up behind Mount Torrance, she found herself on the steep slopes that wound around it.

She knew then that she was being taken to the Apache stronghold situated high on this mountain.

Her heart pounded like thunder inside her chest as she clung to the warrior who sat in the saddle in front of her. She glanced down the side of the mountain, where rocks were tumbling as the horse's hooves loosed them from the narrow path.

She closed her eyes and clung more tightly to the warrior, opening them only when she felt the horse steadying on a less steep slope.

Now that it was light enough for her to see, she saw that she was on a horse directly behind Chief Falcon Moon's. He carried his sister on his lap.

Wylena was concerned because Bright Star still appeared to be asleep. There had been hushed whisperings among the sentries who stood watch over her and Bright Star about soldiers within the fortress who had come down with a fever. She had stiffened in dread when they spoke the word smallpox!

That meant that Wylena and Bright Star had possibly been exposed to that treacherous disease.

Someone already weakened could get the disease more easily than someone who was strong and well. She was anxious to see if Bright Star had a fever.

She clung harder to the warrior when again he turned the horse onto a narrow path that led right alongside the steep drop-off at Wylena's left side. She swallowed hard and prayed that she would survive traveling on this mountain.

Suddenly her meandering thoughts were replaced by wonder when, up ahead, through a break in the trees, she saw a long line of tepees silhouetted against a backdrop of rocky columns and beautiful aspen trees. The tepees all faced east.

She had been so lost in thought, she had not noticed that the long procession of horses carrying warriors, herself, and Bright Star had turned away from the sheer drop-off. They were now traveling on flat land, where a path leading to the Apache stronghold had been cut through the trees just wide enough for horses and man to travel.

As they approached the village, she noticed sentries perched high on the canyon wall. These warriors were scarcely clothed, wearing only sparse breechclouts and moccasins, their long, sleek black hair held back by headbands.

Suddenly the quiet midmorning air was broken by the voices of children as they came running and shouting their fathers' names, proving how they had missed their fathers while they were away.

Then she saw the women as they came into view, walking proudly in their beautiful fringed dresses and knee-high moccasins. They all wore their hair in lone braids down their backs. As each caught sight of her man, a smile broke out on her lovely face, but the women did not run to meet the men or cry out any of their names.

It was the children who came now and ran alongside their fathers' steeds, their eyes showing their pride as they gazed into their fathers' eyes.

Wylena noticed that no children greeted the chief, nor did a woman, but she knew why. Her brother Joshua had said that he was a young, unmarried chief, who put his full attention on his duty. But her brother had also told her in passing that he knew that the chief was soon to begin looking for a wife, for he had told Joshua that he hungered to have children, especially a son.

If a proud chief could admit such a thing to a white man, then surely he wanted these things twofold inside his heart!

She had noticed many glances from this handsome young chief. Sometimes his eyes had lingered so long on her, she had felt her face grow hot with a blush. She had not seen any sign of resentment when he had looked at her in that way, but instead . . . wonder.

She had felt strange pangs inside her belly whenever their eyes had momentarily met, pangs that were new to her, and strangely, sweetly delicious. She had never been attracted to any certain man before, for she had not had the opportunity to meet many. Her time had been spent on the farm; she'd rarely even gone into the nearby town of Harrisburg to get supplies with her parents.

Her father had kept her hidden at home, for he needed her help in the garden and kitchen too much to let her offer such help to any other man.

She would never forget the long hours of sweating over a hot stove in the summer as she stood beside her mother canning vegetables from the garden and fruit from their orchards.

On the day of the tornado all of those things had been swept from the face of the earth, along with the house, the barn, and her parents!

Their bodies were never found.

No, there was not even a grave marked with their names because no matter how long and how far the survivors of that horrendous day had looked for them, the bodies had not been found.

It was as though those vicious winds had fallen down to the earth long enough to wipe away every trace of her parents and their farm from the face of the earth.

The surviving neighbors gave Wylena money for the journey from Illinois to Arizona—money she would never be able to pay back. But they had insisted they never wanted repayment. It was all they could do to help her get past the sadness of losing so much in her young life.

Finally arriving at the village, where she now saw even more tepees, which stood in a semicircle away from the long line that she had originally seen, she noticed how clean everything was.

In the center of the village stood a large, roaring fire, and around it sat many elderly men who were talking among themselves, surely sharing tales of their past lives, their fortunes, and their misfortunes.

They stopped and looked over their shoulders when they realized their chief had returned with his sister.

They nodded at Falcon Moon, then resumed their chatting, as though nothing in the world mattered to them but those moments with one another, moments that surely would be gone soon, for Wylena had never seen such old men as they. Their eyes, noses, and lips were almost lost midst their wrinkles!

Wylena's attention was drawn back to herself when the warrior she was riding with led the horse to a more isolated tepee.

He dismounted, then reached up for her. He led her gently enough inside the lodge, where there were blankets stacked along one side and a fire pit with a slow-burning fire in the middle of the tepee. Colorful mats were situated all along the floor of the lodge, and just as she was told to sit down beside the fire, a middle-aged Indian woman came in, carrying a pot of stew she placed on a tripod over the fire.

The woman turned and gave Wylena a questioning look, then stepped outside and entered again, carrying a bowl, a ladle for dipping the stew from the pot, and a spoon for eating.

"Eat," she said gruffly, then left and did not return, as the warrior still stood there, his arms crossed, his eyes never leaving Wylena.

Feeling self-conscious under such scrutiny, Wylena could not get herself to consume the stew, although her stomach was growling unmercifully from hunger. She felt so dirty and unkempt, plus she had not been allowed to do her very private duty for some time now and felt as though she might burst, she needed to go so badly.

She gazed shyly at the warrior.

She couldn't remember his name.

To her all of the Indian warriors' names sounded alike, except for Falcon Moon's. She would never forget his name, nor him.

The longer she was near him, the more intrigued with him she became.

Although he saw her as an enemy, he treated her kindly now. He rarely frowned as he looked into her eyes, as he had right after meeting her. She had to believe that he had mulled over what she had said about Joshua being her brother. Oh, surely he did realize that she couldn't make all of that up!

But for now, her main concern centered around his sister. She wanted to know Bright Star's condition, whether she was feverish.

Wylena stood suddenly and looked the warrior squarely in the eye. Without mincing words, she told him what she had to do, surprised when he complied with her request by taking her outside and pointing to a thick stand of brush back away from the tepee.

Noticing how he placed his hand on his knife sheathed at his right side, she realized that he was giving her a silent warning not to go farther than that, or he would come after her.

She was glad when he turned his eyes away from those bushes. She hurried into them, and soon emerged a happier person. She saw a stream not that far away.

Approaching the warrior again, she gently touched him on the arm.

He turned and gazed into her eyes in a friendly fashion that made her feel as though she could request one more thing from him.

"I would love to wash up," she murmured, searching his eyes for a reaction. "The stream. Can I go there and wash my face and hands?"

He gazed at the stream, then looked into her eyes again, and nodded.

She hurried to the water and knelt beside it. She sighed with pleasure as she splashed some on her face, then cupped water in her hands to drink.

After dousing her hair in the stream, even though she had no soap to wash it completely, she started walking back to the waiting warrior, but stopped when she saw Chief Falcon Moon standing outside a large tepee.

When he felt her looking at him, Falcon Moon turned his eyes to Wylena. They both stood there for a moment or two, just looking at each other, waiting for the other to make a move. And then suddenly Falcon Moon came over to Wylena.

He looked at her wet hair and her soiled blue silk dress.

He reached out a hand to touch her, then quickly drew his hand back again, as though he'd had second thoughts.

"How is your sister?" Wylena blurted out.

Today it seemed that his mind was on more things than whether or not she was evil, or attached to that terrible Mexican general.

When she saw that he was still having trouble responding to her, Wylena stepped closer to him. "Please let me know how Bright Star is," she said, practically begging. She thought about the smallpox at the fortress. "Does she have a temperature?"

"Yes, she has a fever," Falcon Moon said, his eyebrows forking. She did seem to sincerely care about Bright Star.

"I'm sorry to hear that," Wylena said, sighing deeply. She looked more intensely into his dark eyes. "Chief Falcon Moon, I have to tell you something that you might not want to hear."

Falcon Moon's insides tightened at those words. Was this woman playing games with him after all? What could she mean?

"What are you not saying?" he said, his voice tight. "What do you have to say about my sister that you are hesitant at saying?"

"There were some soldiers at the Mexican fortress suffering from the terrible disease called smallpox," Wylena said cautiously, worried about how he would take what she had to say.

She could see his bare, muscled shoulders stiffen, and his hands turn into tight fists at his sides.

"Truly, Falcon Moon, I would not lie to you," she blurted out. "I am concerned about your sister's welfare and your people's, too. If your sister has a fever, then she might have smallpox. She should be isolated from everyone else or many of your people could get the disease if she has it. They could die."

She swallowed hard, lowered her gaze, then looked into his midnight-dark eyes again. "I would never tell you this unless it were true," she murmured. "Why would I? I gain nothing except knowing that I have done what I can for you and your people by telling you about the smallpox. I truly hope Bright Star doesn't have it. I shall pray that she doesn't."

"You will pray for my sister?" Falcon Moon said, searching her eyes to see if she was being truthful. He thought she might just be telling him things that would make her look good in his eyes in order to get him to trust her.

"I have already prayed for her," Wylena murmured. "Please take her far from the others."

"You were at the fortress at the same time as my sister, so you might also have smallpox," Falcon Moon said, studying her face.

He knew about smallpox and its symptoms because there was an outbreak among his people when he was a mere child.

"I don't feel like I am coming down with anything, and I certainly don't have a fever," Wylena said reassuringly. "But your sister came in contact with more soldiers than I. They were around her while she was out in the courtyard after the evil general had her placed there. The soldiers came and went, laughing and poking fun."

She didn't tell him the worst . . . that some of those soldiers had even spit on Bright Star!

"Go inside your tepee while I care for my sister," Falcon Moon said. He glanced over at the sentry. "Brown Horse, you do not have to stay inside with the captive. Just stay outside. She deserves some privacy."

Wylena wasn't sure if he was doing this out of kindness, or because he didn't want his warrior to have any more contact with her in case she had been exposed to smallpox. She understood his caution about spreading the disease in case she had been exposed, and was just glad that he had paid heed to her and would now go to his sister and see that she was taken care of.

Wylena went inside the tepee and eagerly ladled stew into the bowl. She ate ravenously, but could not get Bright Star or her brother off her mind.

Even now, as she thought of Falcon Moon, she felt sensual heat in her belly, and she knew that warmth was not from eating the stew!

Chapter 8

The cope of Heaven seems rent and cloven
By the enchantment of thy strain;
And on my shoulders, wings are woven
—Percy Bysshe Shelley

Falcon Moon could not ignore the possibility that his sister had contracted smallpox, although he still didn't know if he should believe a white woman.

He immediately moved Bright Star so she was isolated from all of his people except himself and their shaman, Free Spirit, who was needed to see to his sister's welfare.

Although many warriors had already had contact with Bright Star, he still could not leave her where others might, too. Everyone loved her and would want to go to her and give her their best wishes and love.

Falcon Moon knew he couldn't allow Bright Star to spread the disease among their people. Thus far, no markings had surfaced on her lovely, soft copper skin.

Having delayed seeing his grandmother for too long already—after arriving at the village with so much else to see to—Falcon Moon went now and entered her tepee without announcing himself. It was that way between him and his precious grandmother. They never needed to warn each other that they were entering their lodges. Trust and love were strong between them.

"Grandmother, I am sorry that I could not come to you earlier," Falcon Moon said as he knelt on his haunches beside her before a softly burning fire in her fire pit.

The women of the village saw to her food, and even now something delicious-smelling cooked over her fire in a smoke-stained black pot acquired from a trading post many moons ago.

"I understand you have many important duties as chief, my grandson," Falling Water said. Smiling, she reached a quivering, bony hand out for him and touched his handsome face.

She gazed directly into his eyes, squinting in order to see him with her weakened vision.

"Word was brought to me that Bright Star is very ill," she said, slowly bringing her hand away from him to rest on her lap. She sat cross-legged on thick, rich pelts as close to the fire as she could get in order to feel the warmth on her face. These days she seemed to be much colder than usual.

Around her frail, bent shoulders she wore a blanket made by her younger hands many moons ago.

"Yes, she is ill," Falcon Moon replied, his voice drawn with concern.

He settled down on the pelts near the fire, which were wide enough for two people to sit on them.

"I was told that she might have contracted the white man's deadly disease called smallpox," Falling Water said, reaching up and flicking a lock of gray hair from her eyes, where it had fallen out of the knot above her head.

"That is so," Falcon Moon said. "We will have to wait and see what Ussen decides for my sister. Free Spirit is working his magic over her as we speak. I feel assured, myself, that she will be well soon."

"It is shameful why she was taken to that Mexican fortress," Falling Water said, her eyes flashing angrily at the very thought of her delicate and sweet granddaughter having become involved with a man that some of the Apache called a white devil.

It didn't matter that he was the brother of a holy man, loved by the Bear Band of Apache. Their people had seen too often how one brother could be good and loved by everyone who knew him, while his brother could be someone with whom no one wanted to associate.

It was so wrong that someone like Bright Star could give her love to such a man as Jeb Schrock. By having done so, she had gained only her capture by the Mexican soldiers and now an unknown sickness.

"Yes, it is a disgrace that my sister was treated so unjustly by the Mexican general," Falcon Moon said thickly. "But she is home now, and when she becomes well, I will make certain she never sees that white man again. Once the Mexican general takes someone in his heart as his enemy, that person cannot escape the vengeance planned for him. This time, because the Mexican soldiers could not find the scalp hunter who so many hate, it was my sister who paid for the white man's crime. No vengeance could be worse than what my sister has suffered, except death."

"I am going to go be with Bright Star," Falling Water said, her voice breaking with emotion at the thought of what her beloved granddaughter had endured at the hands of the Mexican general. She started to rise, but stopped when Falcon Moon placed a loving hand on her shoulder.

"I advise against it," Falcon Moon said, slowly easing his hand away from her shoulder once she was sitting back down on the pelts. "You are too frail, Grandmother, to chance catching my sister's illness, if she is suffering from something. She might be feverish from exposure to the cold. When she was not out in the sun, on the ground, made to stay there by the evil general, she was in a cold, damp cell. If she has a disease brought on by chill, that can be cured. We must pray that is all it is, but, Grandmother, again I say, you should not tempt fate by going to see Bright Star."

"I am our people's Holy Woman," Falling Water said, squinting again to gaze into her grandson's midnight-dark eyes. "I do not fear death for myself, but I do for our people. And . . ."

She paused, causing Falcon Moon's eyebrows to arch with question. "And?" he said when she still did not finish what she seemed ready to say. "What else were you going to say to your grandson?"

"I had another vision early this morning," Falling Water said. She reached out to take one of Falcon Moon's hands. "It was another vision of an earthquake. It came and destroyed our homes, along with everything down and away from our mountain. In my vision, I saw the Mexican fortress all but swallowed up by Mother Earth."

"You have had many visions such as this and we still have not had a serious earthquake," Falcon Moon said gently, so as not to disrespect his grandmother's faith in what her visions forecasted. "But I did recently feel the earth tremor. It made me recall your visions of an earthquake."

"You know, my grandson, that though revenge

is a part of the Apache philosophy, we believe that eventually Ussen, the Great Spirit that watches over us, will take vengeance upon our worst enemies. Like I have warned you before, after I saw another vision, Ussen will send some catastrophe of nature, such as an earthquake, to destroy our enemies, and there will be no necessity for any of our Apache people to raise a hand when Ussen deems the time is right for the killing."

Although Falcon Moon had heard all of this before, he listened quietly, as though this was the first time she had told him about this vision.

"My grandson, this catastrophe that I speak of might kill our people, too, but do not fear it happening," she softly reassured him while gently patting his hand. "Falcon Moon, four days after the catastrophe occurs, all Apache will be raised from the dead, to again possess our land. The buffalo will return to the plains, and the deer to the mountains, and life will be as it was—before the coming of the white people to land that once solely belonged to people of red skin, before the arrival of those Mexican soldiers who live way too close to our mountain, and who have gone too far this time in their interference among our people by having stolen away one of our innocent, beloved maidens . . . your sister."

She sighed, lowered her hand, and rested it on her lap, and gazed into the flames of the fire. "Yes, life will be good for our people and this good life will last forever with no more interferences from anyone who is not of our beloved Apache!"

Falcon Moon said nothing in response. Although he wanted to believe his grandmother's latest predictions, of having a new life with plentiful herds of buffalo, and no more whites or Mexican soldiers to deal with, he knew they would remain as only that: predictions from an elderly woman who wished to be powerful enough to bring about these things that would bless their people.

He knew that none of her predictions would come to pass. The buffalo were all but gone now, and he knew there would be no more. The white eyes were too hungry and greedy for things that were once solely the red man's to ever turn away from those things and allow them to be the red man's again. Yes, the whites had tasted the good life that once had been solely the red man's, and hungered for more!

"Falcon Moon, I do expect the earthquake to come, for you know how our people have feared the Mexicans' digging in sacred Mother Earth, because such diggings will cause an earthquake," Falling Water said, again watching the flames of the fire. "I see the earthquake as the Mountain Spirits, who are servants of Ussen, causing the shaking to avenge the desecration of Mother Earth."

She looked slowly over at Falcon Moon. "My grandson, the time is near when that earthquake will happen," she said thickly. "It will be as no others felt by any of us before. It will be one of devastation."

She slowly pushed herself up from the pelts. "Grandson, help me to Bright Star's tepee," she said. "I must see to her welfare myself."

"Grandmother, you will be risking everything to be with my sister," he said as she stood, resting her quivering hand on his shoulder as she urged him to his feet.

He took her by the hands and turned her to face him so that they could look into each other's eyes.

"Grandmother, if my sister does have smallpox and you get it, there will be no question as to whether or not you will survive," he said. "Your body is too weak to endure such fever as comes with the disease."

"Grandson, must I again remind you of my age?" Falling Water said. "Must I remind you that I survived the attack from renegades that took your mother's and father's lives? I was left for dead, but I survived. I am here now, am I not?"

She smiled as she reached up and gently patted his cheek. "Grandson, although I am almost blind, my body old, wrinkled, and ugly, I have outlived most of my age. I outlived my shaman husband, as well. If it is now time for me to go to my ancestors, so be it."

Falcon Moon saw that she was too determined to be with Bright Star for him not to take her

there. He slid an arm around her waist and ushered her from her tepee, then walked her to
where Bright Star lay on a bed of blankets and
pelts in a tepee far from any others.

Free Spirit smiled up at them, then resumed
caring for Bright Star.

Falcon Moon helped his grandmother rest on
pelts at the opposite side of his sister from where
the shaman was sitting, then slowly backed away,
and was soon on his way to his own lodge.

Falcon Moon sat down beside the fire in his
own tepee and became lost in thought about all
that his grandmother had said.

He thought over what she had said about her
prophecy of an earthquake. Now he believed that
it would happen, because although sometimes it
took a while, her visions were rarely false.

"I will accept Ussen's bidding, however it will
be done," he whispered to himself as he gazed
upward through the smoke hole, toward the blue
heavens.

He did hope that part of the vision was wrong.
He did not want to see all of his people taken, for
he could not envision the world changing as his
grandmother predicted.

Sighing, torn over how to feel about any of
this, especially the white woman whom he had
brought among his people, he stood and left his
tepee again.

He felt guilty for his doubts now that he
believed his grandmother's prophecy, but he

wondered whether it could happen as extensively as his grandmother said that it would.

But no matter how large or small it would be, he felt that perhaps he should go and warn Father Joshua. If Wylena was who she said she was, should he not take her home at the same time he went with his warnings to the priest?

He found himself drawn to the tepee where Wylena was being held captive.

Just as he stepped inside, Wylena appeared at the entrance, her eyes pleading with him.

"Please let me go home to be with my brother Joshua," she asked softly. "If you truly care about my brother at all—you say he is your friend— then surely you wouldn't want him worrying needlessly over something that could be corrected by sending me home to him. Was it not enough that I was made a hostage of that horrible Mexican general? Why should I be held as captive of the Apache when I have done nothing to warrant it?"

Falcon Moon saw and heard sincerity in her voice. It made him consider again that she might be telling the truth.

Yet he was still too angry at having seen her standing over Bright Star, not trying to help her in any way, to believe that she could be a sister to such a kind and caring man as Father Joshua.

He turned quickly on his heels and left the tepee, leaving Wylena standing there in shock.

She fell to the floor and cried, wondering where this would end.

Her heart pounded hard with fear. She crawled over to sit beside the fire and gazed heavenward through the smoke hole.

"Lord, please reach inside this young chief's heart and show him the truth," she sobbed. "Please, or I am not certain what my fate will be."

She recalled her mother reading Bible verses to her. They had offered her comfort during a time when she never knew what her father might do next. Suddenly she felt better, as though her mother were there, reading those verses to her again. It was as though her mother truly was there, in spirit!

"Thank you," she whispered, slowly smiling. "Thank you."

Chapter 9

Feeling quite lonely with both Wylena and Jeb still gone, Joshua stepped out into the darkness of night. He had spent the entire day in prayer.

He wrapped his arms around his waist as his eyes searched through the darkness.

He had decided that if Wylena had not returned by morning, he would chance going alone up Mount Torrance to see Falcon Moon and seek his help.

He hadn't taken this course of action yet because he knew that although he was a friend to the chief, Falcon Moon was the only one of that Apache band that he could trust not to harm him. Falcon Moon had taken his people in hiding high on the mountain for a purpose: to keep them safe from both white people and the Mexicans.

It was true that Joshua had gone there once without being harmed, but since then things had changed. His brother was a hunted man, and not only because he was rumored to be the scalp hunter, but because of Falcon Moon's sister.

Joshua was afraid that the Apache might believe the twins thought alike, as they were so alike in outward appearances. Therefore, could they not blame one brother for the other's sins?

"But Falcon Moon knows I am a man of God, of peace," Joshua whispered, walking slowly toward his garden. Although the soil was not the best, he had many vegetables that were ripening and ready to be picked.

If not for the strange circumstances of the past two days, he would have been out there gathering the fruits of his labor. Since his sister had arrived to live there, he expected her to harvest the vegetables and can them. He had watched his mother and sister canning at the end of every summer back in Illinois. He would never forget how hard they had worked.

But the canned foods always tasted especially good in the middle of the winter, so neither his mother nor his sister had ever complained about preparing them for the family under the undesirable circumstances of the summer's heat.

"Now am I to have to live without my sister, after already losing my sweet mother?" Joshua asked aloud. He reached his hands up toward the sky. "Dear sweet Lord, why has this happened?"

The sound of a horse arriving brought Joshua quickly from his prayer and troubled thoughts. He squinted into the darkness, as clouds had slid over the moon and taken away the light.

"Who is there?" he shouted, straining his eyes even more as he tried to see who was on the horse.

"It is I, your brother," Jeb shouted back at him.

A keen relief splashed inside Joshua's heart at hearing that at least one of his siblings was still alive.

He felt like giving his brother a lecture over worrying him needlessly, yet he decided to give in to the keen relief he was feeling and put any frustrated anger behind him.

Jeb rode up and drew a tight rein a few feet from Joshua. The clouds were slowly moving past the moon, giving Joshua a full look at his brother. He was relieved to see that he looked unharmed. That must mean he had had no serious confrontations while he was away from his safe haven.

"I'm sorry if I worried you," Jeb said as he dismounted. He slung his horse's reins around a hitching rail, then went to Joshua and gave him a gentle hug. "I'm sorry I worried Sis."

He stepped away from Joshua and looked toward the mission. He looked at the open door, hoping to see his sister standing there, also anxious to see him safely home.

"Our sister is gone," Joshua said flatly, causing

Jeb to look quickly at him. "She's been missing for as long as you've been gone." He hung his head, swallowed hard, then gazed into his brother's dark eyes again. "I have no idea where she is, Jeb. No idea whatsoever."

"What do you mean?" Jeb asked incredulously. "Why don't you know? What's happened?"

"Come with me," Joshua said, reaching a hand out toward his brother. "Come inside. We'll talk beside the fire. It's getting chilly out here. First it's so stifling hot, and then so cold you'd think you were in Illinois again. It's strange weather here, in the shadow of the mountain. Mighty strange."

They both went inside and sat down on their rocking chairs before the fire, Jeb anxiously awaiting an explanation for Wylena's absence, wondering how on earth his brother had allowed it to happen.

"So?" Jeb said, leaning his face closer to Joshua's. "Why don't you know where our sister is? Why did she leave, and when? Good Lord, Joshua, you know the dangers of a lone woman being out there where there are savage renegades lurking everywhere. Not to mention the white men who are the worst of criminals and have come out here to hide from the law they escaped from back in a more civilized land. And there are those Mexican soldiers."

"I noticed you gone at the same time as our

sister," Joshua said, his voice drawn. "I don't know when she left, or why, where she has gone, or with whom. I just know that she wouldn't be absent for this long on her own initiative, because she wouldn't want to worry us. So, Jeb, that could mean only one thing. She must have gone outside for a leisurely walk after our talk the other evening and someone must have grabbed her."

"When I left, I saw no one, not even her," Jeb said, forking an eyebrow. "So she must have gone outside before I chose to leave myself."

"Where have you been, Jeb?" Joshua asked, looking his brother squarely in his eyes. "Don't you know how I worry about you if you are not safely at home when daylight arrives? I thought you might have been caught and taken prisoner."

"I went as close to the Mexican border as I thought safe, then rode high onto a cliff that gave me a full view of the activity at the fortress down below," Jeb said, sighing heavily. "I didn't see Bright Star. I have no idea if she is even still alive."

He lowered his eyes, then looked at Joshua again. "I couldn't risk going any closer," he said thickly. "You know that she was being used as a decoy in order to lure me there to save her. I'd have been handing myself over to them on a silver platter had I gotten any closer."

"And so all the while you were out there on

your horse, you didn't catch any sight of a group
riding with a hostage?" Joshua asked drily.

"I saw no one but the Mexican soldiers inside
the fortress walls, and those who leave it to dig
for gold in a canyon on their side of the river,"
Jeb said. "You should've seen the packhorses
they use for transporting the dug-up gold. God
almighty, you'd not believe the amount of gold
they must be digging up. Makes me want to go
and grub, myself, but I know that's impossible. I
wouldn't get anywhere near it before being shot
dead for trespassing, even before they realized it
was me, the man they call the scalp hunter."

"Jeb, please don't use such language in my
presence," Joshua said softly. "You are taking the
Lord's name in vain each time you do that."

"Sorry, Joshua," Jeb uttered. "Sorry."

"At least you're home," Joshua said softly. He
pushed himself out of the chair. "You must be
tired from all the traveling you've done. Let's go
on to bed. Tomorrow is another day. If Wylena
isn't home by then, we've got to figure out a way
to get to Chief Falcon Moon's stronghold to see if
he will help us search for her."

"You can't be serious about including me on
that," Jeb said. He rose from his rocker. "I'd not
last a minute once I am spied on that mountain.
Nope, Joshua, I just can't do that. I like my hide
and hair too much to tempt fate by going anywhere near the Apache, especially in broad daylight on their mountain."

Jeb gave Joshua a manly hug, then left his
brother standing there watching him as he lifted
the tapestry aside that hid the stairs to his hideaway. He turned and gave his brother a lingering
look, then descended the stairs to the small space
that he called his room.

Joshua sighed heavily before starting for his
own room at the end of the short corridor. He
had to reach out for a chair to keep himself from
falling when the floor shook beneath his feet.
"An earthquake," he gasped, still holding on to
the chair until the tremor stopped.

He looked heavenward and thanked the Lord
that it was not a bad quake.

Then a thought came to him that made him
turn cold inside.

Jeb!

He was down in the dugout room. It could so
easily cave in on him, even with such a slight
tremor.

"Jeb!" he shouted, running and yanking aside
the tapestry.

He was glad when he saw Jeb standing at the
foot of the steps, holding a lit lantern and smiling
up at him.

"The devil didn't get me this time," Jeb said,
laughing deeply.

"Jeb, don't joke about such a thing," Joshua
said, sweat pearling on his brow in the aftermath
of the shock of thinking his brother might have
died so easily. "I think the time has come that

you should stay up here and chance someone coming before you can get hidden. It's not safe down there anymore, Jeb, if it ever was."

"I'm fine, Joshua, fine," Jeb said. He gave his brother a smile that he knew always won him over. "Go to bed, Brother. Like you said, tomorrow is another day. I'm certain I'll be seeing it with you. And until my name is cleared, it's not safe for me to be anywhere but here."

Joshua returned his brother's smile, dropped the tapestry in place, then went to the door and gazed up at the mountain that shadowed his home. Now he wondered if it was even safe enough to go up the mountain pass after this slight earthquake. Some of the paths closest to the edge might well have disappeared.

"Only Chief Falcon Moon and his warriors would know how else to come and go on that mountain if their usual passages were destroyed tonight," he whispered to himself.

He was torn with what to do, and when to do it. He was finding it harder and harder to accept that his sister was missing. He did not even know if she was still alive!

The thought of her death sent Joshua quickly to his knees. He again prayed for mercy for his sister.

He then gave thanks that his brother had at least found his way home again, safe and sound.

Chapter 10

O, what a war of looks was then between them!
Her eyes petitioners to his eyes suing
—William Shakespeare

Trembling, Wylena stood outside her assigned tepee. While she was sitting on pelts and mats beside the fire, she had suddenly felt everything beneath her tremor, and she knew immediately what had caused it.

Several years ago back home in Illinois, an earthquake had surprised everyone early one morning, even though they had been warned that Harrisburg and the land surrounding it lay near a fault line.

The day the ground shook in Illinois, much of her parents' crops were uprooted, and their chimney, made of stone, had crumpled to the ground as though it had turned into a pile of dust.

Tonight she had felt only slight tremors.

She knew a huge earthquake could come at any moment and cause the canyon walls that lay behind the village to collapse atop the tepees. Still trembling, and unable to go farther than just outside her tepee since the sentry was there to stop her, Wylena had never felt more alone.

She wondered if the slight earthquake had affected her brothers in any way. Had it been worse there at the foot of the mountain? What about Jeb down in his underground hideaway? Could . . . it . . . have caved in on him?

That thought brought tears to Wylena's eyes, blinding her so that she didn't see Falcon Moon hurrying toward her.

When he felt the ground move, he had looked from his tepee and seen Wylena, distraught and crying, run outside her own. He had not forgotten witnessing her moments of fear when she stepped into the cobwebs.

Realizing that she was the sort of fragile person who apparently feared things easily, he could not help but go to her and reassure her that she had nothing to fear, that he would make certain that nothing happened to her.

Yet how would he tell her that without revealing his true feelings about her?

He knew now that he could not help but have feelings for this woman. He cared for her. He truly could not contemplate now how she could be guilty of having played a role in his sister's abduction by the Mexican general. He also doubted that she could have been the general's woman— she struck him as too virtuous.

"Come back inside the lodge," Falcon Moon said as he took her gently by the elbow and led her through the entranceway. "You are safe. We have occasional ground tremors on our mountain, but only since the Mexican soldiers began digging in Mother Earth for gold."

"Why would that have anything to do with what just happened?" Wylena asked, deeply touched that this powerful Apache chief was taking the time to ease her fear. She knew she should mean nothing to him. She was only there as a part of his vengeance against the Mexican general. Hopefully, in time, he would come to realize his error and perhaps even apologize to her. But she doubted he would ever do that. Apologizing to a white woman, or perhaps anyone for that matter, might belittle him too much in the eyes of his people.

It truly didn't matter to her, though, whether he apologized. All she wanted was her freedom so that she could go and see if her brothers were all right.

"Sit," Falcon Moon softly urged as he helped her down onto the cushion of pelts.

Once she was sitting, Falcon Moon took the time to add a log to the fire in the fire pit before sitting down beside her.

Crossing his legs before him, he gazed over at her, drawing her eyes to him. Like the Apache women's, the white woman's eyes were dark and beautiful, with thick lashes shadowing them. He was glad that she no longer had tears in them. He must have succeeded at reassuring her and lessening her fear.

He wanted to make certain that nothing made her afraid, especially of him. Soon he would tell her that he had thought long and hard and reached the conclusion that he was wrong to have taken her. Although, by having done so, he had saved her from such a man as the Mexican general. In that, he was glad he had chosen to take her when he saved his precious sister.

He fought the urge to reach over, take her into his arms, and show her just how much he cared that the earthquake had frightened her so much.

He wanted to comfort her in that way, but he had no rights to her. He must quell the urges that were suddenly in his heart.

He would kiss her now if he could see any way around frightening her all over again by making her think he had come there not to help her in her time of fear, but to take advantage of her.

He cleared his throat nervously when he realized that too much time had passed without either one of them speaking. Their eyes had held on to each other's for much too long. Falcon Moon couldn't help but take pleasure from the way she gazed back at him. She did not do so any longer with fear, or even anger.

He felt that without actually saying the words, he had helped her realize that he was there for her in any way she would have him.

"You were about to tell me why you think the Mexicans digging for gold might have caused the tremors in the ground tonight," Wylena said, her heart throbbing inside her chest over how he had looked into her eyes for so long. She had seen something in the way he looked at her that touched her heart.

Had he suddenly realized that she had nothing to do with General Zamora? Did he believe her about being Joshua's sister?

Oh, Lord, she hoped all of these things were true, for she could not help her loving feelings for the handsome, young chief. She was certainly intrigued by him, but it was even more than that.

She had never desired a man's touch before, but every time this man touched her, even slightly, she felt a euphoria claim her that was new to her.

"It is true that the Mexicans are to blame for the uneasiness of the earth," Falcon Moon said, trying to keep emotion out of his voice.

"How could they be?" Wylena asked, hoping that he could not hear how hard her heart was pounding from her being this close to this man whom she now saw as a man, instead of her captor.

A captor did not go to a woman to try to make

her less afraid after a slight earthquake terrified her.

The way he looked at her told her that things had changed between them since he had roughly taken her from that dungeon at the Mexican fortress. At the time, she was glad to have been saved from a madman, yet afraid that she might be at the mercy of another. Now she knew that this man was anything but a madman. He was a man of heart, of courage, of all things that were good, not bad!

"Each time the Mexicans dig for gold, they weaken the mountain and earth even more," Falcon Moon said thickly. "Our people's Holy Woman, who is my grandmother, has foretold a large earthquake and I do not doubt it will happen. Gold is taboo to our people for this reason— we do not want to be the ones responsible for such a tragedy an earthquake would bring upon innocent people."

He looked away from her and gazed into the flames of the fire. "An Apache may pick up nuggets from the dry bed of a stream, but he is forbidden to 'grub' in Mother Earth for it. Mother Earth is the symbol of the sun and hence sacred to Ussen."

"What is Ussen?" Wylena asked, drawing his eyes back to her.

"Ussen is our people's Great Spirit, the same as the white people have their own God they pray to," Falcon Moon said. "If you are who you say you are, the sister to Father Joshua, then you are very aware of your God and the blessings that come from him. We gain blessings from Ussen."

"I *am* Joshua's sister," Wylena said. "Please believe me. He must be so worried about me. You could send someone to question my brother if you still do not believe me. He will tell you that I am his sister and he will ask you to bring me home to him."

Believing that she was sincere, Falcon Moon was still not one to leap too quickly into things, so for now he put what she said in a far corner of his heart. He would consider her statement when he was alone and could act on her request one way or the other.

A part of him didn't want to take her anywhere, even if he did know that she was Joshua's sister and that Joshua would be sick with worry about her. For now, he would enjoy having her company at least a while longer, for once she was gone, they would probably never see each other again, except for rare moments when he visited Joshua.

Up until now, he had never wanted to become closely involved with anyone of white skin. But now? He would mull it over some more and then decide.

"The Mexican soldiers grub in the body of Mother Earth on the Mexican side of the river, but it still causes our mountain to dance and shake his shoulders on the Apache side," Falcon Moon said. He noticed that she sighed loudly over his ignoring what she had said about her brother.

He shifted his legs, raised his knees up before him, and wrapped his arms around them. "I do not know if you are aware of this, but Mother Earth has already opened up more than once and swallowed some of the soldiers as they were digging for the gold," he said, looking slowly over at her when he heard her gasp of horror.

"This time the earth's trembling was only a warning," he continued. "The next time it could be much worse."

"The ground on your mountain trembled tonight," Wylena said tightly. "If your Ussen only wants to frighten the Mexican leader and his soldiers who work under him, why would Ussen cause your mountain to be involved at all?"

"Ussen is wise in all things," Falcon Moon replied, upset that she seemed to doubt the love of Ussen for the Apache people.

"Falcon Moon, please listen to me when I tell you that I am afraid for my brother Joshua," she said. Wylena knew she should refrain from mentioning Jeb in any respect. As far as anyone knew, Jeb was no longer in this area. "Please let me go to him and see if his mission was affected by the earthquake."

Falcon Moon rose slowly to his feet. He stood over her for a moment and gazed into her eyes.

Fighting off his wonder at how she was entrancing him, he turned and quickly left the lodge.

Just after stepping outside, he saw Bull Nose lurking behind a nearby tepee, staring at the one that housed Wylena.

Anger spurring him on, Falcon Moon hurried to Bull Nose and roughly placed his hands on the man's shoulders. He spoke heatedly to him. "Forget whatever you are thinking about the white woman," he growled. "She is my concern only!"

Bull Nose glared at Falcon Moon, yanked himself free of his grip, then stepped away from him quickly and hurried to his own lodge.

Falcon Moon stared at Bull Nose's tepee. He knew now, without a doubt, that he could no longer trust him and that the time was near when he must tell his people that Bull Nose was no longer a man of importance to them, that he did not deserve anything special. He certainly did not warrant ever one day being their chief.

But for now, Falcon Moon had something more important to tend to. He felt guilty for having spent so much time with the white woman when he should be spending more time with his beloved sister.

He walked toward the lodge where Bright Star was being isolated from everyone else. He was eager to see if she had improved in any way. He wanted to rest a hand on her brow to see if she still had a fever. He would also check her lovely copper face for any signs of smallpox.

If he saw even one tiny sore erupting there, he would die a slow death inside, for he would know that not only would his sister be doomed, but also his entire people!

Chapter 11

I will have my revenge,
I will have it if I
Die the moment after.
            —The Spanish Curate,
    John Fletcher and Philip Massinger

Finally settling down after the slight earthquake and seeing Falcon Moon, Wylena stretched out on her bed of plush pelts and blankets beside the soft, glowing embers of the fire in her tepee. Having not realized she was this tired, she was surprised to find herself ready to fall asleep.

With Falcon Moon on her mind—she wondered why he had left the tepee so quickly earlier, as though she had said something wrong—her eyes began to close.

Then a slight, strange scratching sound beside

her on the tepee wall caused her eyes to fly wide open again.

What she saw not far from her made her freeze with fear. She was so afraid she couldn't even scream as she watched four huge tarantulas crawl along the inside of the tepee toward the warmth of the fire. When one lost its footing and fell close to Wylena, she finally let out a scream that rattled her through and through. She scrambled to her feet and ran from the tepee.

Bull Nose smiled wickedly when he saw her, glad he had thought of something that would cause her to leave the tepee and fall right into his arms.

Yet she was running not toward him but instead to Falcon Moon. He must have heard her scream, for he had come quickly to see what was causing her such alarm.

Bull Nose grumbled to himself as Wylena fell into Falcon Moon's arms, clinging tightly to him as her whole body shook from the force of her sobbing.

With his plan gone awry, Bull Nose slunk away before his chief or the sentry assigned to stand outside the white woman's lodge could see him. He was determined to try again. He knew where he could get more tarantulas.

He had known about Wylena's fear of spiders since she had walked through the thick cobwebs that one time and been so shaken up.

He hurried to his lodge, relieved that no one,

not even the sentry, had seen him place the tarantulas inside the woman's lodge. He had managed to lift the buckskin fabric at the back of the
tepee and let the tarantulas out of the bag, onto
the side wall.

Now in his own tepee, he pulled his entrance
flap aside slightly, enough so that he could see
Wylena with his chief. A keen jealousy grabbed
him at the pit of his stomach when he saw Falcon
Moon holding the woman in his arms, as though
she belonged there!

"She belongs with no one but me," Bull Nose
grumbled. "She will be mine!"

Falcon Moon's heart was racing from his near-
ness to Wylena. Although he had tried, he had
not been able to rid himself of his attraction to
her. And now, the way she was clinging to him,
finding solace in his arms after having been
frightened, he did not want to let her go.

Her body against his felt so right!

Her eyes implored him as she gazed up into
his through her tears. His heart raced even faster.

"Falcon Moon, there are huge spiders in my
tepee," Wylena sobbed out as the saltiness of her
tears fell across her lips. "They are tarantulas.
How could they have gotten there? Had I not
seen them . . ."

She visibly shivered. "If I was asleep, they
might have crawled over my body," she said. "I
might have been bitten by not only one but all
four of them."

"Tarantulas?" Falcon Moon said, forking an eyebrow. He glanced quickly over at his sentry, who was looking back at him with a quiet apology in his eyes for not having been able to help her in her time of trouble.

Then Falcon Moon gazed into Wylena's eyes again. "I have no idea how they could have gotten there," he answered. "We have not been plagued by such spiders in our village. They are known to be elsewhere, along the canyon walls and beyond, but not ever in our village. You see, they are as afraid of humans as most humans are afraid of them."

"Then how . . . ?" Wylena asked. She felt a sensual warmth inside her belly when Falcon Moon reached out a hand to wipe her face dry of tears with the flesh of his fingers. "Where could they have come from?"

Falcon Moon had his own idea about this. He glanced toward Bull Nose's tepee just as Bull Nose dropped the entrance flap closed. He didn't want to believe the young man was capable of this, but it was hard to understand that young warrior's logic anymore.

Did he resent Wylena being there? Was that why he did it?

Or was it something else?

Did he think that he would look courageous by saving her once she discovered the spiders in her lodge?

No. He did not want to believe it. What was

important was making Wylena comfortable with her surroundings once again.

She must be made to feel safe in her own bed.

He had supplied her with some of the richest pelts that he had among his own for her to sleep upon. A body as fragile as hers needed more softness than others.

He looked over at Brown Horse, the sentry assigned to stand guard beside Wylena's lodge tonight. The sentry was no longer required to keep her captive, but to keep her safe from those who might want to harm her, such as the one who had placed the tarantulas in her tepee tonight.

"Brown Horse, go inside and remove the tarantulas," he shouted at him. His people were coming from their lodges, to see what was causing the commotion at a time when most were comfortably midst their blankets.

He looked around at his people and smiled. "It is nothing to worry yourselves about," he reassured them. "It is being taken care of."

"But what caused the woman to scream and leave her lodge?" one of the women asked curiously.

"Like I said, it is nothing to worry yourself over," Falcon Moon reassured her. He looked around him at his people. "Go on back to your beds. Warm yourselves beside your night fire. It is quite damp and cold tonight on our mountain."

Everyone seemed to nod in unison and soon the only ones who were left outside were Wylena and Falcon Moon as they waited for Brown Horse to exit the tepee.

"Is the warrior going to kill the spiders?" Wylena asked. She eased herself from Falcon Moon's arms and turned toward her tepee. Again her thoughts returned to the horrible sight of the spiders crawling along the inside wall of the tepee.

"No, they will not be killed," Falcon Moon said. "Those spiders do not harm humans, only frighten them."

Again he gazed over at Bull Nose's lodge. He knew in his heart that someone must have planted the spiders inside Wylena's tepee. He could not get past thinking that Bull Nose might be responsible. His attention was quickly drawn back to Brown Horse as he came from the tepee carrying a blanket with the spiders wrapped gently within the folds.

The sight of the blanket made Wylena visibly shiver again.

She watched as he took them away to set free.

"I hope he takes them far, far away from here," Wylena said loudly. She looked up at Falcon Moon. "What if there are more and I just didn't see them? What if Brown Horse didn't see them, either?"

"He is wise in all ways, one of my most loyal warriors, and I depend on him for many things,

so you can be assured that if there were more
tarantulas there, he would have found them,"
Falcon Moon reassured her. He gently reached
an arm around her waist. "Come. We will return
to your lodge. You can sleep now, knowing that
you are safe. I will even sit with you until you are
fully asleep."

Wylena gave him a look of wonder. She was
stunned to know that he could be this caring of
her. She wondered if he could see, and feel, her
attraction to him.

Although she had been brought there as his
captive, he had never mistreated her in any way.

"Thank you for making me feel safe," she
murmured to him.

He nodded, then ushered her inside the tepee.
He led her over to the bed of pelts and blankets.
"I will stay until you are asleep," he said softly.
"I want you to know that you can relax now and
sleep."

"Yes, I do feel as though I can," Wylena whispered, her heart racing at the thought of him sitting next to her as she fell asleep, so close she
could reach out and touch him.

She did so badly want to do more than just
touch him, but reminded herself all over again
that any such thoughts about him were mis-
placed.

She had to admit to herself that a part of her
never wanted to be separated from this man,
whose dark eyes mystified her.

As he sat down beside the fire, she went to her bed and curled up on its softness.

She felt somewhat ill at ease with him there. She did not fear him, but instead longed for him to touch her, kiss her, hold her, and never let her go!

She knew she shouldn't let her mind wander and indulge in these fantasies. The fact that she was there after being taken captive was truly enough.

When she returned home, things would be different, yet she would always remain his captive in one sense . . . a captive of his heart!

As he sat there gazing into the curling flames of the lodge fire, Wylena had the opportunity to look at him more directly before allowing herself to fall asleep.

She gazed at his powerful, muscled shoulders, his sculpted facial features, his beautiful, long, black hair that hung down to his waist. His belly was flat. His chest had no hair.

She had read somewhere that Indian warriors plucked each and every hair from their faces and chests every day. Knowing that this had left the chief's copper chest and face so smooth made her ache to run her hands over both!

She turned her gaze to the necklace he wore around his neck. "Why do you wear a necklace with a lone tooth hanging from it?" she blurted out, surprising herself with the suddenness of her question.

She blushed as he looked quickly over at her, but he did not seem disturbed by the personal question.

"I wear a tooth from a bear because the bear is my power; it is my medicine," he said quietly.

"I see," was all that she could think to say, but in truth, she was seeing more and more things that were mystical about this man, and his Apache people. She was more intrigued by the Apache every minute.

"Also, my people are of the Bear Band of Apache," he quickly added.

He reached out and gently touched her cheek as he smiled into her eyes. "Sleep," he said thickly. "Tomorrow is not that far away."

"But you need sleep, too," Wylena said, trembling from ecstasy at the feel of his hand resting on her cheek, hoping he couldn't tell the effect he was having on her.

"I shall sleep," he said, slowly easing his hand away from her. "After I see that you are asleep, so then I shall return to my lodge to sleep, too."

Wylena smiled at him, felt her eyes drifting slowly closed, then fell into that black void of sleep as Falcon Moon continued to watch her.

He studied everything about her, but especially her face and its sweetness.

He just knew that a woman like her could not love a man like the Mexican general. How could he have, even for one minute, thought that she could?

She was all sweetness, while the general was all ruthlessness.

Yes, Falcon Moon did believe her.

He would soon send someone to ask Father Joshua if his sister had come to live with him. Then Falcon Moon's doubts, as slight as they were now, would be gone.

Once that happened he would be free to love this woman. He hoped she would love him, too. He was encouraged by the emotion he saw in her eyes and her behavior. He reached over and smoothed the blanket over her. He leaned down and brushed a soft kiss across her lips, then rose and left quickly, before he did something reckless that he might regret later.

He hurried to his feet, and was gone without looking back.

Chapter 12

The sun was just barely visible along the horizon when Falcon Moon was awakened by a troubled voice. He recognized it as belonging to Brown Horse, the warrior he had assigned to stand outside Wylena's tepee.

Falcon Moon hurried from his bed and slid into a breechclout and his moccasins. As he came through the entrance flap, he flipped his hair back from his eyes and put a headband in place.

When Brown Horse spoke Falcon Moon's name again, this time in a more frantic tone, Falcon Moon stepped outside into the cool morning air, where fog was just beginning to lift from the land and tepees.

"My warrior friend, what brings you to your chief's lodge this early morn?" Falcon Moon asked. Yet he already knew by the look in his warrior's eyes that the man was very troubled about something.

"My daughter has grown ill," Brown Horse said, his voice drawn. "My wife, Pretty Sun, came moments ago and alerted me. I need to be with them. Our shaman, Free Spirit, has been summoned. I want to be there to hear what he says about my daughter's illness."

He swallowed hard as he glanced over at the tepee in which Bright Star still lay in isolation, then turned back to his chief with a frenzied look in his eyes. "My chief, my daughter might have the same ailment that causes your sister still to sleep," he said, his voice breaking. "Smallpox. What if . . . my daughter and your sister have that dreaded, deadly disease?"

"There have been no signs except the fever that Bright Star might possibly have that disease." Falcon Moon tried to reassure him as he rested his hand on his friend's shoulder.

"Your sister has had the fever for so long," Brown Horse said, searching his chief's eyes. "Surely you are beginning to believe she might not . . . survive whatever has downed her."

"Her mistreatment at the hands of the Mexican soldiers, as ordered by their general, is why my sister is so ill," Falcon Moon said, lifting his hand away from Brown Horse. "So go now to your daughter with less concern because I do not believe she has anything that will take her life.

Children are prone to fevers from time to time. You know that, my friend, because as children we had our own fevers that worried our mothers and fathers."

"Yes, I recall many times when my skin was hot, yet still I am concerned for my daughter's welfare. But I will not think any longer that it is caused by the white man's disease, for if Bright Star shows no signs of smallpox, then surely she does not have it," Brown Horse said, sighing heavily. "I must go now to be at my daughter's bedside. I want to hear our shaman's words that will lessen my worries even more than you already have."

Suddenly Brown Horse embraced Falcon Moon. "You are a good chief," he said thickly. "You are a good friend."

Falcon Moon returned his embrace, then watched as he broke into a soft trot toward his tepee, where soft spirals of smoke lifted from the smoke hole of the lodge.

Realizing that Wylena had been left vulnerable without a warrior standing outside her lodge, but reluctant to disturb any of his warriors this early in the morn, Falcon Moon hurried to her assigned lodge and went inside without speaking her name.

He expected her to still be asleep and did not want to alarm her by suddenly awakening her.

But he didn't want to stand outside, either, when he could be inside with her, watching her sleep.

He thought that when he saw her beginning to awaken, he would slip quickly from the tepee, so that she would not know that he had been there, gazing upon her loveliness, though he still warred inside his heart over who she was.

As he sat down beside the fire, not far from where Wylena peacefully slept, her dark hair spread out on the blanket beneath her like fine silk, he watched her sleep.

He recalled the first time he had seen her as he was high above the Mexican fortress, spying on how his sister was being treated.

He had puzzled over how she could just stand there looking at his sister, who lay out in the sun with flies buzzing around her bloodied mouth, and not offer her any assistance. He also recalled how she had set the bowl of food on the ground near his sister's mouth, but not awoken her to tell her that food was there for her to eat. His hate for the white woman had been instant.

After hearing her explain that she was forbidden to help Bright Star, Falcon Moon believed that she was Joshua's sister and had been taken for the same reason as his sister.

"I wish that I could see inside your soul and know your innocence with certainty," Falcon Moon whispered. "If you are Father Joshua's sister, he must be feeling the same as I felt when I first knew that something had happened to my sister, when she did not return home as expected."

It was time to find the truth behind Wylena's words—he would send a warrior to the mission to question Father Joshua. Then Falcon Moon would know!

He did so badly hope that what he wished would be true. He cared for this woman deeply and ached to hold and kiss her.

If he found that he was truly free to do so, he would approach her with his feelings, and see how she felt about him.

He did think that she must not hate him for what he had done, for she spoke gently to him when they were together, and he saw too much in her eyes that made him know she had feelings for him.

When Wylena stirred in her sleep, Falcon Moon stiffened. He knew that it was not appropriate for her to find him sitting there observing her as she slept. He stood quietly and gave her another questioning look, then turned and left the tepee just as his shaman stepped up to him with news that sent rushes of happiness into his heart.

"My sister is awake?" Falcon Moon asked, searching Free Spirit's old eyes. "Bright Star . . . is awake?"

"Bright Star is awake and is asking for you," Free Spirit said, nodding. "Come. She is so anxious to see you. And she no longer has a fever. Her skin is cool to the touch. Her eyes are bright."

They walked together to the tepee where his sister had spent her time in isolation after arriving back in the village.

He hurried inside the tepee and found Bright Star sitting up and feeding herself some soup from a wooden bowl. That alone made Falcon Moon realize just how much better she was.

With the disappearance of the fever had come the return of her strength, at least enough for her to sit up.

"Bright Star," Falcon Moon said as he went and knelt down before her on his haunches.

He reached a hand out and tested her flesh for hotness. He smiled broadly when her skin felt cool to his touch. He also saw how bright and eager her dark eyes were as she smiled at him between bites.

"You are a miracle, sister," Falcon Moon said, laughing softly. "The miracle is that you were so ill yesterday and are so well today."

He looked over his shoulder at his shaman. "Thank you," he said sincerely. He looked past him at the entrance flap, then into his shaman's eyes again. "You are needed now in Brown Horse's lodge. His daughter is quite ill."

"I know, and I was already there before I came to you with the news of your sister," Free Spirit said. "I knew that you would want me to go where I was needed most. Brown Horse came to me and spoke of his daughter's illness. I hurried to her and made medicine for her. She is already better and sleeping sweetly. When she awakens, she will be well enough to make her parents smile again."

"I am in the presence of two miracle people, it seems," Falcon Moon chuckled. "My sister and my shaman!"

"I will leave you now and go to my own lodge," Free Spirit said. He gathered into his large buckskin bag the materials he had used to heal Bright Star. "I must prepare more medicine for whoever needs it next."

After his bag was filled with his healing materials, he slung it across his frail, bent shoulders, smiled from Falcon Moon to Bright Star, and left.

"That is all that I can eat for now," Bright Star said. She handed the half-emptied bowl to Falcon Moon. "But I shall want more later."

First he set the bowl and the spoon just outside the entrance flap for the maiden who'd brought them to pick them up for cleansing. He went back and sat down beside Bright Star as she drew a brush made of cactus fiber through the long, thick strands of her beautiful hair, unsnarling the ends. She then twisted it into two long braids.

Falcon Moon knew the women of the village had been taking turns tending to her hair and body while the shaman had gone outside to visit with his friends around the fire.

Falcon Moon's sister smelled clean, like river water, and she was dressed nicely in a fringed and beaded dress—a dress she had made with her own hands. It was brought to her by a woman who knew she would rather wear her own clothes, even while she was sick.

"Tell me how you rescued me," Bright Star requested, sighing as she stretched out again on her bed, only now realizing that she might be rid of the fever, but not the weakness that had come with it. She turned on her side and faced Falcon Moon. "Thank you for coming for me. I . . . I . . . would not have lasted for much longer."

She hurriedly leaned up on an elbow. "My brother, there was a woman in the same cell I was placed in who became my friend," she rushed out. "Her name was Wylena. Do you . . . could you . . . know what might have happened to her? You see, she was there for the very same reason that I was taken there. It was because of her brother Jeb. We were both there to lure Jeb to the fortress to rescue us, for you see, he is being accused of being the scalp hunter everyone hates."

While she was talking, saying things that made Falcon Moon's heart race with gladness to hear that Wylena was truly who she said she was, he could hardly hold himself back from going to her immediately.

She was who she said she was.

His heart raced more as his sister told him all she could remember happening at the fortress. He grabbed on to Wylena's name as though it were a song in his heart each time his sister mentioned her.

He was eager to leave this lodge and go to the other, where he could see the white woman he now knew that he loved. He wanted to look into her eyes and tell her how sorry he was for ever having doubted her.

He wanted to take her into his arms and hold her to his heart, and then if she would allow it, he would kiss her.

The very thought of her lips on his made a sensual, almost painful warmth stir in his gut.

He had never loved before. He had put his people first at all times. Always!

But now he needed Wylena with every beat of his heart. He only hoped he could have her.

He held himself tightly at bay as he waited for his sister to give him the moment he needed to go to Wylena and look upon the face of true, adorable innocence!

Suddenly he remembered something that made the color drain from his face.

He had left Wylena to come to his sister in haste. After hearing the good news of Bright Star's recovery, he had left without assigning anyone to watch over her and keep her safe!

Chapter 13

Under the arch of life . . .
I saw
Beauty enthroned; and though her gaze struck awe,
I drew it in as simply as my breath.

—Dante Gabriel Rossetti

Bull Nose held a corner of his entrance flap slightly aside, just enough for him to look outside. He was watching the activity at Wylena's lodge. He hoped to find an opportunity to sneak in her tepee and threaten her with the possibility of more tarantulas if she didn't cooperate with what he wanted of her.

He smiled slyly to himself as he saw Brown Horse leave, hurrying to his lodge for some reason, with Falcon Moon then going inside Wylena's tepee. But Falcon Moon had not been there long before he left again, having been summoned to his sister's lodge.

Since then, no one else had entered nor stood outside to guard Wylena.

His heart pumped wildly inside his chest—he finally had the opportunity he needed to go there and get from her what he desperately ached to have.

It was not so much that he had been attracted to her, a woman whose skin was white. It was because his chief, who had scorned Bull Nose in front of their people more than once, obviously had feelings for the woman. He chuckled under his breath to think that once his chief discovered that this woman was soiled by another man's hands, he would no longer want her.

Falcon Moon would cast her aside as though she was no more than Bull Nose, whom Falcon Moon no longer saw fit to follow him into chieftainship.

Yet he would never allow his chief to know that it was he who had taken away this petite woman's virginity.

Bull Nose would love to take credit but did not want his chief to have the ammunition that Falcon Moon would need to send Bull Nose from his Apache people, a banished man.

It would be sufficient for Bull Nose to know that he had done this to his chief. He could enjoy ensuring that his chief finally did not receive something he wanted so badly. As it was, anything Falcon Moon wanted, he got. His Apache people, who adored him, made that happen.

Only Bull Nose would know the secret of how Wylena had been robbed of her virginity. He would threaten her with her life to keep her silent.

He knew that he had to move in haste, for he could not allow anyone to come to Wylena's lodge while he was there or see him leave with her.

He had been preparing for this the moment the chief chided him in the presence of many of their people. At that time, he had not known how he would get back at Falcon Moon for embarrassing him so heartlessly in front of an audience.

It was when Bull Nose became aware of Falcon Moon's special feelings for the white woman that Bull Nose had set his plans in motion. Some time ago, while exploring, he had found a cave far from the village. He knew that there he could have full privacy away from everyone.

He had established a second home there with blankets, food, a rifle and knife, and a fire pit already prepared with wood. The most important supply that he had stored in the cave was his collection of spiders that he had caught, among them tarantulas.

One look at them and Wylena would be completely at his mercy. He needed to assure her silence for when he released her to return to Falcon Moon's arms.

No, she would not dare reveal what he did to her, or she would know that she would die by lethal spider bites!

Yes, he would take the white woman there and he could have his private moments with her with no one being the wiser . . . especially his chief!

He knew that Falcon Moon would be at his sister's tepee long enough for Bull Nose to take Wylena.

As for Brown Horse, Bull Nose knew how ill his daughter was. Brown Horse would not return to his post outside Wylena's lodge anytime soon.

Bull Nose had placed a spider inside Brown Horse's child's blankets, a spider whose bite made one seriously ill, but usually would not kill.

Bull Nose was knowledgeable of spiders, from having studied their activity when he was alone in the forest on his mountain. He had watched insects caught in their webs and noted how long it took the spiders' venom to take effect. If the bite only paralyzed the insect, then Bull Nose knew that particular spider was not a lethal one.

Afraid that he had already taken too much time, with every moment precious now that he had decided to carry out his plan, Bull Nose clutched the bag holding the tarantulas close to him and crept slowly from his tepee. He stopped and looked carefully from side to side, and then forward, to see if anyone was watching.

When he saw that everyone was too involved with their own personal morning activities to pay heed to the lodge that housed the white woman, he made a mad dash inside Wylena's tepee.

Wylena was sitting beside the fire, in deep thought over her feelings for Falcon Moon, wishing he were there with her, but she jumped in alarm when she heard someone come into the tepee.

She looked over at the entrance and grew pale when she saw Bull Nose standing there. In his eyes she saw a wickedness she had never seen before on anyone, not even the cruel Mexican general, or her own father.

Bull Nose was breathing hard and clutched a bag to his right side.

She grew cold with fear as she considered why he might be there. His demeanor, his eyes, the strong pulsebeat at the side of his neck, told her he had plans for her that were not pure. She could not believe that he would chance coming there like this, knowing that his chief could arrive at any moment and find him there.

"Why are you here?" Wylena asked as she slowly rose from the blankets and pelts. "What do you want?"

"I do not have a lot of time for small talk," Bull Nose said, and inched closer to her. "Listen carefully to what I tell you. Then do as I say, or else."

"What are you . . . going . . . to make me do?"

Wylena said, her voice breaking as she slowly stepped away from him, then tripped over a log she had placed there only moments ago, ready to put it on the fire.

She fell hard on her back, then had no time to get up, for Bull Nose was there, straddling her, with a look in his eyes that made Wylena realize why he was there. He did not have to tell her. It was in his every move, in the quivering of his lips as he set the bag aside and reached a hand up inside her dress.

"Do not scream, or do anything that will draw attention and bring someone to your rescue, or I will let loose the tarantulas I have in this bag," Bull Nose said, chuckling when he saw the terror in her eyes as his hand brushed against her.

"Please . . . don't . . . ," Wylena begged, feeling disgustedly ill as one of his hands stroked her where no man's hand had been before. His other hand still held on to the bag. "I beg you. . . . Please don't do this. Falcon Moon will know. He will kill you."

"For taking a white woman's virginity?" Bull Nose said angrily, lust in his eyes. "I think not. Do you not know that you are our people's enemy? You are an enemy captive. It is only right that I have free rein of you, even though my chief has warned me to stay away from you."

He leaned his face closer to hers. "I have wanted your body from the moment I saw you," he said huskily. "And so I will have you. By doing so, I will achieve two goals. One . . . my chief's disappointment in you when he discovers you are not a virgin. Two? I will best a chief who has humiliated me by telling me I am no longer worthy of being chief after him. But I'm not seducing you here. I will take you elsewhere."

"You surely know that you can't get away with this," Wylena hissed. She glanced at the bag of tarantulas, now realizing who had put the others in her tepee to frighten her.

Then she glared up into Bull Nose's eyes. She had to make a choice, and quickly.

"I can see your mind working," Bull Nose said. He grabbed her by a wrist, still holding her in place with his body. "I could be banished for what I am about to do, but just you remember this. I will find you later. I will not bother placing tarantulas on your body, but spiders I know will kill you instantly. Now do you dare cause trouble for this Apache warrior? Or will you cooperate and let me have my way with you?"

"I will not allow this to happen," Wylena exclaimed.

She put her fears of spiders behind her as she raised a knee and sank it deeply into his groin. He let out a howl of pain so loud, she knew that everyone in the village had to have heard.

She saw the pain she had caused to him by the look in Bull Nose's eyes and how he had rolled away from her, grabbing hold of himself.

Breathing hard, knowing that she had to move

quickly, she rolled farther away from him. She scrambled to her feet, ran to the entrance flap, and shoved it aside. Just as she got outside, she collided with a hard body. She bounced backward a fraction, then fell to the ground just outside the tepee.

"Wylena?" Falcon Moon asked, looking down at her incredulously, and then at the closed entrance flap. He had heard someone let out a cry of pain, and knew it was not Wylena, for it was a man's voice.

"He's in there," Wylena sobbed as Falcon Moon gently helped her up from the ground.

"Who?" Falcon Moon asked, his eyebrows forking.

"Bull Nose," Wylena said. She watched the entrance flap, waiting for Bull Nose to try to make a fast exit.

There was silence everywhere around her as the people who had been outside tending to their morning chores stopped and were now staring at her. They watched as Falcon Moon rushed inside her tepee. Wylena tensed as she heard the sounds of knuckles hitting against flesh, and then heard the same yelp of pain she had heard only moments ago when she had gotten the best of Bull Nose.

She just could not believe that the warrior could be so daft as to think he could get away with what he had tried. He had not counted on her being brave or strong enough to fight him off. She smiled, flipped her hair back from her face, then stood there proudly when Falcon Moon dragged Bull Nose by his hair outside the tepee for everyone to see.

Falcon Moon leaned into Bull Nose's face. "You just made the biggest mistake of your life," he growled.

"I do not understand how," Bull Nose had the courage to say back to his chief. "The white woman is an enemy . . . a captive. Why should the chief of a powerful Apache people care so much for a white woman?"

"No matter the color of her skin, she is a woman wrongly being manhandled by a man. A man who was supposed to set good examples for the youth of our village," Falcon Moon said strongly. "You, the one chosen to be my successor, have just proven, not only in my eyes, but in the eyes of all of our people, that you are not worthy. I have had enough. Our people have had enough. You must leave, Bull Nose. You are banished."

Wylena stood stiffly watching Bull Nose's humiliation as Falcon Moon told everyone why he had entered Wylena's tepee.

The Apache people followed Falcon Moon as he continued to drag Bull Nose to the far edge of the village, past the corralled horses and the large communal garden.

Falcon Moon dragged him until they reached the cliff side that made a sharp drop on one side of the mountain. A tiny path wound around the other side of the wall and led to the bottom of the mountain.

Bull Nose looked pleadingly at Falcon Moon as his chief finally removed his hand from Bull Nose's hair.

"Leave," Falcon Moon grumbled. He stood broad shouldered in a buckskin shirt and breeches, the fringes of which fluttered in the soft breeze. "Take your shame with you. Do not turn your eyes back toward us. Once gone, always gone."

While all of this was happening, Wylena kept thinking about Bull Nose's warning about the spiders, and how he said he would find her and kill her the next time they met face-to-face. She wondered if he truly would come for her once she left the mountain.

He knew where her brother's mission was.

It would be so easy for him to sneak up one night and let loose several poisonous spiders into the mission while she and her brothers slept—spiders that would kill them all.

She also felt uneasy over being, in part, the cause of Bull Nose's banishment. Surely there were those among this band of Apache who would blame her, not Bull Nose, for the chief deciding to banish him. Had she not been there, surely whatever differences he had with his chief could have been worked out.

But attempting to rape a woman? That was a very different sort of crime.

The more she thought about it, she could not help but be filled with fear of what this banished warrior might do. He surely could not hate anyone now as much as he hated her. When he stopped and gave her a look over his shoulder that sent chills up and down her spine, she began to tremble with fear. She could not hold in the tears that splashed from her eyes.

When Falcon Moon turned to her, he saw her tears. He realized she must be afraid of the look that he had seen Bull Nose give her before going down the mountainside with no belongings, aside from his damaged pride.

Falcon Moon knew that look had shaken Wylena, and he understood. Surely she feared Bull Nose's need for vengeance against both of them.

Forgetting that he had a large audience, as his people still stood there, Falcon Moon went to Wylena and drew her gently into his embrace.

"I deeply apologize for all that has come into your life since the moment I chose to use you as a way to avenge what happened to my sister," he said thickly. He held her still. "My sister. She told me everything. You are innocent of all that I accused you of. I will make it up to you, especially what almost happened today. Had he succeeded . . ."

"But he didn't," Wylena murmured, clinging to him.

She felt protected. Oh, Lord, she needed his

arms. She needed him. She was a woman whose heart was lost to this wonderful Apache chief.

When she again remembered Bull Nose's threat she brushed the thoughts away.

Surely that man would not try any of the things he had warned her about. He had to be afraid of the wrath of his chief!

Yet if he was daft enough to have gone into her tepee today, with his chief only a short distance away in another lodge, wouldn't Bull Nose probably chance anything to harm her?

She brushed such concerns from her mind as she eased herself from Falcon Moon's arms. She gazed up into his eyes. "You said that your sister is awake?" she murmured. "And she told you everything?"

"Everything," he said, placing an arm around her waist to usher her away from the crowd. They began to disperse and return to their normal daily duties. Except for two people.

Bull Nose's parents.

They were on their knees close to the path where their son had left the village. They looked heavenward, pleading with Ussen to keep their son safe and to forgive him for all of the wrong that he had done his chief, and therefore his beloved Apache people.

Wylena heard their prayers. She looked over her shoulder at them, pitying them the loss of their son. It was the same for them as if he had died.

Falcon Moon saw her look back toward the mourning mother and father. "In time they will get past their mourning and accept that they did all that they could to guide their son along the right path of life," he said softly. "One can only do what one can. The rest is left to the child. This child had everything, but as a man he chose to walk the wrong path—that made him lose all that he might have had. He is unworthy of your concerns."

Wylena knew that once she returned to her brother's mission, she would be vulnerable without Falcon Moon to protect her.

"Come with me," Falcon Moon said, interrupting her troubled thoughts again. "I will take you to my sister, and then I will return you to your brother."

A part of Wylena was anxious to see both her brothers, but she also hated leaving Falcon Moon. She was afraid that she would never see him again once they went their separate ways.

She gazed up at him, wishing there could be more between them that would assure he would never forget her. She smiled uneasily at him, for despite her best efforts, she could not quickly cast Bull Nose's threats aside!

Chapter 14

Leaving the stronghold and going down Mount Torrance was much different for Wylena from her journey up the mountain. She had been blindfolded all of the way as she traveled up this dangerous pass. But she had been aware of the dangers of the climb up that pass, anyway, as the horse's hooves scattered rock, sending it down the sides of the mountain.

Wylena was on Falcon Moon's horse with him now, sitting behind him, her eyes wide as she held on for dear life to his waist, as the pass grew narrower every few feet. She tried not to look, but when she heard more rock falling and hitting the sides of the mountain, her eyes were drawn there to see just how dangerous it was. She gasped, feeling the color drain from her face when she saw just how close to the edge they rode.

"I can tell by the way you are holding on much more tightly than before that you are afraid," Falcon Moon said. He glanced over his shoulder at her. "Do not be afraid. I have traveled this pass countless times. My horse has, too. My stallion understands the danger that lays so close. He always gets me safely where I want to be when we travel up and down this same pass."

"How much longer until we reach a wider stretch of land?" Wylena asked, her voice sounding foreign to herself; it was so filled with fear.

She imagined how only one slip of a hoof would cause herself, Falcon Moon, and his white steed to tumble down the mountainside.

"It is near," Falcon Moon said, looking straight ahead again and steadying his reins as he watched every step his horse took.

He recalled an incident one fateful day when one of his warriors' steed had lost its footing. He would never forget hearing the cry of terror as his warrior fell through the air. Then the sound of silence that ensued after both his friend and the horse had hit solid ground down below.

Wylena knew that she must get her mind off

the cold fear that grabbed at her insides. Falcon
Moon might try to reassure her, but she still
could not help but be terrified over where she
was.

She tried to focus on other things besides a fall
down the mountainside to help get her past this
horrendous fear. She focused her eyes on Falcon
Moon's bare, muscled back as she sat there so
close to him and smelled the familiar scent of the
young chief.

He always smelled of fresh river water and
something else akin to the smell of pine, the
scent she had enjoyed back in Illinois when she
was with her family in their wagon traveling
through a pine forest.

She also gazed at Falcon Moon's hair.

As it fluttered against his back, the scent of its
cleanliness wafted to her. And, ah, how beautiful
his hair was as it hung in place from the beaded
headband he wore around his brow.

Like so many times before, in the short
amount of time Wylena had spent with Falcon
Moon, he wore only a breechclout and moccasins.

He carried no weapon today other than his
rifle, which was safely stored in its gun boot at
the right side of the stallion, and a knife sheathed
at his waist. Because she was sitting so closely
behind him, there had been no way he could position a quiver of arrows at his back, so he had
left his bow and his arrows behind at his tepee.

She wished she were free to run her hand up and down the sleekness of his back, to revel in his closeness. She could even envision placing her lips there, and kissing his copper flesh!

She blushed at where her thoughts had taken her, but she could not pretend she didn't care for him. If she was honest with herself, she had to admit it went much further than just caring.

She loved him.

She was so afraid that once he left her at her brother's mission and they went their separate ways, she might never see him again. She wished there could have been more between them while she was at his village to assure her that he would never forget her.

"I am so glad that your sister is doing so well," Wylena exclaimed. She knew talking was smarter than allowing herself these fantasies about a man she surely would never be with again. "I am so glad that she told you I was innocent of all that you accused me of. I do regret not being able to talk with her and tell her good-bye before leaving the village."

"She is much better, but still she needs rest," Falcon Moon said, again glancing back at her over his shoulder. "She was awake long enough to tell me the truth about you. She also managed to eat some nourishing soup. But she was soon asleep again, although this time I knew it was to rest. I knew for certain that she would awaken again, whereas before, as she slept so soundly in

that strange sort of sleep, I had no idea if she
would awaken, or die."

"I am so very happy that she is doing much
better," Wylena murmured. "How I wish I could
have seen and thanked her."

"I shall tell her that when I return to the
stronghold," Falcon Moon said. "She did speak
highly of you. And she was so glad to know that
you were freed from that horrible dungeon
where you both were imprisoned by the Mexican
general."

"I only wish that they would have treated her
with more kindness," Wylena said with a catch in
her voice as she recalled seeing General Zamora
beat the tiny, innocent maiden with a whip. "Your
sister gave the general no reason whatsoever for
him to have treated her so inhumanely. And I understand how it must have looked to you to have
seen me unscarred and well, while your sister was
scarred and bloody from her mistreatment. I . . . I
still do not understand why they made such a difference between us."

"It was because my sister's skin is red and
yours is white," Falcon Moon said thickly. "The
Mexican general would rather my people be
wiped from the face of the earth. He would do so
himself if he had the chance. He has the same
feelings for the red man as most whites have."

"I am white and I have no ill feelings toward
your people," Wylena murmured. "Nor do my
brothers."

That brought a glare from Falcon Moon as he looked quickly at her. "One of your brothers is even worse, in my way of thinking, than the Mexican general," he said, his voice drawn. "A man who goes around the countryside killing and scalping innocent people is not a man at all. He is an animal, one that should be shot at first sight."

Hearing the hate in his voice, and what he wished to do to her brother Jeb, brought a new sort of fear to Wylena's heart . . . fear for her brother's welfare.

"Jeb is an innocent man," she cried out. "What people are saying about him is horrendously untrue. He is a man of God. There is no way he could be responsible for all that is being said about him. And your sister loves him. Does that not tell you something? Bright Star is so sweet and pure. She would not love a heartless killer, now, would she?"

"It is because she closes her eyes to the truth, the same as you do, that makes her defend that man who wanders the night, killing and scalping," Falcon Moon said, slapping the reins of his horse as flat land finally stretched out before them and they left the mountain behind them.

"I was raised with both brothers, and our mother read the Bible to us children every night before we went to bed, so how can anyone even consider that one of us might have turned out to be so evil?" Wylena asked.

She wondered whether defending her brother so fervently to Falcon Moon was in effect destroying any chance of ever seeing him again.

She now wished wholeheartedly that she had never begun this dialogue with Falcon Moon about her brother. It had wasted her precious remaining time with him, which Wylena had wanted to spend making memories she could cling to when she was no longer with him.

Now that was ruined! Absolutely ruined!

She saw the mission up ahead. The steeple reached heavenward like a beacon that was leading her home to her brothers. They rode in silence the rest of the way to the mission.

When they were only a few feet away, Joshua caught sight of them and left the mission in a run, his black robe almost tripping him as it twisted around his legs in his haste to reach Wylena. She could see him smile radiantly at her, his relief evident on his face as he reached his hands out toward her.

"Wylena!" he cried, not taking his eyes off her. "Wylena, oh, Wylena, my prayers have brought you safely home to me!"

When Falcon Moon drew a tight rein beside Joshua, Wylena slid quickly from the horse and fell sobbing into her brother's arms.

"There, there." Joshua gently stroked her back. "You are home. You are safe."

"I am so sorry that I worried you," Wylena said, her voice catching as she leaned away from him so that they could gaze into each other's eyes. "It all happened so fast, Joshua. I . . . I . . . was taking a walk in the moonlight because I was finding it hard to sleep, and then . . . then . . . suddenly a hand was clasped across my mouth, to keep me quiet, and then I was silenced by a gag wrapped around my mouth."

"And?" Joshua said, his eyes searching hers. Falcon Moon was forgotten for the moment. He slid from his saddle and stood closely behind Wylena holding his reins.

"I was taken to the Mexican fortress and put in a dungeon. For a while I was imprisoned against the wall, my wrists in irons," Wylena said. Her voice broke again as she remembered her first moments at that horrible place. "But Falcon Moon came and saved both me and Bright Star."

"Thank God you are all right," Joshua said. He looked over his shoulder at Falcon Moon, unsure of how he should feel about that young chief now that he had kept Wylena with him for a time, instead of bringing her home immediately. Yet he was so happy that Falcon Moon had saved her.

"I wasn't treated as unjustly as Falcon Moon's sister," Wylena continued, taking a step away from her brother, turning, and giving Falcon Moon a solemn glance at the mention of his sister and how she was treated.

"It is all behind us now," Joshua said, drawing Wylena closely to his side, an arm holding her there safely next to him. "Falcon Moon, thank you for bringing my sister home to me."

"I apologize for not having brought her sooner," Falcon Moon said solemnly. "But I was not certain what role she played in my sister's abduction. At first, when I saw her in the court-yard at the fortress, I thought she might be the general's woman. And even when Wylena told me over and over again who she was, I still could not put it from my mind how much better she had been treated by the Mexican general than was my sister, so I could not believe anything other than she was special to the general."

"And so when you rescued your sister, you also took Wylena, thinking she was something to the general?" Joshua asked incredulously.

"I was wrong and I apologize, but your sister has come home to you, unharmed, so you should not feel any ill will toward me," Falcon Moon said. "I cannot say as much for my sister. She is still not well after being mistreated so unjustly by General Zamora."

"I am so sorry to hear that about Bright Star," Joshua murmured. "Is she still as ill, or is she re-covering?"

"She is still ill, but her health is not as bad as it was when I rescued her from the Mexicans," Falcon Moon said. "I pray daily now to Ussen for Bright Star's recovery. The first time I prayed for her, after holding her safely in my arms at my stronghold, the white wolves across the canyon howled and I knew that Ussen was going to take care of Bright Star. If Ussen hadn't, I would have understood that Ussen saw it was not to be. But had my sister died, I would have lost my Spirit Guide, and I would have been unhappy."

"What is a Spirit Guide?" Wylena could not help but ask, intrigued more and more by this handsome young chief and his beliefs.

"It is similar to a Christian guardian angel," he said thickly. He gazed over at Joshua, who was smiling, and Falcon Moon understood why. Joshua was glad that Falcon Moon had listened to him while he told Falcon Moon about many of his own beliefs, among them the explanation to the young chief about guardian angels.

"That is beautiful," Wylena could not help but say.

"Falcon Moon, when I say good-bye today— after thanking you again for bringing my sister home to me—it will be our last good-bye," Joshua said quietly. "I was wrong to ask my sister to come to a land with so many dangers that she must face, day by day. I will abandon my mission and take my sister back home to Illinois. I can set up a church there and be as happy as I would have been to succeed at this mission. But as it is, no one comes here to seek the blessings of the Lord. The land is too dangerous for people to travel from their homes."

Wylena sucked in a wild breath. She looked with wide eyes at her brother. "Illinois?" she said shallowly. "You are actually giving up your dream to have this mission and returning to Illinois?"

"Your safety surpasses all else," Joshua said. "We will begin our journey back to Illinois as early as tomorrow. After leaving my home in Illinois, there has been one tragedy for the family after another. I will return now and make all wrongs right."

Wylena did not want to return to Illinois. Once there she would never see Falcon Moon again. And so far, no one had even mentioned Jeb. What of him?

He would be a sitting duck as the three of them traveled to Illinois.

She knew it would be better to find a way to clear Jeb's name! That should be most important to their family, not taking her back to Illinois because of what had happened to her.

Falcon Moon's heart had also skipped a beat when he heard what Father Joshua was planning to do. He gazed in wonder at the woman who had stolen his heart. How could he have discovered true love only to lose it?

He could not help but think back to those wasted hours and days when Wylena was at his village—when he could have tried to encourage her to stay with him forever.

Instead, he had spent that time mistrusting her, even though his heart had ached for him to have her as his own!

Ah, what wasted time, which he would live to regret until the day he died, unless . . .

His eyes glistened as he gazed now into Wylena's, for he knew that he could not allow her to leave. He would find a way to make certain that she would be with him for eternity.

He had already seen children borne of their love in his mind's eye!

Chapter 15

She is a woman: one in whom
The spring-time of her childish years
Hath never lost its fresh perfume
—James Russell Lowell

Wylena watched Falcon Moon ride away to return to his village. Everything inside her silently cried out to him not to go so soon. She needed to spend more time with him.

She couldn't believe that she had fallen in love with an Indian—and not just any Indian, but a proud, important Apache chief.

Back when she was in Illinois, if she heard even the slightest mention of the Apache, word spread in the newspaper of another atrocity they were accused of doing, she had truly thought those Apache must be nothing more than animals who killed for killing's sake alone.

But now? She had met an Apache chief and discovered that he was the kindest, gentlest man she had ever known besides her brother Joshua. Thinking of Joshua made her realize that he was standing there silently watching her as she pined away over a man she had just bidden sadly good-bye, a last good-bye.

When she turned to Joshua, he would read her feelings for this chief in her eyes, especially if he saw the tears that were threatening to fall.

She sighed heavily, forced herself to be braver than she was feeling about loving someone who was in a sense forbidden to her, then turned slowly. But she didn't see Joshua at all.

He had returned to the mission without taking her with him. Joshua had obviously seen how she was behaving over Falcon Moon's exit and had gone on inside, to give her the moments she might need to re-collect herself.

Yes, her brother Joshua was a wonderful man. Understanding, kind, and loving.

He knew that she would not see Falcon Moon again, so he had given her these last moments to accept the knowledge alone.

She gasped and her eyes widened when Jeb stepped up to the door, standing in the shadows in case Falcon Moon might turn his head to take a last look at whom he was leaving behind.

Surely Jeb had been watching slyly from a window all along and had seen both his sister's behavior toward the young Apache chief and Falcon Moon's attitude toward her.

Wylena knew he must have been as worried about her as Joshua. Yet she would never forget how he had shied away from going to save Bright Star from the Mexicans and would have done the same if he found out that she was a captive of the Mexican general, as well.

She just wouldn't allow herself to think about that.

She believed that if he knew how much danger she was in, he would have stopped at nothing to save her!

Smiling, eager to have his arms around her, she lifted the hem of her dress and ran hard to the door, and when she reached Jeb, she flung herself into his arms.

"Jeb, oh, Jeb, I worried so much about you while I was gone," Wylena cried. "The Mexican general won't rest until he has your hide. You know that, don't you?"

"Yep, but he won't get a chance at it, ever," Jeb said, returning her eager hug.

Then he placed his hands at her waist and gently pushed her away from him so that his eyes could travel over her.

She could see his disgust in how she looked, her clothes dirty and in such disarray, even ripped and torn in places.

The dress had some of Bright Star's dried blood on it from when Wylena had taken Bright Star into her arms at the Mexican fortress once they were reunited in the dungeon.

Her hair was clean and fresh, though, as was her skin, for she had been brought a clean basin of water for bathing each day she was at the Apache stronghold. All of the dirt and filth on her clothes had gotten there while she was imprisoned at the fortress, not while she was among the Apache.

"Look at you," Jeb said, visibly shuddering. "At least the chief could've lent you a squaw's dress to wear while you were at his village."

He dropped his hands away from her when Joshua approached and stood beside him.

Wylena could see the questioning looks in both her brothers' eyes and knew they were anxious to hear all that she had to tell them. But most of all she saw their relief and joy that she was safely with them again.

"Let's sit," she said, and motioned with a hand toward the three rockers that faced a slow-burning fire on the grate of the fireplace. "It was quite an experience coming down the mountainside on a horse. I had to close my eyes several times in order not to see the dangerous drop-offs. One slip of the horse's hooves and I would've been a goner."

She sat down and began rocking slowly back and forth, then looked from brother to brother as they sat in their own chairs with their anxious eyes fixed on her.

"First let me say, Jeb, I worried about you every minute I was gone," she said, her voice breaking with emotion. "I now know the Mexican general will go to any length to find you and kill you. You know, that is why both Bright Star and myself were captured and taken to the fortress. It was to lure you there. General Zamora thought you would come and try to rescue us."

She saw Jeb's eyes lower momentarily, then look up again into hers. "I am so glad that you didn't," she sighed. "As it was, we got out of there safely without you having to place yourself in danger."

"Had I gone there, I wouldn't have lasted a minute once I got anywhere near the fortress," Jeb said drily. "The sentries would've ended my life without even taking me to the general first. All the general is interested in is seeing me dead, no matter how or by whom."

He turned to Wylena. "I'm so glad you understand," he said, and his voice broke. He turned to Joshua, then looked back at Wylena. "My life hangs by a thread as far as that general is concerned. Until the true culprit is found and I can prove my innocence, I will still have to be very careful."

"I wasn't harmed by the Mexican general," Wylena murmured. "But it wasn't the same for Bright Star. She was treated horrendously.

She . . . was . . . beaten. I even witnessed the general hitting her in the mouth with his fist. I wasn't able to help her, or . . . or . . . I probably would've been shot on the spot."

Jeb got up from his chair so quickly it toppled sideways and landed on its side. His eyes were filled with fire. His hands were tight fists at his sides. "I'll make him pay," he growled. "Somehow, someday, I will make that son of a bitch pay."

"Jeb, I will have no such language at my mission," Joshua gasped. "If you must speak like that, do it somewhere else. But watch your manners, Brother. You are not only in the house of the Lord; you are in the presence of our sister, who is all sweetness."

Jeb knelt before Wylena. He reached and took one of her hands. "I'm sorry, Sis," he said quickly. "I wasn't thinking. It was just that when I thought of sweet Bright Star getting mistreated, I could not hold my rage inside me."

"But she is all right now, Jeb," Wylena reassured him as she reached a hand to his cheek. "I was afraid for a while that she might not make it. But her shaman immediately saw to her injuries and fever. Also, for a while I thought she might have smallpox, for there are some at the fort who are downed with the nasty disease. But no sores ever rose on her flesh. The fever was surely from being exposed to the dampness of night when she was made to sleep outside on the ground."

"On the ground . . . ?" Jeb repeated. The pain in his voice proved how much he was hurting over the mistreatment of the woman he loved.

He rose to his feet, went to stand over the fireplace, and watched the dancing flames. "And I'll never see her again, to tell her how sorry I am that she was treated that way, and explain how I could not have gone to her rescue," he said with his voice drawn.

He turned and gazed down at Wylena. "I do see the rationality of returning to Illinois," he said. "We must, each of us, put all of this behind us, especially our feelings for those we have been drawn into loving. I saw it in your eyes and behavior, Wylena, how you feel about the Apache chief."

"Yes, I am intrigued by him," Wylena said softly.

"Tell us about your time at the stronghold," Joshua interrupted her.

He didn't want to hear her go as far as to tell them that she was in love with the Apache chief.

He knew that if she was, she had to leave her feelings in Arizona, because he was most definitely taking her back to a world that was sane and safe.

Illinois.

He should never have allowed her to come to the Arizona Territory. He should have gone to her the moment he heard that their parents were dead.

"Tell you?" Wylena said, wincing at the thought that neither brother had any idea that she had been taken to the Apache stronghold as a captive, with a sentry standing guard outside the lodge where she was held.

"Yes, we would like to know why you were taken to Falcon Moon's stronghold instead of home to us." Joshua leaned forward to look more squarely into her eyes.

"You truly don't want to know," Wylena said, lowering her eyes. "You might not understand."

"What's there to understand?" Jeb said, his voice growing louder. "What do you mean?"

"Now, don't either one of you get angry from what I am about to tell you, because everything has turned out all right," Wylena murmured. "I am home. I am with you. We are together, a family. That is all that matters."

Jeb righted his rocking chair and sat in it again as Wylena told her brothers how she had been taken from the fortress, blindfolded, as Falcon Moon's captive.

She explained away her days and nights with the Apache by reassuring them that she had never been harmed, except for the time one of the Apache warriors placed tarantulas in her tepee.

"Tarantulas?" Jeb repeated, his eyes darkening with anger. "Who did that?"

"His name is Bull Nose," Wylena murmured. "He and Chief Falcon Moon clashed a lot, even

though for a while Falcon Moon meant to train
Bull Nose to become chief after him. But the man
proved untrustworthy. And when he did this ter-
rible thing to me, that was the last straw as far as
Falcon Moon was concerned. He ... banished
Bull Nose."

"He actually sent him away?" Joshua said. His
eyes widened. "I have heard Falcon Moon speak
so kindly of that young man. I wonder when it
all changed."

"It happened before my arrival, so I am not to
blame for the young man's misfortune of having
been sent from his village and people," Wylena
said softly.

Then she visibly shivered. "But now that he is a
banished Apache, without a home and people,
that makes him even more dangerous, as far as I
am concerned," she said. "I am afraid I will have
to keep a close look around me at all times, for I do
believe he has it out for me and will not stop at
anything until he gets his vengeance against me."

"Why would you have anything to do with
how Bull Nose feels?" Joshua asked, forking an
eyebrow.

Wylena lowered her eyes. She knew that she
had to tell her brothers everything for them to
understand. She did so quietly, spelling out how
Bull Nose had threatened her and almost abducted her, and when she was through, she saw
anger in the eyes of both her brothers, even
Joshua, who was usually so gentle.

"That does it," Joshua said, and rushed from his chair. "I was beginning to think that perhaps we didn't have to leave Arizona as quickly as I had originally planned, especially since we have Chief Falcon Moon on our side. He surely would not allow the Mexicans to harm you, Wylena, once they hear that you are safely with me again at my mission. But now that I know about Bull Nose, it still stands that we leave tomorrow for Illinois. All three of us."

Wylena winced as though she had been hit, to know that they were leaving tomorrow, meaning she would certainly never see Falcon Moon ever again.

"We must start packing now," Joshua said, and walked away in a rush, the skirt of his gown fluttering all around him in his haste. He looked over his shoulder at Jeb. "Get what you want to take and place it beside the door with what I plan to take."

Without turning back to look at Wylena, he spoke to her, anyway. "Wylena, you hadn't yet totally unpacked from your journey from Illinois, so you don't have much to do to get ready to leave. Do you hear me? Get your things together."

When he didn't get a reply, he stopped and turned to gaze at her. He saw her standing at the window, peering at the mountain, and he was certain that he heard her sobbing.

And he knew why.

Her eyes had said it all while the Apache chief was there. He had even seen it in the young chief's eyes and behavior as he had looked back at her.

They had fallen in love.

Joshua realized that he must keep an eye on her all night to make sure she didn't flee to go be with Falcon Moon, or that the chief didn't come and claim her himself, while everyone else slept.

Chapter 16

And this maiden she lived with no other thought
Than to love and be loved by me.

—Edgar Allan Poe

Falcon Moon smiled at his sister, who was now in her own tepee, but still was not strong enough to be up and moving around. He wasn't very concerned.

He knew that even though his sister was petite, she had the will and courage of an eagle!

She would soon be soaring amid their people, laughing and happy again, after her horrible ordeal at the hands of the Mexican general.

Vengeance was like a hot poker inside Falcon Moon's belly—he badly wanted to go make the general pay for what he had done to his sister.

But Falcon Moon knew it would be best to let

this go, for he had his whole Bear Band to protect. Making war with anyone right now was not an option. It would be the worst thing for them all. As it was, they were safely hidden up on their mountain with sentries posted at enough strategic places to keep anyone from coming and interfering in Falcon Moon's people's lives.

Bright Star had made the mistake of leaving the security of their mountain to meet with the white man whom Falcon Moon despised.

"Bright Star," Falcon Moon blurted out as he sat beside the lodge fire with her, close to where she lay on her bed of plush pelts. "You must never leave our mountain again unless you are escorted. Of course you know that. You have paid dearly for having done it one time too many in order to be with that man who has spoken lies to you and made you vulnerable."

"Brother, I understand how you feel about Jeb, and my having met him secretly, and I see now why you warned me about leaving the mountain, not only because you do not want me to meet with the man I love, but also because going from our stronghold places me in danger of those who would use me wrongly," Bright Star said. She reached over and gently touched his arm. "My brother, I have paid dearly for not having listened to your warnings. I promise not to leave our mountain again unless escorted."

"Do you think that the scalp hunter will chance being caught by those who hunt him because of his evil deeds, to meet you? That he will meet you in the company of one of my warriors?" Falcon Moon said.

Dressed in a lovely, soft doeskin gown, Bright Star slowly sat up. The blankets fell from around her to rest on her legs. She brushed her long black hair back from her face and gazed into the slow-burning embers of the fire. The late-afternoon light was fading as the sun moved lower in the sky; it filtered through the smoke that spiraled upward through the smoke hole.

"I do not know how it can be done," she murmured. She looked quickly at Falcon Moon. "I know that you have instructed your warriors to capture Jeb if he is seen, so, no, I cannot chance meeting with him, for I would be leading him into the hands of danger. I understand how you persist at believing that he is the scalp hunter. Until you have been proven wrong, no, I can no longer meet with him. It is only a fantasy when I speak of going to him again. Nothing more. I cannot chance being grabbed again by our enemies any more than I can chance my darling Jeb being grabbed. And sad to say, his enemies are not only the Mexicans but also, our Bear Band of Apache."

"It is good to hear you speak more reasonably about what you would and would not do when it comes to that man," Falcon Moon said sternly. "One day it will be proven to you that this man is not being falsely accused. I just cannot understand how you do not see that now, because you are the only one, besides his sister and brother, who believes he is innocent of the crimes I know he is guilty of."

"How can you know for certain?" Bright Star softly argued, her eyes flashing into her brother's. "Have you actually seen him scalp someone? Have you seen him with scalps? Until he is proven guilty, by association with the scalps he would have with him were he the scalp hunter, then I will believe that he is innocent, and I will love him from afar until we are able to meet out in the open after he is proven innocent."

"That will never happen," Falcon Moon grumbled. He leaned his face closer to hers. "Sister, I will never understand how you can speak so kindly of a man who is guilty in almost everyone's eyes. Why can you not see the evil in this man?"

"How? Why?" she said, her jaw tightening. "Because I know the true man he is and that everything he is accused of doing is false. He has promised me time and again that he is not the man most see him as. He is a man of God. He prays to his God, as we pray to Ussen!"

"If I told you that I have absolute proof that this man has done the deeds he is accused of, will you finally believe me and remove him from your heart forever?" Falcon Moon saw her eyes waver at his conviction about the man she loved so dearly.

"What sort of proof can you have?" Bright Star said. She lay on her side to face her brother, her eyes imploring him not to tell her that which could destroy her, for were she ever to be shown, for absolutely certain, that Jeb was a scalp hunter, it would totally devastate her.

"Only recently, while you lay ill in our shaman's lodge, Jeb was caught scalping an Apache youth from another band, and when Jeb saw a warrior from this same band approaching him on his horse, Jeb got off the first shot from his firearm and downed him," Falcon Moon said stiffly. "The warrior fell from his steed and lay quietly on the ground, only injured. With blood spilling from the wound on his chest, he pretended to be dead, all the while having his hand on his sheathed knife. He waited breathlessly for Jeb to come to him, to scalp him. He was ready to plunge his knife into Jeb's heart, but Jeb was apparently afraid that there might be other warriors close behind this one. He did not take the time to scalp him. That he was dead was good enough for him this time."

"Again, it was a mistaken identity," Bright Star softly argued. "There is a man out there who resembles Jeb and is taking advantage of the similarities in appearance by killing and making it look as though Jeb is responsible."

"The only person in this area who resembles Jeb is his twin brother, and everyone knows that he is a godly man, who would never take another man's life," Falcon Moon said. Yet he suddenly realized that his sister might still be too weak to endure the strain of arguing with her brother.

He started to stand, to leave his sister to rest before her evening meal was brought to her, but her hand on his arm stopped him.

"Brother, did this warrior who was shot by the scalp hunter die, or did he make it home to his shaman and was made well again?" Bright Star asked softly. "Was he able to deliver the body of the scalped youth to his family?"

"He did take the youth to his family, and he then went to his chief. He lived long enough to tell his chief who had fired the lethal bullet into the young brave's heart," Falcon Moon said, taking Bright Star's hand, gently holding it. "The warrior known as Proud Wind lived only long enough to describe the assailant and he swore to his chief that the guilty person was none other than Jeb Schrock. He told his chief there was no mistaking who the murdering, scalping, evil man was. He had at one time met with Jeb's brother, his identical twin, so he would not have mistaken the scalp hunter for Jeb if it were actually another man."

"Oh, surely he saw wrong through the haze in his eyes that comes just prior to one's death," Bright Star said with a sob lodging in her throat. "It . . . could . . . not be Jeb!" she cried. "He is so gentle and caring with me. He has always treated me as though I were his fragile flower. How could a man who is so gentle be that evil?"

"There is always a portion of good in even a man who is evil," Falcon Moon said thickly. "The portion that is good in Jeb Schrock was reserved to love such a sweet, delicate woman as you. But, Sister, the rest of him is all evil. He is a man who lies even to his own brother—who is a true man of God, a priest. Jeb's days on this earth are surely numbered, for although he uses a hiding place now, he cannot stay well hidden forever. As he almost got caught and killed when he downed the young Apache youth, he was again almost downed. If only Proud Wind had been quicker with his rifle, the scalp hunter would have been killed. One day soon, he will finally be made to pay for his sins against mankind."

"I would rather not talk any further about Jeb," Bright Star said. "I would like to know about Wylena. You were able to take her safely home?"

"She is safe now with her brother Joshua," Falcon Moon said, his mind now solely on this white woman who had stolen his heart.

He felt guilty for having ever accused her of anything and for having kept her hostage.

He wanted to make it up to her, somehow, and he wanted to find a way to keep her brother from taking her from the Arizona Territory!

The thought of never seeing her again created

an emptiness in the pit of his stomach, a feeling of despair that was new to him.

No other woman had ever caused such feelings within him. No other woman had ever stolen his heart away!

"I am so glad that she is home again with her brother Joshua," Bright Star said softly. "It is sad that she cannot be reunited with her other brother, as well. It is so sad that Jeb must live like a hunted animal when he has kin who need him in order to fill that one last empty space in their lives. Family should be together. Maybe one day they will be reunited."

"Father Joshua told me that he is leaving the mission and returning to their homeland in Illinois," Falcon Moon said. "They are leaving tomorrow."

"They are?" Bright Star said, leaning up on an elbow as a thought struck her. Her heart reeled with the pain of possibly losing the one she loved. "That must mean that somehow Jeb will go with them. He will surely join them somewhere along the line. That means I will truly never see him again."

When Falcon Moon saw her start to get up, with a wildness in her eyes, he placed a heavy hand on her shoulder. "Do not even consider what I believe you are thinking of doing," he ordered her. "You are not well enough to walk far, much less get on a horse and try to find Jeb, to see him before he leaves. My sister, accept what must be. Accept that you were not meant to be with that man. He is not worthy of your love."

She fell back down onto the blankets. She brushed tears from her eyes. "I do realize that I cannot leave my bed just yet," she said, her voice breaking. "And, yes, I realize that I must accept my loss. It hurts, oh, it hurts, but I do know now that I will never see my love again."

"Can I trust that you will stay in your bed and truly not attempt to leave the stronghold?" Falcon Moon asked her. "You see, Sister, I am trying to find a way to stop Father Joshua from leaving. I feel that he is needed on this land, where there is too much evil lurking in shadows. The white people are coming more and more each day on land that once belonged solely to the red man. A white holy man can perhaps talk sense to these people. He will help keep them from wanting to annihilate all red men from our land."

"It is not only for that reason that you will go and speak with him, is it?" Bright Star said. Smiling slowly, she continued, "It is because of Wylena. I can hear something different in your voice when you speak her name."

"I do have feelings for her, that is true," Falcon Moon said. "Early this evening, when I go to talk with Father Joshua, I plan to take a special gift to her. I feel that a gift is needed in order to help erase from her mind those times when I was not so gentle and kind to her. There is a necklace I traded for some time ago that was meant to be our mother's. But she is gone now. And you have many necklaces of your own. I will take this one to Wylena. Perhaps it will prove my despair over how I initially treated her."

"When you speak with her, will you give her my love?" Bright Star murmured. "She was all that was good during my imprisonment at the Mexican fortress. We became friends, although we were parted more than we were together. I hope that one day I will see her again."

"That can only be so if I manage to convince Father Joshua that leaving his mission would be a mistake," Falcon Moon responded.

"There is one thing you are not thinking about," Bright Star said, leaning up on an elbow to look into her brother's eyes. "If you truly believe that Jeb is the scalp hunter, would it not be best if Joshua and Wylena were to leave? Would that not mean that Jeb will be gone, too? He would not remain behind, to scalp and kill."

"That is so," Falcon Moon said, searching her eyes. "Sister, do you realize what you just said? You just expressed that at least a part of you knows who this man Jeb is."

Bright Star's eyes widened. Then she fell down onto her bed of pelts and turned her back to her brother. As she awaited his departure, she scarcely breathed.

Falcon Moon gazed a moment longer at his sister, then left in a rush of footsteps.

When he returned to his tepee, he reached inside a buckskin bag and took from it a lovely turquoise necklace. When he acquired it, he had envisioned it adorning his mother's neck.

Now he pictured his woman wearing the necklace.

Yes, he did see Wylena as the one for him.

He must find a way to encourage Father Joshua not to leave, even if that meant it would keep Jeb—the scalp hunter—in the area. In a sense, that was good, for it would give Falcon Moon the opportunity to finally find and kill him for the crimes he had committed.

He walked over to where his horse was tethered and gently stuffed the necklace inside his travel bag, then went over to two warriors who were standing talking nearby.

"I am leaving," he said, looking from one to the other. He turned and gazed at his sister's lodge, then at his warriors again. "I will be gone for a while. Watch that my sister does not leave her lodge. She is too weak. She must stay in her tepee for proper rest and nourishment."

As he spoke he saw Pretty Rain, the maiden who was assigned to care for his sister until she was well enough to do so herself, enter Bright Star's tepee. She carried a pot of soup for his sister's evening meal.

After securing his warriors' promise, Falcon Moon mounted his white stallion and rode away, hoping that he was in time to stop the woman he would always love from being taken from him, for what if Father Joshua chose to leave tonight instead of tomorrow?

He shoved his heels into the flanks of his steed and rode in a hard gallop toward the pass that would take him from his mountain.

Chapter 17

Wylena was in her room, slowly placing her clothes in her travel bag, which she had only recently unpacked. She had failed to persuade Joshua to reconsider his decision about going back to Illinois.

As evening moved into night, the moon high and casting shadows through her bedroom window, she stopped what she was doing and went over to the window. She loved moonlit nights like this.

If she were back home in Illinois, she would have nothing to fear should she want to go outside and take a leisurely walk beneath that moon. As it was, the one time she had done this after arriving in Arizona, she had been abducted.

In a sense, she felt like a prisoner again, for she

didn't like having guidelines about what she could or could not do.

Yes, it was true that back in Illinois she could be free to come and go no matter what time of day or night it was.

But she still didn't want to return there and leave Falcon Moon behind.

She suspected he had feelings for her that matched her own for him, and now she would never know where those feelings might have gone. Could she have eventually been his wife?

Would he even actually want a white wife?

Had he not been so kind and gentle with her? That meant that he was not against people with white skin. He had room in his heart for those he saw worthy of befriending.

Oh, surely she could have been, or already was, something special to him.

Disgruntled at her brother for not listening to reason when she promised she would never again venture into the night without him beside her, she slowly shook her head back and forth.

"What else can I say or do to make him understand that I just don't want to return to Illinois?" she said in a low, frustrated whisper.

She slammed a dress into her travel bag, not bothering to fold it neatly. Drat it, she didn't care about wrinkles. All she wanted was to be free to love and be with Falcon Moon!

Her spine stiffened when she heard the sound of a horse approaching the mission. Since she had been there, no one had come after dark to the mission for any reason.

"Falcon Moon?" she whispered, her face filling with color at the mere thought of his return.

Her heart thumped wildly inside her chest as she ran out to where both brothers were sitting in their rockers, relaxing before the fire.

"Don't you hear?" she cried, seeing the alarm in their eyes as they rose from their chairs and gazed at her. "A horse! A horse is arriving!"

"No, we didn't hear it," Joshua said. He quickly took Jeb by an arm and ushered him toward the tapestry. "We were busy talking."

"Oh, Jeb, I wish it wasn't necessary for you to hide like a scared puppy every time we hear someone approaching the mission," Wylena said, sighing heavily. "It just isn't fair. Why can't they find the true scalp hunter?"

He gave her a strange look, then disappeared behind the tapestry, down to where he could hide.

"I shall go and see who it is," Joshua said, hurrying toward the door. He looked over his shoulder at Wylena. "Go to your room. There is no sense in you putting yourself in danger should whoever it is be here for the wrong reasons."

Again Falcon Moon's face flashed before Wylena's eyes. She wondered if it really might be him.

He knew they were leaving on the morrow. What might he want with her brother Joshua?

For surely that was why he would come again so soon—that is, if it was Falcon Moon.

"No, I'll stay here," Wylena murmured.

As her brother went to the door, Wylena clasped her hands together and looked heavenward in prayer that it was Falcon Moon and not someone else who meant her family harm.

Another thought came to her suddenly. The Mexican general!

Oh, Lord, could he be the one who was making an early-evening call?

Was he coming for her?

She started to turn, to run to the tapestry and rush downstairs and hide with her brother, yet before she had the chance, Joshua had the door open. The person standing there was most definitely not the general, nor was it an enemy to their family.

"Falcon Moon?" Joshua asked with raised eyebrows as he gazed at the Apache chief in the light of the moon's glow. "What brings you back to my mission?"

Falcon Moon looked past Joshua and saw Wylena standing on the far side of the room, her face flushed, her eyes wide as she gazed back at him.

Wylena saw then how his eyes roamed slowly over her. Surely he saw how different she looked in clean clothes, with her hair brushed to perfection as it hung long and clean down her back.

She saw approval in his eyes, then knew that

was true when he gave her a slow nod of hello,
smiled, then turned his gaze back to Joshua.

"I have brought something for your sister,"
Falcon Moon said, smiling again at Wylena, then
at Joshua. "It is a gift of apology, for having
wronged her. May I give her the gift?"

Joshua's eyes widened as he gazed at Falcon
Moon in wonder, then looked at the buckskin
bag that he carried. He quickly turned and
looked at Wylena, whose face was flushed from
embarrassment. Or excitement?

"Father Joshua, do I have permission to give
your sister the gift?" Falcon Moon repeated,
searching the priest's eyes for a positive answer.

Joshua turned back to Falcon Moon, wondering what might be inside the bag for his sister. He
knew that whatever it was, it was a gift from the
heart of a man Joshua saw as kind and generous,
a man of peace.

Joshua looked into Falcon Moon's eyes once
again. "Please come in," he said, stepping aside
for Falcon Moon to enter the living room of the
mission. "Yes, if you wish, give her your gift."

Wylena's knees felt rubbery and weak when
Falcon Moon came over to her and stopped just
before her, his midnight-dark eyes gazing intensely into hers.

"I am so sorry for having wronged you by
holding you captive," Falcon Moon said thickly.
"Will you accept my gift as an apology?"

Stunned by this new turn of events—having

only moments ago, in the privacy of her room, ached to see this man again—Wylena felt the heat of a continuing blush on her cheeks as she tried to find the right words to say to Falcon Moon.

By the way he looked into her eyes, she understood that he was there for more than just giving her a gift as a way to apologize to her.

She could see that he loved her.

It was the look of sincerity in his eyes that spoke to her of such a love, and she could not help but feel the same way about him. She wondered if he could see it in her eyes, too.

Knowing that he and Joshua were awaiting her answer, Wylena nodded. "Yes, I would love to accept your gift," she murmured.

"That is good," Falcon Moon said, smiling broadly. He opened the bag and reached inside.

When he brought out the necklace, he heard Wylena's gasp and saw the wonder in her eyes as she gazed at it.

"Why, it's so beautiful," she murmured, staring at the silver necklace on which hung many turquoise stones. She looked up at him. "You truly want me to have this?"

"It would look beautiful around your neck," Falcon Moon said. "May I put it on you?"

Wylena could feel her blush deepen. She lowered her eyes bashfully. "Yes, please do," she murmured, suddenly unaware of anything else. For the moment, no one but her and Falcon Moon existed.

He stepped behind her and she lifted her thick black hair, growing wonderfully warm inside when Falcon Moon touched her neck as he fastened the necklace. Then he stood back away from her as she lowered her hair to her shoulders again.

Her pulse racing, having never felt so special before, Wylena went to a mirror on the wall and gazed into it. She sighed to see the loveliness of the necklace, and Falcon Moon's reflection behind her in the mirror as he watched her, his eyes expressive of so much that reached clean inside her soul.

Her pulse still racing, she turned to Falcon Moon. "Thank you," she murmured softly. "I have never seen anything as beautiful as this. I shall wear it with pride, always."

Joshua could hardly believe his eyes, or his ears, as he stood silently by, observing what was transpiring between his sister and this young Apache chief.

It had to do with more than a mere gift.

He saw their interest in each other.

"Falcon Moon, thank you for your kind gift," he said quickly, his voice betraying a nervousness he did not want to reveal. "We must bid you farewell now, though. We are rising early on the morrow to leave for Illinois."

"Leaving is not necessary," Falcon Moon said quickly as he turned and faced Joshua. "Wylena will never be done wrong again. I, personally, will see to it."

"It isn't your place to assure my sister's safety," Joshua said, feeling rattled at the young chief's true feelings for his sister.

He knew that he must certainly take her away, for their love would be a cause for concern.

And there was Jeb.

Joshua could not allow the young chief to come around like this without Jeb eventually being caught at the mission. Joshua was protecting, not only his sister, but also his brother by leaving!

"But I wish to protect her," Falcon Moon said, confused by Joshua's sudden strange behavior toward him.

But Falcon Moon quickly understood. It was because his friend the priest did not want to share his sister with a man with red skin. It insulted him, yet he would not show such feelings to Joshua or Wylena. There were other ways to convince this priest that Wylena belonged there with Falcon Moon, not with her brother!

"Falcon Moon, hear me well when I say that I am Wylena's brother, and when our parents died, I took on the role of her parents, and I believe she will be better off in Illinois," Joshua said firmly. "We shall leave tomorrow."

Falcon Moon saw that there would be no reasoning with Joshua. He would have to go about this another way. But first he would leave in order not to say things that would make Joshua an enemy. He gave Wylena a long gaze, then Joshua, then left.

Wylena's heart sank as he walked out and she clutched a hand to the necklace. It would be a reminder, always, of how she had suddenly fallen in love, and then was denied that true love by a brother who thought he was doing what was best for her.

But as she saw it, Falcon Moon was what was best for her, and now she had lost him! She started to run to her bedroom, but Joshua reached out and grabbed her by an arm, stopping her.

"Sis, it is best that we leave," he said, searching her eyes, which were suddenly filled with tears. "You are being foolish to feel something for Falcon Moon, even though I myself realize what a good man he is. But in the real world, Wylena, it is not best for a white woman to fall in love with a man with red skin, not even a man I see as good, through and through. It is taboo, Wylena. Taboo."

"If you see him as such a good man, oh, how could you deny him to me?" Wylena cried. "I love him. He loves me. We are meant to be together!"

"Wylena Schrock, listen to me when I tell you this one last time that we are leaving for Illinois tomorrow," Joshua said flatly. "It is the best course for our entire family. Have you forgotten so quickly the danger your brother Jeb is in? When we get out of this area, he can live like a human being again, not like a mole living underground."

"I won't go," Wylena said, her hands sudden fists at her sides, her jaw tight. "And as for Jeb, in time his name will be cleared. I know it. He is innocent. He will be proven innocent."

"Wylena, we . . . are . . . going home," Joshua said in a flat tone. "All three of us are going home tomorrow. Jeb will hide beneath blankets at the back of the wagon until we are out of the area where someone might recognize him. Then we will all be able to sit together up front."

Having never heard her brother so determined about anything—he was actually giving her orders—Wylena just stood there, her eyes wide, as he walked away from her, leaving her alone with her thoughts.

She didn't know how to change his mind, but knew she must. After all, she was in love, even if it was taboo for her, a white woman, to love an Indian!

Chapter 18

Completely devastated by her brother's stern decision, Wylena went to her bed, on which she had left her half-packed travel bag. With an anger that came rarely to her, with one mad sweep of a hand she brushed everything from the bed to the floor.

She turned her back to the mess and stood at the window, sobbing. The moon whitewashed everything outside with its beautiful sheen. There were muted shadows everywhere she looked—innocent shadows of trees. Even the large steeple made its shadow along the land, a reminder again of what would happen on the early morrow.

Her brother Joshua was forced to leave everything because of her!

Had she not left that night and made herself vulnerable to those who were evil at heart, her brother would not have had to make such a decision. She knew it went against everything he truly wanted to do.

He had traveled this far, to this land, for a purpose. He had wanted to spread the word of the Lord to those people who came to settle in a place where much evil lurked everywhere. There were renegade Indians who watched and waited for those they could prey on, and kill. There were evil white men who came to new settlements, with cheating of all sorts on their minds.

And then there were the Mexican soldiers not that far across the border who were ready to make war with anyone who threatened them, particularly now, with the gold mining near their fortress. Gold that was going to make them rich, especially the general.

Wylena's brother Joshua had been told of plans to build a new fort in close proximity to the mission, which had been abandoned before her brother's arrival by other priests who gave up on saving lives as they had planned to do when they chose to make their homes there.

And now? It was not like her brother to give

up on his plans to do the same. It was only because of his sister that he felt he must leave.

"It isn't fair to him, nor me," Wylena sobbed
as she looked out on the peacefulness of the land
that could be so brutal.

"The mistake I made led me to the man I will
always love," Wylena said. She wiped her eyes
clean of tears with the back of a hand. "And now
I must leave him, and my brother must leave his
mission, all because of a mistaken identity . . .
because someone believes my brother Jeb is the
scalp hunter!"

The thought of anyone believing that made
her furious all over again, almost as furious as
she felt over being made to abandon this new
love, which had not been able to mature further
than a mere touch when Falcon Moon placed the
necklace around her neck.

Oh, but that touch had been so magic, so elec-
tric!

She knew from that moment that she had been
right to believe that something had developed
between her and the kind, handsome Apache
chief.

As she reached a hand up to touch the necklace, to imagine that she was touching Falcon
Moon, she stopped and leaned forward, closer to
the window, when she thought she saw movement beyond, in the very edge of the trees that
grew close to the mission.

A sudden fear grabbed at her heart. It might

be Mexican soldiers returning for her, or to attack the mission in the hope of finding Jeb there!

She had wondered why they hadn't done that earlier, and concluded that it was because this was a house of God, and if they didn't believe in much else, they had enough faith to stop them from desecrating the place of godliness.

She started to run and warn Jeb, but stopped dead still in her tracks when she saw movement again. This time she knew that she wasn't imagining things.

"Falcon Moon?" she whispered. She placed a hand to her necklace, again clutching it, as she watched Falcon Moon edge his white steed farther out of the shadows of the trees. The moonlight revealed that he was gazing intensely at the mission.

As he sat there, so noble and tall in his saddle, with the moon splashing its lovely white sheen onto his copper face, Wylena's heart throbbed with a need she had never felt before. She wanted to go to him!

He must want her to come to him, or why else would he sit there in the moonlight, so close to the mission that her brothers might see him there?

She thought briefly that perhaps Falcon Moon was watching for Jeb to come from the mission, and she prayed to herself that Jeb would not take that moment to leave as he sometimes did at night.

Her heart thumping wildly, her face flushed with excitement, she opened the window, and without another thought, she climbed from the window and ran under the moonlight toward Falcon Moon.

She saw how quickly he dismounted and stepped toward her. Yet he did not go farther, but waited for her to come to him.

When Wylena reached him, she did not even consider what she was doing.

She just did it.

She flung herself into Falcon Moon's arms, and what happened next made her knees buckle; the sweetness inside her heart was so over-whelming as he brought his mouth to hers in a kiss so all consuming, Wylena almost fainted from the wonder of it.

When he moved his lips away, and they stood there gazing into each other's eyes, the moon's glow bringing them closer tonight than she had imagined could ever happen, she smiled at him bashfully.

He returned the smile and gently reached up and lifted the necklace he had given to her into his hand. "This looks beautiful on you," he said. His voice sounded so vastly different than Wylena had ever heard it. There was a hoarse huskiness to it.

"I love the necklace," Wylena murmured.

She was afraid that if she blinked her eyes, she would be back in the bedroom, packing her clothes for the long journey ahead that would take her away from Falcon Moon's arms forever.

But she knew that this was real, that every sweet, breathtaking moment of it was truly real. He had come back to announce his love for her, as she had so badly wanted from the moment she allowed herself to love this man, who had first seen her as his enemy, and now saw her as much more—as a woman he desired with every fiber of his being!

"I do love it so," she said, smiling into his midnight-dark eyes.

He moved his hand from the necklace and instead placed it gently on her cheek, where its warmth bled sweetly into her flesh. "I love you," he said, searching her own dark eyes.

"And . . . I love you," Wylena found herself saying.

He swept his arms around her waist and drew her tightly against him as he kissed her with a heated passion that made her dizzy with want, a want that was new to her, a want that felt wonderful and joyous!

And then he drew his lips away from hers and swept her fully into his arms. He carried her into the deep, dark shadows of the trees, where only slight ribbons of moonlight occasionally found their way through the thick foliage overhead.

She did not question where he was taking her, or why. At this moment there was only Falcon Moon. The rest of the world was far, far away, even her brothers—who thought she was in bed, safely away from all harm, and the man she loved.

She did not want to think about how they would react were they to discover where she actually was!

She had been raised by the guidance of a mother who read the Bible every morning and every night, especially after she had been hit by an abusive husband, the brownish purple bruises on her face proof of how this man ruled all of their lives.

For the most part, though, Wylena had been an exception. Her father had never raised a hand against her. He had seen her as a frail, fragile thing that he thought might break if he hit her.

She felt blessed for that, and also because she now knew that his abusive ways had not rubbed off on her and ruined her forever. She had worried more than once that she might never be able to love any man because of the one who'd never shown any kindness toward anyone.

But after being around Falcon Moon for even a short time, she knew that he was an exact opposite of her father.

He was kind.

He was gentle.

He was even sweet.

She loved him, and would love him until the day she died.

"I know of a place where no one will pass by

and see us together," Falcon Moon said, erasing all the ugly thoughts from Wylena's mind, bringing her back to this precious moment and how wonderful it felt to be in the arms of this man. She pressed her cheek against his powerful, bare copper chest.

She could hear and feel his heartbeat and knew that it beat faster because of the moments that lay ahead of them.

She knew that they would make love. It would be her first time.

Although her brother was adamant about leaving the area tomorrow, she knew that she must find a way not to go. She was meant to be with Falcon Moon. This moment proved it!

Wylena looked away from Falcon Moon when she became aware of a soft splashing of water and saw a stream. The moon's glow reflected in the water as though there were many moons tonight, not only one. She smelled the scent of nearby flowers, but she could not see them.

Falcon Moon stood her on her feet on what felt to her like velveteen grass, it was so soft. His eyes seemed to burn with passion as he gazed into hers. Once she was standing before him, facing him, he framed her face between his hands and brought her mouth to his in another passionate kiss that rendered her weak.

She clung to him as he used his body to press her down onto the heavenly grass. Strange new sensations were born inside her as he slid a hand slowly up the skirt of her dress and stroked her in a spot that felt suddenly alive.

Deep down she knew that she should perhaps be alarmed by this sort of brazen touch, but instead, she trembled with an ecstasy unknown to her as he slowly caressed her there, gently, yet surely. Wylena gasped as pleasure spread within her. Her answering heat and excitement seemed alarming and dangerous to her, yet she could not deny him anything, not even this.

As he straddled her, resting on his knees, Wylena clung to his sinewed shoulders and he lifted the skirt of her dress much higher, until that private part of her body tingled with readiness.

A delicate madness seemed to engulf her when she held her arms out away from her and allowed him to unbutton her dress, then lift the skirt.

The night was cool, yet the breeze felt like a soft caress. Wylena experienced bliss that she never knew could exist when Falcon Moon leaned down and flicked his tongue across one of her rose-tipped nipples. She shuddered sensually as his tongue danced along her body, and when he knelt even lower over her, his tongue sought the part of her that now seemed to have a life of its own. Her womanhood throbbed almost unmercifully with an ache that was new to her. She closed her eyes and did not try to deny him what he sought. She allowed his tongue and lips on that place that made her senses reel with such pleasure, she thought she might faint from its blissfulness.

As he flicked and licked, she tossed her head back and forth, moaning, the delicious shivers of desire overwhelming her. And then he stopped.

She opened her eyes just as he stood over her, dropping his breechclout away from himself. Wylena felt the heat of a blush when she saw that part of him that she knew was made for making love with her. She had been raised with brothers, yet she had never seen that part of their anatomy, ever. Their house was large enough for everyone to have their own private places. She was glad about that, for she would not have wanted this moment ruined, when she saw the man she loved naked, his muscled body a copper sheen beneath the moonlight.

Her heart pounding, consumed with this need she had never known before, she smiled at him and reached her arms out for him. He returned the smile, then stretched out over her.

She could feel his strong thighs against her legs.

She could feel one of his knees gently part them. She moaned as she felt his manhood probing her.

"You are the first," she found the sense to say. He drew himself gently away from her. He framed her face between his hands again, and his eyes searched hers as though he was silently asking permission to go on with this sweet seduction beneath the moonlight.

"You are the first because I want you to be," Wylena murmured, reaching a hand to caress his cheek. "My love, I do want you. I will always want you. You will be my first and my last. I will love you, only you, forever."

"The first time there is some discomfort," Falcon Moon said, then brushed soft kisses across her lips. "But it will be brief and then you will feel the same wondrous sensations that I will be feeling. We will find paradise together tonight, my love. And also forever, for you must find a way to persuade your brother not to leave."

"I don't want to even think about that," Wylena said softly. "I only want to think of now and how we are sharing such wonderful moments."

He ran his fingers through the soft glimmer of her hair and gazed in awe at her loveliness. Then when a sudden onslaught of passion gripped him again, he forgot all tomorrows and concentrated only on tonight, this moment, this woman!

He swept his arms around her and held her tightly against him as he began his entrance into her warm place, her body giving way to his slow approach inside her. And when he felt the proof of virginity, he held her more tightly against him and kissed her passionately as he gave one shove that gave him the entrance that he desired.

Wylena felt an instant of sharp pain, and then

she felt nothing but the wonders of his lovemaking as he thrust himself farther into her, his strokes long and even as he withdrew and then thrust again, all the while kissing her with a kiss of total demand.

She sought out the sleekness of his back with her trembling hands and went lower, and rested them on his buttocks.

Her hands stayed wrapped around him as he continued his rhythmic thrusts within her. Then she felt something even more pleasurable building inside her as she lay there in a drugged passion.

It spread as his kiss deepened and he pushed himself more deeply inside her. He groaned as his body quivered and shook against hers, just as she found paradise, too, when a silent explosion swept through her senses, as though stars were flashing inside her consciousness as the wonder of pleasure overwhelmed her. She clung to him until the final throes of passion were behind them.

He clung to her, his heart pounding like a thousand drumbeats inside his chest. And then he rolled away from her and lay on his back in the cool grass, his whole body still feeling the wonderful sensations that being with her had given him.

Wylena lay on her back, looking heavenward at the stars and the moon, yet seeing none of them. All she could see was his face as he had found paradise at the same moment as she. It was a mask of such pleasure, pleasure that she was responsible for, and she was proud that she had not disappointed him.

She wanted him to want and love her forever, even though if things didn't turn around for her, these might be her very last moments with this wonderful Apache chief.

"I just can't let it happen," she blurted out, turning to face him. "What can I do to convince Joshua that his place is here, not in Illinois? He came here for a purpose. How can he turn his back on it?"

"He has a full night to sleep on it," Falcon Moon said, reaching and taking one of her hands in his. "After he thinks about what he is leaving behind—his dreams, his mission—he will surely change his mind."

"When my brother makes his mind up about something, nothing can change it," Wylena said sullenly. "Oh, Lord, were he to know what I am doing tonight, he . . ."

Falcon Moon reached over and placed his arms around her waist and drew her up to sit beside him.

He held her close to ward off the chill of night as much as possible. "My woman, I cannot have just found you, only to lose you again," he said thickly. "Something will happen to change your brother's mind."

"And if it doesn't?" she asked, turning her

face up to his, searching his eyes. "Then what should I do? You have seen the kind, gentle side of my brother, but there is a stubborn side, too."

"If he does not change his mind, I will change it for him," Falcon Moon said, drawing a gasp from Wylena.

"What do you mean?" she asked softly.

"I will watch and wait, and if I see you leave by wagon tomorrow, I will come to your brother then, and tell him that I cannot lose you," Falcon Moon said. "I will take you from the wagon. Your brother will have to accept it."

"I don't know," Wylena said, swallowing hard.

If Falcon Moon came that close to the wagon to claim her, he might catch sight of Jeb somehow. If Falcon Moon was going to be that vigilant, awaiting an opportunity to take her from the wagon, might he not be watching the mission as they left it? Would he not see Jeb sneak beneath the blankets? Could her having fallen in love with this wonderful man mean the demise of her brother?

Just then Falcon Moon drew her closer and kissed her.

For now, for this precious moment, she could not allow herself to think of anything but Falcon Moon and being with him.

Chapter 19

Wylena sat beside her brother Joshua in the wagon, the morning air crisp and the sun brilliantly bright as it rose behind them in the early-morning sky.

Their destination was still Illinois. She hadn't been able to change Joshua's mind no matter how much she had argued with him as they packed their belongings in the wagon.

His mind was preoccupied with worries about the possibility of Jeb's capture as they traveled.

Just one person stopping the wagon to search it was all it would take for Jeb's life to end. Knowing this, Wylena had finally stopped arguing with Joshua about his decision to return to Illinois.

As she sat there beside him on the seat of the wagon, she did so with a quiet, frustrated anger.

Had they remained at the mission, as she would have preferred, Jeb would not be hidden under a blanket with the sun beating down onto him.

Wylena made a concerted effort not to look constantly at the blanket, knowing that if anyone saw how nervous she was about it, and decided to investigate, she would be the cause of her brother's demise.

"Joshua, this is so foolish," Wylena suddenly stated as she gave him a troubled stare. "Turn around. Take this wagon back to the mission."

She reached up and repositioned the straw bonnet she wore when a wheel careened down into a small ditch, causing the whole wagon to shiver and shake. She checked the ribbon that secured the hat in place, and tightened the bow beneath her chin. She lowered her hands to her lap and rested them on the leather skirt that she had chosen to wear on the first leg of this long journey. She also wore a long-sleeved, white cotton blouse and leather boots, the same boots that she had worn so often while horseback riding in Illinois.

She had decided that she would detach one of the horses somewhere along the way and ride for a while on it instead of the hard wooden seat. Not only would that help her by giving her sore, aching bottom some reprieve from the seat and the wobbliness of the wagon, but it would also give her a way to work off her frustration. Riding a horse always gave her a quiet peace inside her heart.

"Sis, do I have to assume that I am going to hear you fuss at me all of the way to Illinois?" Joshua said, stopping her before she continued with what he had heard countless times already that morning about returning home. He gave her a soft look. "I'm doing what is best for what is left of our family. Why can't you understand that?"

"If I knew we'd make it safely home, without anyone's interference, then I'd stop worrying out loud," Wylena said, her voice breaking.

She so badly wanted to tell him how she truly felt! Yes, she was concerned about getting Jeb safely out of this area, where too many people thought that he was the scalp hunter, but she was also being forced to leave her heart behind. She still could hardly believe what had transpired last evening between her and Falcon Moon. She could still feel his hands and mouth on her, making her shiver sensually each time she remembered what sorts of feelings he had awakened inside her.

From the moment they had left the mission, she had been watching for Falcon Moon to ride up and demand they turn back and return to the mission—and forget going to Illinois.

She expected him to reveal to Joshua just how he felt about her, that he wanted her for his wife. Although he had not openly said that to her, she knew that it was his intention to marry her, or why would he be so adamant about her not leaving the area?

"Sis, your mind has wandered again," Joshua said, interrupting her thoughts.

She blushed as she looked over at him, not having heard what he had last said to her. It was hard not to think about Falcon Moon and how she regretted having to leave him after discovering he truly loved her.

Suddenly Wylena saw movement out of the corner of her eye. She looked quickly to her far left, and upward. Her stomach tightened when she saw a long line of Indians on a ridge, moving slowly, keeping up with this wagon's speed.

"Mexicans," Joshua blurted out, drawing Wylena's eyes to the right, where she saw many Mexican soldiers on another ridge, opposite where she had seen the Indians. Fear filled Wylena's heart, for she quickly recognized General Zamora at the front of the long line of soldiers.

How could she ever forget those horrible hours she had been forced to endure at the fortress? Not wanting to think about that, she looked abruptly at the Indians. Her heart skipped a beat when she realized who was at the lead. It was Falcon Moon!

"We could be in a pack of trouble," Joshua said, looking over his shoulder where Jeb still lay hidden. His gaze fell on the rifle that was close to

Jeb, so he could grab it were they suddenly attacked by the Mexicans.

Wylena was so afraid, she couldn't speak. She wanted so badly to cry out for Falcon Moon, to ask him to help her and her brother, but she knew that the best thing for them all to do was just to keep riding onward and wait for Falcon Moon to make his move. Wylena knew that he would not allow the Mexicans to get anywhere near the wagon.

"Look," Joshua said, nodding toward the ridge where the Apache and their horses moved along at the same pace as the wagon. "There are more Apache."

Wylena quickly saw how many more Apache Indians appeared on the ridge, surely from other bands, come to accompany Falcon Moon and his warriors on this mission. They all made one long line of black against the blue horizon.

Then Wylena gasped and her insides tightened when the Apache began riding hard down the slope, war cries following along with them as they headed away from the wagon and toward the Mexicans.

Joshua drew a sudden tight rein and stopped the team of horses.

Wylena watched with a thundering heart as the Mexicans began to scatter in all directions to try to avoid being killed by the Indians. Suddenly there was total silence and no sight of the Mexicans anywhere.

Thank God, Wylena thought to herself. There were only the Apache, who now stood back from the wagon as Falcon Moon, alone, approached it.

Wylena watched with a racing pulse, her face flushed, as she made eye contact with Falcon Moon, who came closer and closer, his rifle now slid into his gun boot at the right side of his steed.

He wore only a breechclout and moccasins, and his hair hung loose down his muscled back, the headband keeping it from his face.

Wylena almost swooned at the sight of him as he stopped directly beside the wagon, on the side where she sat, his sculpted, copper face passive as he looked past Wylena and at Joshua.

And then everything suddenly changed.

Falcon Moon grabbed Wylena and soon had her sitting with him on his horse, positioned on his lap. Nestled there, she felt so happy, so protected, but waited anxiously to see how he would explain his sudden action to her brother. She prayed that Jeb would stay hidden.

One wrong move and he could have an arrow in his heart!

"Father Joshua, I am taking your sister with me," Falcon Moon said, his voice steady and determined. "I promise to watch over and care for her. I will marry her."

Joshua seemed at a loss for words. He waited for Wylena to say something, but all he got from her was a soft smile.

"This is what I want," she murmured. "Joshua, turn back. Go to the mission. By doing so, we can still see one another often. If you go to Illinois, as you had planned to do, I know that we shall never see one another again."

She had to force herself not to look at the blankets, afraid that some of the Apache might follow her gaze and realize that she was looking there for a purpose.

"Sis, I know that your heart is lost to this Indian chief, and I also know there is nothing I can say or do to make you change your mind, so go on with Falcon Moon," Joshua said, searching her eyes. "At least I know that you will be safe there, perhaps safer than were you to stay with me."

"Thank you for understanding," Wylena replied. She found it hard to believe that this was truly happening. She was going to be taken back to the stronghold and become a part of it as Falcon Moon's wife. Had anyone told her, even a month ago, that something like this would happen to her, she would have said that person was daft.

"Joshua, please return to the mission," Wylena softly begged, all the while worrying about what would happen to Jeb were he to stay in this area. She could only hope that one of these days someone would find the true scalp hunter and everyone would owe her brother an apology.

The world would be good then. Both her

brothers could come visit her at the stronghold and she could go openly visit them at the mission.

"Please, Joshua?" Wylena quickly added. "Please turn around and return to the mission. You know that is where you would rather be. That is where you belong. It is your home. It is your chosen house of God. One day you will be able to help those who come to this land and settle here. You know it's already happening not all that far from here. Nothing can stop the influx of white people, especially now, if they hear about the gold that the Mexicans have discovered. Gold is something that people would die for. But if you stay at your mission, you can preach the word of God and explain the evil of gold, for nothing good has ever come from people going West to pan for it."

"I am going to stay," Joshua told her. "I would not be able to say a final good-bye to you, not now that we have been reunited again after so many years apart. Go with love, Wylena. I know that you are in safe hands."

"Thank you, Joshua," Wylena murmured, close to tears. "Thank you so much."

"May God be with you," Joshua said, already turning the wagon back in the direction of the mission. He had to make different plans now for Jeb. Tonight, under the cover of darkness, he would encourage Jeb to go alone to Illinois, where he could be safe, for no one there would ever know that he had been accused of being a scalp hunter.

Wylena untied her bonnet and tossed it into the wind, then snuggled close to Falcon Moon as they rode off with his warriors.

When they reached the summit of the ridge, he stopped and placed her on a horse that had been brought for her. Together, side by side, they rode into the foothills of the mountain.

Joshua snapped the reins and sent his team of horses faster toward his mission. When Jeb spoke from beneath his cover of blankets, Joshua's heart turned cold.

"Joshua, I know what you're thinking," Jeb said loud enough for only Joshua to hear. "There's no way in hell that I'm going alone to Illinois, especially not as long as our sister is with that savage. Falcon Moon will pay for taking our sister from us, and in the worst way possible."

Joshua's heart sank to hear the venom in his brother's voice. There was something in that voice that made Joshua believe that Jeb might not be the man Joshua thought he was, and that just perhaps he might have something to do with the scalpings and killings, after all.

It gave him a sick feeling at the pit of his stomach to let his mind wander to such possibilities, when all along he had truly felt that Jeb was being framed by the real scalp hunter.

"You will do nothing about what happened today," Joshua said in a flat tone over his shoulder to Jeb. "Our sister went with the young chief because she wanted to. While she was with Falcon Moon at his stronghold, she fell in love with him. Face it, Brother, she is going to marry the man, and if you do anything to try and stop it, I swear, Jeb, you will have me to answer to."

He waited for Jeb to respond, glad when he didn't. Joshua snapped his reins and rode harder toward the mission, very relieved when he saw the tall steeple not that far ahead.

Jeb lay there filled with anger, with a dark need for vengeance that not even his holy brother would be able to quell.

In time, he would make everyone pay, not only for how he was being made to hide away like a scared puppy, but for taking his sister from the sort of life she should live, not a life that would make her look like one of the Apache squaws as she dressed like them and married their chief. For now, he lay there in a pool of sweat, swearing anew with each breath taken, glad when he heard his brother finally draw the horses to a halt inside the barn.

"We're home," Joshua said softly. "Jeb, I'll hurry inside. Then you come inside when it gets dark."

Jeb grumbled and climbed from the back of the wagon just as Joshua left the barn.

Jeb stayed hidden in the barn until night fell with its dark shroud over the land, then rushed to the mission and ran on inside. He smiled when his brother handed him a large glass of cool water. He gulped it down as Joshua began to walk away from him.

"Jeb, I must leave you now and go into the chapel and continue to pray," Joshua said over his shoulder. "I am torn with how to feel toward you in light of the rumors about you."

"My own brother doesn't believe me?" Jeb asked, then placed the empty glass aside and hurried to his hideout beneath the mission.

Once inside the chapel, where candles burned softly above the altar, Joshua knelt before a statue of Christ. While gazing at the heavenly, peaceful face of his Lord, he began praying.

"Be with Wylena and, Lord, most of all, be with Jeb," he said, tears streaming from his eyes. "I truly believe now that Jeb needs my prayers the most."

Chapter 20

We have made no vows—there will none be broke,
Our love was free as the wind on the hill
—Ernest Dowson

Wylena awoke from one of the most peaceful nights of sleep since before the sudden deaths of her parents in Illinois to hear the sound of women humming contentedly. When she went to bed after arriving at the Apache stronghold, she had not been alone. She had fallen asleep in Falcon Moon's arms, too exhausted to stay awake for long after climbing into his plush pelts.

Before going to bed, she had washed the day's grime from her body. She had watched him wash, as well, from a wooden basin of water, desiring him with every fiber of her being, yet too tired to even think about making love with him.

And he had understood. He had climbed onto the pelts, as naked as she, and had drawn soft blankets atop them, then had held her endearingly close as she closed her eyes, so contented she would never forget that moment.

She had not awakened once during the night. She turned from where she lay on her side and saw Falcon Moon sitting beside the bed, his eyes watching her, a slow smile quivering across his lips.

"How long have you been awake?" Wylena asked, brushing fallen locks of hair back from her eyes as she sat up slowly, the blankets falling from around her, leaving her breasts bared to her lover's feasting eyes.

"I have gone for a swim, have brushed down my steed, fed him, then came back with a pot of food that a maiden made for our breakfast," Falcon Moon said, reaching and cupping one of her breasts with a hand.

The exquisite sensation that aroused in Wylena made her feel as though she were melting. She closed her eyes, swallowed hard, then slowly opened her eyes again when she felt his hand no longer there.

"Falcon Moon, I was amazed yesterday when I saw how many of your Apache friends were with you high on that ridge, gazing down at me and my family," she murmured.

Her throat went dry when she realized that she had just made a reference to her "family," not only Joshua. Had Falcon Moon understood the meaning behind what she said? Would he now realize that Jeb was on that wagon with her and Joshua?

"I sent word to many of my friends' strong- holds in the region, asking their assistance in coming for you," Falcon Moon said.

"Why would you have done that?" Wylena asked, shoving the blanket away from herself. She scooted closer to Falcon Moon, so close she could smell his fresh, river smell, his hair still somewhat damp from his recent swim.

She wanted to move her hands over his pow- erful, muscled chest, and even lower on his body. Although he had said that he had left the tepee for a swim, and to tend to his horse, she knew that he had to have been clothed to do those things.

But now? He was very much nude, revealing every inch of his powerful body to this woman who ached to have him take her away, again, to paradise!

"One of my scouts brought word to me that the Mexican general was going to watch for you after hearing that you would be leaving the area," Falcon Moon said. Pausing for a moment, he touched her face. "I immediately sent word to my friends, who have their own private strong- holds. I requested their assistance in getting you from your brother, to take you back to my home, to be my wife," he continued. "They all know of

Father Joshua's goodness, and did not want to see him harmed in any way."

"It was such a sight to see," Wylena said, trembling with a building ecstasy as Falcon Moon searched her body with his hands, finding and touching her every vulnerable, sensual place. "You on one side, with so many of the Apache warriors, and the Mexican general with his men on the other, whose number did not match yours."

She laughed softly. "It was so good to see the Mexicans turn and run scared back to their fortress," she said, then sucked in a wild breath of anticipation when Falcon Moon came to her, lifted her into his arms, and positioned her on her back.

"I did not want an all-out confrontation with the Mexicans," Falcon Moon said, his voice growing husky as he brushed his hands along her naked flesh, stopping here and there to caress her where he knew it aroused her the most. "When he saw the strength of we Apache, the great number there were on our powerful steeds, he knew that he did not have a chance at coming anywhere near you or your brother. Now he knows that in a short time, I could always have such a force behind me when I beckon to my friends for assistance."

She wanted so badly to ask him if he realized that he had been so close to Jeb. If he had thrown back the blankets in the wagon, he would have seen the man he called his enemy.

She believed that he, as astute and smart as he was, must have known that he was near Jeb, yet had chosen to claim her as his before the watchful eyes of her brother Joshua, over taking the other brother hostage.

All of this was best left unsaid. In time she would know what he would finally do about Jeb, for surely he knew that this brother was not all that far away.

"I am anxious to see Bright Star today," Wylena said. Her voice caught when he spread himself over her, that part of his anatomy already grown tight and ready for making love with her.

"My sister is up and about now," Falcon Moon said as he brushed soft kisses from one of Wylena's breasts to the other. "But, my woman, I have only you on my mind, along with the plans we will make to finalize our togetherness as man and wife."

"I so badly want that," Wylena said, slowly roaming her hands over his back. Then she daringly reached out and touched his manhood.

It was so hot.

It was so tight.

And now it pressed gently into her as she spread her legs wider apart to assist that desire that drove them both this morning.

As he shoved fully into her, drawing a gasp of pleasure from deep within Wylena, he whispered to her against her parted lips.

"Marriage is something from the heart," he said huskily. "It is not only words mumbled. We will have a four-day feast, and at the end of that fourth day, at sunset, the marriage ceremony will finish without vows spoken as I have heard they are spoken in the white world. To we Apache, marriage is sacred and permanent. I know that some whites do not cherish their vows and go from man to man, woman to woman. But once an Apache man has taken a wife, and an Apache woman has taken a husband, it is forever, until death do they part."

"I shall never want another man," Wylena whispered back against his warm mouth. "You are my everything. I want only you, my love. Only you."

"Tomorrow will be the first day of the four-day feast and celebration," Falcon Moon said, stroking her where her heart seemed to be centered at the juncture of her thighs, drawing tiny moans from her. "I shall send word to your brother Joshua today that he is welcome to share this special event with us."

She did not allow herself to think of Jeb and how he would be left out of perhaps the most wonderful days of her life.

"It would be wonderful if Joshua could come and enjoy himself with us," she murmured, yet she doubted that he would, for he would not chance leaving Jeb alone for that long. "But he has his daily prayers that must be spoken in his chapel. Perhaps he can come for one day, but not all four."

"One is enough for me if it is for you," Falcon Moon said, stopping his thrusts long enough to gaze into her eyes and marvel over this moment. He had the woman he wanted forever with him again, and she would be with him now until they were old and gray and had many grandchildren running up to them.

"Let us make a child today," he whispered into her ear. "Do you want children?"

"I want many," she whispered back, shivering sensually when he again began his rhythmic thrusts inside her. She felt so alive and receptive of his warmth there. Each thrust brought more desire into her heart, more peace and love! She clung to his neck as he pressed his lips against the hollow of her neck, and then moved lower, where he went from one breast to the other, his tongue flicking the nipples and his teeth nipping her.

So totally overwhelmed by the pleasure that was spreading through her, Wylena closed her eyes, sighed, and let herself enjoy these precious moments, for although she and Falcon Moon had spoken so endearingly of becoming married, she knew that at any time something could happen to change it. That was the way of the world as she had always known it.

Falcon Moon's body was beginning to feel like a hot flame, burning with a passion that overwhelmed him. Until now, until he fell in love with this special, sweet woman, making love to a woman had never meant anything to him except for a gratification that came with being a man.

He had had many women of his own color sharing his bed with him at night, but none had ever awakened the deep sexual excitement that he had found the first time he made love to Wylena.

He had felt it even before they had lain down together. Just being near her had caused his heart to react as at no other time in his life. He did not want to think it was wrong to allow himself, a powerful Apache chief, to choose a white woman over one of his own color. It was the heart that spoke of whom to choose as the one he loved. Not a need to love and marry someone of his own people!

This woman he was holding today had entered his soul that very night he had taken her from the Mexican fortress. Although he had taken her for a different purpose from having her as a bride, he knew the moment he looked into her eyes that he loved her. He had had to fight those feelings until he knew that she was nothing to the Mexican general. He felt so blessed once he had finally discovered who she truly was, the sister of a holy man.

"I love you so," Wylena whispered against his lips when he brought them to hers for a passionate kiss. "My love, oh, my love."

She clung to him and he kissed her over and over again, until suddenly she knew that she could not hold back her full needs any longer.

As he drove into her, more swiftly and surely, and he held her tightly against his powerful body, Wylena shuddered, arched, and cried out as she felt her climax throughout her body, just as she felt him begin trembling while he shoved himself more deeply into her—almost frantically—and he moaned out the pleasure he was receiving.

And then they lay quietly together.

His body was like a torch, burning brightly from inside him, his manhood still quivering from what he had received at the final plunge within her.

"My darling," Wylena whispered, kissing him, her body still on fire with the pleasure she had just felt. "Can we . . . can we . . . do it again? Is it too soon? I feel that I can. Can . . . you . . . ?"

He didn't respond verbally. He shoved himself into her even more deeply this time and again he moved within her in steady strokes as she clung to him, their lips trembling with fiery kisses.

Outside the tepee, hidden in the thick brush, Bull Nose listened to the sounds emerging from Falcon Moon's tepee.

Bull Nose had not gone far when he was made to leave his village in shame. He had circled around, eluded all sentries, and gone to his cave.

He was glad that he had stocked it well enough with supplies. He had never thought that he would be living there full-time. He never truly believed that his chief would dislike him enough to actually banish him.

He wanted his chief dead and he wanted his woman!

His loins were on fire after listening to Falcon Moon and Wylena's activities inside the tepee; their moans and groans filled him with such need. His hand went to his tight groin, trying to stifle the urges that were plaguing him, yet he had Wylena in his mind's eye. He stroked himself through his breechclout until he finally found some relief. As his body lurched with pleasure, it was not enough for him. Only the woman inside Falcon Moon's tepee could complete him.

His face flushed, his breechclout soiled, he ran farther into the dense brush and found a small stream. He hurried into the water to cleanse himself and his clothes, yet his mind would not let go of his sexual desire.

He stretched out beside the stream, plucked some berries from a bush, and began eating them, smiling to himself as he envisioned Wylena's naked body.

Chapter 21

Tell me not, in mournful numbers,
Life is but an empty dream!
—Henry Wadsworth Longfellow

Dressed, but still reeling over what she had just shared with Falcon Moon—she discovered new things about making love each time they were together—Wylena wondered if he noticed how she was beaming as they ate the morning meal.

She had never known that being intimate with a man could be so wonderful. She had never seen her mother react in any special way at any time with her husband, so Wylena did not believe that her mother had ever enjoyed her time alone with him.

The act was surely forced on her by a ruthless, unkind husband, who thought only of his own needs, forgetting his wife's.

She lowered her eyes at the realization that she could be thinking such private things about her parents. Lovemaking was never discussed between her and her mother, who should have been the one to prepare Wylena for such things after she met a special man.

She realized now that people could not teach about something they knew nothing about themselves. So she felt a deep sorrow for her mother now.

Her mother had taught her about the good in life, not the bad, but since she had not enjoyed her husband, love between a man and a woman had been omitted from her teachings.

"My women make delicious soup, do they not?" Falcon Moon asked. His words broke into Wylena's deep thoughts of things she wished not to dwell on when she was feeling so lighthearted and gay.

"I will soon be the one making your breakfast meal, and all others, and I hope you will compliment me, as well, on what I place on your plate," Wylena said, offering a gentle smile to Falcon Moon.

"You will never disappoint me, whether or not your cooking matches that of others that I have known," Falcon Moon said, chuckling. "I wish my mother were alive to show you the ways of my people's cook pots, but when Bright Star feels better, she will show you."

"Yes, I am certain I have much to learn, espe-

cially about the different meats your hunts will
bring home for our meals," Wylena said. She ate
a piece of rabbit meat from her wooden spoon
along with some delicious, rich broth.

When the wooden bowl was empty, and her
belly was full, she shoved the bowl aside and re-
laxed beside the fire. "At my home, our meals
were mainly of chicken and pork, for my father
raised chickens and pigs," she murmured. "We
had cows, too, but only for milk and butter."

"Our meals do vary much from yours," Falcon
Moon said. He had only just heard not so long
ago about the chickens the white men had
brought into Arizona country from their homes
far away. He had also heard mentioned that
white people ate the eggs the female chickens
laid.

He had never eaten pig's meat, and something
told him that he did not want to. What he hunted
and brought home, not only for eating, but also
for making clothes and tepees, would please him
well enough still, and he hoped it would be
enough for his wife, too.

"My woman, today is special in many ways
now that you are with me and my people to
stay," he said, changing the subject from food to
what he felt was more important. "Wylena, I will
first go and check on my sister and tell her about
the upcoming nuptials, and then I will go sit
with my ailing grandmother and tell her, as well,
about what the next four days will bring into our

people's lives. Although she is not well, she will still be able to enjoy many parts of the celebration that only require her to sit and watch and listen. After I speak with her, I must go and be by myself."

"By yourself?" Wylena asked, her eyes widening. "Where . . . and why . . . ?"

"I must go to my private praying place and spend time alone with Ussen," he said softly. "I will pray to Ussen for our happiness as man and wife. While there I hope also to feel my departed father all around me as I have before. His spirit comes often to me as I pray. It is as though we were never parted from each other—those moments are so real."

"Truly?" Wylena asked, her eyes wide. She knew that there were mystical things about Indians and had hoped to learn about them as Falcon Moon's wife. What he had just said was special and she was glad he had shared it with her.

She wished there was some way she could feel her mother's presence as he felt his father's.

"We Apache believe in communication with our departed loved ones who have gone on before us," he said. "If the one who summons the dead speaks the name of one who is dead, they summon the ghost of that person to them."

He smiled into her eyes. "This person at our Happy Place might be hunting or sleeping at the time they are summoned and may not want to come as beckoned, but they must. It is the way of our people that the one summoned respect the wishes of the one doing it."

"You said the departed might be hunting?" Wylena said in awe.

"Those who reside in our Happy Place in the Cloud Land have bodies such as they had on earth, but they never wear out, tire, or know hunger."

"It sounds so wonderful," Wylena murmured. "Surely your people don't fear death if where they go is so special."

"It is special," Falcon Moon said. "It is much like our earth home. There are trees, grass, game, and one's friends and relatives, who are safe and happy there."

"We whites have no true conception of what heaven offers," Wylena said softly. "But we can envision very clearly what hell offers—damnation and fire forever."

"The Apache have no concept of the white people's queer idea of hell," Falcon Moon said thickly.

"No white people enjoy thinking or talking about it," Wylena murmured. "They especially don't want to end up there."

Falcon Moon reached over and gently touched Wylena's cheek. "I really must leave now," he said. "The sooner I leave, the sooner we shall be together again, but know, my sweet woman, that my absence might continue into the night. But I will return before the morning breaks in its golden colors along the horizon, for tomorrow is for us. The celebration will include our entire people, and some from neighboring strongholds, since I have already sent them word of this special time. It will be a time we shall always remember. At the end of the fourth day, we will be man and wife."

"My darling Falcon Moon, I shall wait with patience and love for your return," Wylena murmured.

She leaned forward. "I just wish that I could join you today," she said, searching his eyes.

"I must do this alone," he said, smiling at her. "But after we are husband and wife, you will share many special moments like this with me and my people, who will then also be yours."

"But there will be times when you will have to leave me," she murmured. "I know that you will have to leave for the hunt with your warriors and that you will have councils that do not include women, not even the wife of a chief. And I will understand all of those times when I will watch you leave our tepee without me."

"There will be times when I will take you from the mountain to visit your brother Joshua, and I would hope that he would come and visit us at our home," Falcon Moon said, reaching out and gently touching her face. "I would like to have your brother here with us during the four days of our marriage celebration."

"Four days is quite a lot of time for my brother

to be gone from the mission," Wylena said, although she knew that he had nothing holding him there besides Jeb.

"My brother Joshua prays every morning and every evening in his chapel," she murmured. "It is like you praying to your Ussen. I am not certain how often you do this, but my brother is dedicated to doing it twice each day. Sometimes he prays more often if he feels the need to do so."

"I pray each morning," Falcon Moon said softly. "You will pray with me once we are husband and wife. If you do not choose to pray to my God, then you can pray to your own. It starts a day with goodness."

"I have never seen you praying." Wylena searched his eyes. "Of course I believe you when you say you do, but you do it in such a private way, I have not noticed."

"It is always done in private whenever possible," Falcon Moon said. "I have done it when you slept. When we are married, we will pray together often, but not during the dawn prayers. That is the fathers' time, alone, to pray.

"Each morning, as the sun first appears on the horizon, the father of each Apache family stands at the door of his tepee, always facing the east, and with his eyes and arms uplifted, he prays to Ussen, not to the sun as some whites believe, but to Ussen. Ussen made Mother Earth and everything on it."

He paused, then said, "With we Apache, religion is a personal thing. It has neither an organization nor minister to interact for us with Ussen, as you whites have priests and preachers. We pray directly to him and he answers us."

He continued. "Ussen does not always answer one's prayers. Sometimes there are things requested of him that he does not think is best for the one seeking it."

He gazed deeply into her eyes. "I have one great regret that troubles me as we prepare to marry," Falcon Moon said, quickly changing the subject.

"What is it?" Wylena said, moving to kneel before him so that they could look directly into each other's eyes.

"Bull Nose," Falcon Moon said, the peaceful gaze quickly erased from his face. "I wish there had been more that I could have done for that young man. He was someone whose beginnings were so different from how he turned out to be. I had seen him as worthy of learning to eventually walk in the moccasins of a chief were I never to have sons who could follow me into chieftainship. Even if I had a son, and Bull Nose had proven his worth to be chief, I told Bull Nose that he would be chief over my son."

He kneaded his brow and lowered his eyes momentarily, then dropped his hand to his lap and looked again into Wylena's eyes. "But when Bull Nose began openly challenging my worth as chief, I had to work quickly to stop it," he said firmly. "You see, my woman, power is a mysterious, intangible attribute—difficult to explain, even by one who possesses it. It is the most valuable attribute of a chief, even above one's courage. Without it, how could he maintain discipline and hold on to his warriors? Unless a chief's people believe he has power, he is no longer worthy of being chief."

He paused, lost in concentration, then spoke again. "A chief's greatest power is in having his men follow him willingly in everything he asks of them," he said. "That is why it was so important to make certain Bull Nose never threatened my power more than he already had tried to do. Sending him away is the best thing that I could have done, for not doing so would have caused calamity among my people. I would have to lower my eyes in shame were that to happen."

Wylena felt the pain in what he was saying, and she could tell that he had truly not wanted this to happen to Bull Nose, yet Bull Nose had forced his own chief's hand.

But something told her that they had not heard the last of that wicked man. She would never forget the threat of tarantulas he had used in order to hold his power over her. She wondered just how far he had gone after his banishment. Something told her that he had not gone far enough!

"My woman, after I meet with my grandmother and sister, I will leave on my steed for my private praying place," Falcon Moon said thickly. He reached for her and drew her into his arms. "My praying time will last as long as it must, and then I shall return home to you."

"I shall miss you," she murmured, melting inside when he gave her one of his warmest, most passionate kisses.

Bull Nose smiled cynically as he sat there, full of all that he now knew. He would not have to chance facing his chief just yet. First he would have his way with his chief's woman.

As soon as Falcon Moon left his lodge, Bull Nose would slit the back side of the tepee with the knife he had placed in the cave before he was banished. He would quickly gag Wylena. Then he would drag her into the dark shadows of the trees, and force her to walk with him to where he knew they could not be seen, for he knew all of the sentries' posts. When he and Wylena reached the cave, he would finally have the woman's body as his.

His heart pounded out the minutes until he knew that it was safe to enter his chief's tepee and steal his woman.

Chapter 22

Wylena stood in Falcon Moon's tepee, wishing she had a mirror so that she could see herself in the doeskin dress embellished with beautiful beads sewn onto the soft white skin in the shape of flowers.

After Falcon Moon rode from the village, Wylena had visited with Bright Star. It had been so good to see her doing much better. It was for certain now her health would soon be fully restored.

Wylena had left Bright Star's tepee moments ago to return to Falcon Moon's. The longer she had talked with Bright Star, the more she felt something special with her, like perhaps she could be the sister Wylena never had.

They shared more than one thing that brought

them closer. Bright Star was Falcon Moon's sister, she was in love with Wylena's brother, and they had shared the worst moments of their lives at the Mexican fortress. Now they wanted to share lovely moments, while at the same time putting those ugly ones at the farthest recesses of their minds.

"And she gave me three beautiful dresses and a pair of moccasins," Wylena whispered to herself as she ran a hand slowly down the front of the one she wore now.

It had been hard to choose, for they each were special in their own way. Bright Star had made them with varied bead designs.

Wylena was anxious to learn how to bead herself, and Bright Star had promised that she would teach her after the upcoming wedding celebration was over.

"I want to wear this one to the wedding," Wylena whispered to herself as she picked up another dress.

She smiled. Wylena was so anxious for Falcon Moon to return and tell her how her braided hair, the dress, and the moccasins had transformed her into someone who could easily pass for Indian except for the color of her skin. After all, her hair and eyes were the color of the Apache people's, and now the dress completed that resemblance!

She smiled again as she recalled something special about her time with Bright Star. Wylena had asked her what she used to make her long, black hair so beautiful and clean. Bright Star had answered that the Apache women gathered the roots of the amole plant, then pounded them into a powder, which turned into a fragrant suds when placed in water. Bright Star had said that when she was well and strong again, she would take Wylena with her to gather amole for their private usage.

Wylena could see why Jeb had been drawn so quickly into loving Bright Star. She was not only beautiful; she was sweet and caring, like their mother had been. Wylena and her brothers missed their mother so much, especially the sweet softness of her voice and her laughter.

Not wanting to feel the sadness that always came inside her heart when she thought of her mother, and how she had died so unmercifully, Wylena turned her thoughts back to Falcon Moon. She was so anxious for him to return home, yet knew that it would be some time now, since she had not long ago heard him leave on his horse to go to his praying place.

She laid the wedding dress aside with the other dresses, then stretched out beside the lodge fire. These past days had been exhausting and had robbed her of the rest she needed after her horrible ordeal at the Mexican fortress. She decided to take a nap and sleep away those hours she had to wait for Falcon Moon.

She settled more comfortably on the pallet of

furs and blankets next to the warm fire that rolled its flames slowly around the logs in the fire pit.

She began watching the smoke slowly spiral up and through the smoke hole overhead, feeling strangely hypnotized by the movement. It reminded her of riding her horse back in Illinois. She would gaze at the chimney of their home; the smoke that spiraled from it always seemed to put her in a slow and seductive trance.

Now her eyes closed and she fell into the soft cocoon of sleep, but was startled awake not long after when she felt a rough hand clasp over her mouth. Remembrances of that other time when a rough hand had swept over her mouth, just prior to her being taken to the Mexican fortress, flashed through her consciousness.

She was afraid the Mexican general had somehow made his way past the sentries and managed to get into Falcon Moon's tepee to abduct her again. But she soon saw how wrong she was when Bull Nose yanked her to her feet and sealed her mouth with a piece of buckskin so that she could not cry out for help.

Her heart pounded as she gazed into his dark, evil eyes and he smiled cynically down at her. Then she glanced to her right side and saw that he had sliced his way through the back of the tepee. She tried to cry out, but all that came from her mouth was strange mumbles.

He held her wrists in his strong grasp. She tried to yank free. That ended quickly when he slapped her across the face. The sting reverberated through her body.

Her nose began to bleed and she could feel the blood run behind the gag into her mouth.

"Do not try anything else or I will kill you," Bull Nose grumbled, speaking loud enough for only her to hear. "The knife is sharp. Do you not see the space made along the buckskin fabric of my chief's lodge covering? It would do the same on your body were you to cause me any more problems as I take you from my chief's home and my people's village."

She wanted to cry out at him that these people were no longer his—he had lost all claim because of his bad behavior. How could he have fooled his chief into believing he was worthy of one day being chief? Even his parents had not seen the evil in his eyes, or heart.

He bent down and spoke into her face. "You will never marry Falcon Moon," he grumbled. "You will not live long enough." He chuckled. "Nor will he live long enough to regret losing you. I will kill you soon, and then go to my chief's praying place and sink this same knife that will kill you into his heart."

The thought of all of this truly happening at the hands of this madman sent chills up and down Wylena's spine. Her knees were rubbery as he yanked her toward the opening at the back. He half dragged her through it once he had stepped free of the tepee.

Wylena again tried to yank herself free and make some noise that would alert someone. But nothing she did made enough sound to travel far enough to be heard. She had no choice but to go with this evil Apache as he continued to drag her, and they were soon in the darkness of the aspen trees that grew tall and beautiful on the mountain.

He forced her to walk with him beneath a steep cliff; she could see rough canyon land beyond, where all sorts of mountain greenery varied here and there, from red shrubbery whose limbs were heavy with berries of the same color, to pine trees that seemed to grow right out of the sides of the towering cliffs.

She recognized his intended destination when she saw the opening of a cave not far now from where they walked amid gravelly white rock. The entrance was half-disguised by more shrubbery, yet visible to her as he took her determinedly toward it.

She had kept a constant lookout for the sentries, who would be watching for intruders on the Apache stronghold, yet she saw none, and knew why. This Apache knew where they were posted and how to elude them.

"This is where we will stay until I know that it is the right time to go and kill my chief," Bull Nose said as he shoved Wylena into the cave.

She looked quickly around her and saw that he had likely been there since his banishment.

He had made the cave comfortable with pelts and blankets. She even saw a rifle resting against the side of the cave. He couldn't have these things unless he had brought them prior to his banishment. He had made himself a home by placing a fire pit far enough back so that the smoke would not spiral from the cave, to alert those who passed by that someone was there.

She gazed overhead and saw small cracks in the rocky cave ceiling and knew that was how the smoke escaped, surely in such small spirals that no one would even notice were they to ride right past this place. There was a rack of meat drying close to the fire. Yes, this man was clever, but in evil ways.

She gasped when she saw a small cage of tarantulas; he must mean to frighten her with them.

Bull Nose threw her to the rocky floor, went back to the entrance, and pulled several limbs across the front, to make the cave look unlived in, in case someone did happen by.

As he did this, Wylena took the chance that she needed to get away from him. She reached for a nice-sized rock. As Bull Nose continued to pull limbs across the cave entrance, Wylena crept up behind him and slammed the rock down hard onto his head. The sound that the rock made as it struck his head, a gushy thud, made Wylena cringe. Blood began rolling from the wound as he turned and gave her a wondering look, then crumpled to the floor of the cave, unconscious.

Her heart beating like drums inside her chest, Wylena yanked the gag from her mouth. Then she stepped past him and began pulling the limbs from the entranceway. Finally freed, she gave Bull Nose one last look over her shoulder, then sprang free of the cave and began running. She hoped to get far away before he awakened.

She prayed that somehow Falcon Moon would sense that she was in trouble and come to her rescue. Her pulse raced. Her thoughts were jumbled—she thought one thing and then another—but mainly she focused on getting back to the village.

Soon, though, she realized that she had no idea which way to go!

She had not paid close enough attention to where Bull Nose had walked for her to realize which way she should go to return to the village.

She stopped and gazed from bluff to bluff, hoping that she would see a sentry, yet she knew that was not going to happen, for hadn't Bull Nose cleverly taken her away from where he knew any would be?

Tears splashed from Wylena's eyes.

She began running as fast as she could, wincing when briars reached through the leather of her dress, snagging it for a moment until she managed to get herself free again. When she slipped and fell, she found herself tumbling head over heels, downward and downward. She reached the bottom, falling hard against a rock, and her head hit the ground with a sickening thud.

And then she fell into a dark void of unconsciousness. Before she reached the full depths of darkness, she prayed that Falcon Moon would hurry home and discover that she was missing, and would soon see how she had been taken, through the back of his tepee, by force. She knew that he was a good tracker. Surely he would find her!

Chapter 23

A long, long kiss—burning, intense,
concentrating emotion, heart, soul, all the
rays of life's light into a single focus.
—Edward Bulwer-Lytton

At the top of a canyon, where he had come many times since he had brought his people to safety on Mount Torrance, Falcon Moon slid another limb from a nearby tree into place in the fire. He had built the fire moments ago at the edge of the cliff where he would pray to Ussen and seek his guidance before he took a wife.

Anytime he made a serious decision, wanting to know whether it was blessed, Falcon Moon came here, a place that he knew was sacred to Ussen because it was so close to his home in the skies. And because it was sacred, Ussen answered prayers that rose from it.

Dressed in his breechclout and moccasins, his horse tethered to a low limb of a tree a short distance back from him, Falcon Moon fell to his knees and looked through the thin, blue smoke of the fire, across the wide, wide chasm that stretched out before him. He then lifted his eyes and arms in prayer, all the while Wylena so close in his heart and mind, her sweetness having touched him so deeply.

"I pray, Ussen, that you bless this marriage and children that will be born from the love that is shared between myself and my woman," Falcon Moon prayed, his voice echoing back to him from the wide spaces around him. "I come today, too, to seek continued blessings for my people, that they will continue to be safe and can prosper at our hidden home on this mountain. I pray that you keep my father's spirit close to me at all times, giving me guidance, as I seek the same from you now and every day. Bless my woman so that she can accept the differences in her life from that which she was accustomed to in her white world. I pray that you keep her safe from such men as the Mexican general and those who might envy my having her. She is all goodness and sweetness. Please see that nothing happens to take that from her, or me, for I share all that she is, and she shares the part of me that comes from the strength you have lent me since the day

I was born into this world—which is so often such a challenge to we people with the skin color the white people resent. My woman is white, but I thank you and I thank her God for giving her the sort of heart that holds no biases or prejudices for those who are not the same as she in color or behavior."

He lowered his eyes and his arms, then gazed heavenward again. "These things I seek today from you," he said thickly. "Be with me and my people in the celebration that will join my life and my woman's, forever, even to be together when we join you and my ancestors in the sky."

He paused again, then said, "Keep my woman safe, always, from those who will see her as a traitor to her people because of the one she chose as her husband." He continued, his voice drawn. "Keep her safe, always, from anyone who will resent or envy her her position as wife to a powerful Apache chief. Also, always, I pray for my sister. Let her be well, happy, and also safe."

A breeze brushed across his face, like a soft caress, and he knew that his prayers had been heard and would be answered.

And then something else happened that made him blink over and over again to be certain that what he was seeing was truly there. How could it be? Yet there it was, something happening before him that was mystical and spellbinding.

His eyes became transfixed on the opposite wall, far away. At first he saw nothing, but gradually a black spot appeared and seemed to grow larger. It looked like the opening of a cave, one inaccessible from where he knelt.

Nothing but a bird could reach the entrance to that cavern, yet as he continued to watch, a thin white cloud descended from the sky and stopped just below the opening in the cliff. Everything within Falcon Moon understood that Ussen was creating this thing that mystified him clean inside his soul.

This was a message from Ussen, for suddenly he saw a face against the backdrop of the cave opening. He scarcely breathed as he continued to watch the face materialize. At times, his father had appeared to him in such clouds to be there for him in times of sorrow and trouble.

But today it was someone else. He could see the full outline now, and it was his woman's! Something gripped him hard at the pit of his stomach when he saw that Wylena wore no smile on her face, as she usually did when she gazed back at him. Instead there was only fear in her eyes.

More of her features became visible to him in the mistiness that wafted, foglike, through the empty space that stretched so far away from him. He could see how she was holding her arms and hands out for him, beckoning to him. And then she was gone in a puff of soft, gray smoke, and all that remained was the image of the cave's opening, which was also starting to fade from his sight.

When all that remained was the tall rock that was there before the vision materialized, Falcon Moon rose quickly to his feet.

He looked wildly from side to side, and then over his shoulder, for he was not certain what any of this meant, but he knew that it could not be good.

Ussen had sent him a vision of the woman Falcon Moon would soon take as his wife, and in that vision she was a woman of much sadness, a woman whose eyes revealed fear. As she beckoned to him, he felt it deeply within his heart.

"Wylena is in trouble!" he gasped. He turned quickly and ran to his white stallion. He grabbed the reins and leaped into his saddle, then began carefully working his way down the mountainside, toward where he knew he had once seen a cave.

He had seen this cave only once, while he and his warriors were exploring this new place after having brought their people there. When the cave was discovered, they had gone inside and found that it could be useful to their people were they ever in the need of a hiding place.

That cave was definitely the one in his vision, but he could not fathom why Wylena was associated with it. He had left her safely at home. Their stronghold was guarded from all angles, so no one could chance getting inside without risking his life.

Should the Mexican general want someone

badly enough—namely, a woman he had imprisoned—and discovered somehow where she was now making her residence, would he not risk anything to have vengeance for her disappearance from his fortress?

And then there was Bull Nose. Could his hate lead him so far as to kill as payback against a chief who banished him? Had not Bull Nose already proven his desire to have Wylena? All of these things kept Falcon Moon riding steadily onward until he finally had the cave in his view up ahead through a break in the trees. When he reached it, he leaped from his steed, and grabbing his rifle from his gun boot, he ran inside the cave.

His eyes narrowed at the remains of a campfire that still had gleaming embers amid the cold ash. He saw meat drying near those coals, then searched for anything that might tell him who had been there.

He immediately saw that it had been transformed into someone's living quarters. Surely not those of Bull Nose. He had been ordered from the mountain. When Falcon Moon saw a small cage of tarantulas and remembered how those spiders had been used a short time ago against his woman, he realized that this cave could belong to only one man. Bull Nose!

His pulse racing, he knelt and ran his fingers slowly through the tiny pebbles of rocks that made up the cave flooring. Falcon Moon found footprints. Some were of a large foot clothed in moccasins, and the others were . . .

"A woman's," he snarled, seeing the tiny size of those prints.

His thoughts suddenly went to Wylena and how small her feet were. He knew she would be wearing moccasins today, for Bright Star told him she would give Wylena a pair of her own.

A rage built inside him at the idea that Wylena had been taken there. Why else would Ussen have sent him the vision of his woman outlined against this same cave? Since the footprints alongside hers were from a man wearing moccasins, he knew it was not the Mexican general who had gotten past the Apache sentries.

"Bull Nose," he snarled. His free hand curled into a fist as his other gripped the rifle even more tightly. "Yes, it had to be you who made this cave a home!

"And he still has her," Falcon Moon said.

He started to leave the cave, but stopped and stared at the dried blood he now saw a few feet from where he had seen the last footprints.

He ran his hands over the blood, then saw a trail of blood that led outside the cave.

"Bull Nose's blood or Wylena's?" he whispered, feeling an ache in his heart. If Bull Nose had brought her to that cave and she had not co-operated, what might have happened to her?

His heart sank. He followed the trail of blood to a small stream. He lost the tracks there and knew that whoever the blood was coming from had surely entered the water there. He splashed his horse through the water to the other side. He found no blood there anywhere. What did that mean? Had the injured party died and floated away in the water?

Not allowing himself to believe that his woman had died so needless a death, and feeling guilty for having left her where someone could take advantage of her, he rode onward. He did not believe that Ussen would have sent Wylena to him in a vision if she was dead. Ussen had sent the vision to him so that he would know to search for her and save her. Yes, that was what he would believe. He could not give up on his woman that easily!

He rode onward, his eyes exploring every crushed piece of grass, trampled brush, and broken twig. He would not give up until he found her, for he did know that he would not find her back at his tepee.

Suddenly Falcon Moon heard the roar of a bear. He tightened inside, but followed the sound. The bear was his power. The bear was his medicine. The bear that he could not see but only hear was leading Falcon Moon to his woman, and maybe to the man who had now betrayed Falcon Moon in the worst way possible. He heard a scream and knew that it was not a man's scream. It was a woman's! Oh, surely it was Wylena.

He was relieved to know that she was alive, yet he knew that she was in jeopardy at this very moment and he hoped to reach her in time.

As he broke through a thick stand of brush on his steed, he drew a sudden tight rein. His breath was quickly stolen away when he saw Bull Nose up ahead, his hair sticky with blood, his breech-clout lying on the ground behind him.

He growled like an animal as he tore away Wylena's clothes while—her eyes filled with terror, her body trembling—she tried to fight off Bull Nose by scratching and kicking him.

It pleased Falcon Moon to see his woman's spirit, her courage, in the face of danger. Judging from the blood on Bull Nose's scalp and hair, she had surely knocked him out, and had gotten this far before he caught up with her.

And now it was Bull Nose's plan to rape Wylena, and most likely kill her, all of which would fulfill his need for vengeance against his chief.

Falcon Moon's heart pounded hard at the scene before him. Bull Nose threw Wylena to the ground, enough of the dress torn away for him to have his way with her.

Wylena caught sight of Falcon Moon standing there just as he dropped his rifle and began running toward Bull Nose.

"You die!" Falcon Moon growled as he grabbed Bull Nose around the throat and dragged him free of Wylena.

Sobbing, she stood up. She smoothed what was left of the skirt of her dress down to hide her nudity and watched Falcon Moon and Bull Nose wrestle along the ground. Then she gasped and covered her mouth with a hand when she saw Bull Nose grab Falcon Moon's knife from his sheath. Bull Nose rushed to his feet and waved the knife threateningly between himself and Falcon Moon.

"You were wrong to teach Bull Nose the art of defending oneself so well with a knife," Bull Nose snarled, his eyes gleaming, his nakedness so stark against the backdrop of trees behind him. "And now you will pay for shaming Bull Nose in the worst way possible by banishing him. I will kill you and then rape and scalp your woman."

"Please don't," Wylena cried. "Bull Nose, you know you can't get away with any of this. Even if you do manage to kill me and Falcon Moon, which I doubt that you can, you will be hunted down and you will pay dearly for it. Listen to reason, Bull Nose. So far you have not actually violated my body, only threatened to do so. All that you are guilty of is—"

"I am guilty of too much," Bull Nose said thickly. "So it will not matter if I am guilty for doing more than I have already done."

"Bull Nose—," Falcon Moon started to say, to try to speak reason with this lost man, but his eyes widened and he jumped with a start when Bull Nose lunged at him with the knife.

Bull Nose found his target and stabbed his chief. Wylena cried out at the blood rushing from the wound that had been inflicted on Falcon Moon's chest. She saw her beloved teeter, as though he was light-headed at the suddenness of the stabbing.

The younger warrior stood back from Falcon Moon, laughing insanely, with his chief's blood dripping from the knife onto Bull Nose's belly.

"You are truly insane!" Wylena cried, feeling powerless to help the man she loved.

The blood still spilled from between the fingers he held pressed against the wound.

Chapter 24

Now was she just before him as he sat,
And like a lowly lover down she kneels
                    —William Shakespeare

Wylena stood as though frozen to the ground as she watched the blood seep through Falcon Moon's fingers, until Bull Nose uttered a strange guttural laugh. She stiffened at the look of triumph in his dark eyes and the way he gazed mockingly at Falcon Moon.

"And so I have proven who is the best of men here today, have I not?" Bull Nose taunted. "I should slam the knife into your heart now and finish it quickly for you, but I have no feelings anymore for you, so why should I give you peace by killing you quickly?"

Wylena hurried to Falcon Moon, stunned that

Bull Nose allowed it. She reached down and ripped the remaining part of the skirt of her dress and held it to Falcon Moon's chest. He eased his hand away from the wound to give her room.

"I'm so sorry that I couldn't find my way home after escaping from this monster at the cave," she sobbed. "This could have been avoided. Now . . . now . . . you . . . we . . . might die."

Falcon Moon's eyes never left Bull Nose even though his beloved woman was so close to him. Her words filled him with remorse and fear combined. He saw just how confident Bull Nose was of the victory he felt he deserved, but being too confident was a lesson Bull Nose had never heeded while Falcon Moon taught him the ways of being a successful warrior.

Although Falcon Moon felt the pain in his chest, he knew that the wound was not very deep. It was most certainly not life threatening.

One big drawback of his life as a warrior was that when he bled, he lost blood more quickly than others. It had always been that way with him. He had learned that as a child.

When he talked with Father Joshua about this malfunction of his body, the priest had explained that sometimes a child is born with such weakness, and that in the white world that person was said to be a "bleeder." Although the condition was potentially life threatening, Falcon Moon had never lost enough blood to die from it.

Nor would he today.

Wylena heard a loud, long roar that brought her head quickly around. She knew that large bears roamed this mountain. When she had first arrived at her brother's mission, he had warned her about always having a weapon with her when she left the grounds.

Of course she would need the weapon to ward off danger from two-legged creatures, but the mountain lion and bear were the most treacherous of the four-legged creatures.

When she heard the loud roar again—this time it seemed to echo all around her—she dropped her hand away from Falcon Moon's chest and slowly turned in the direction of the terrible, threatening sound.

She saw Bull Nose turn out of the corner of her eye. Then she saw something so mystical, she felt sure that she was not seeing it at all. She gasped and stepped closer to Falcon Moon; his arm swept around her waist to give her comfort, as he could feel her fear inside his heart.

Falcon Moon watched only momentarily as the bear appeared more distinctly in the middle of what seemed a swirl of grayish fog. It was standing and walking on its hind legs. The bear's large eyes and claws were the most prominent things about the animal, since all other parts of him seemed lost in the mist. Falcon Moon knew this must seem a strange phenomenon to both his woman and Bull Nose. But to him it was something familiar, since this same bear had come to him many other times when it sensed that Falcon Moon was in danger.

Falcon Moon smiled as he watched Bull Nose take a step away from the slowly approaching puff of cloud that carried the likeness of this bear closer and closer. The bear's feet did not touch the ground. Only Falcon Moon understood that the bear was not there to harm anyone, only to frighten the one who threatened Falcon Moon.

He regretted that Wylena had to be frightened, but soon she would realize there was nothing to be afraid of, and instead something to marvel over. He had been scared the first time this bear had appeared to him in such a way.

"Do not be afraid," he said softly to Wylena, loud enough for only her to hear him. "Look at what I wear around my neck. Do you not see the bear's tooth that I explained to you was my medicine? The bear is my power . . . my protector. It protects me, always, from all dangers. Today it helps me be victorious over my enemy, as it has helped me in the past."

She didn't have time to question him further about it. Falcon Moon stepped quickly away from her, and while Bull Nose was still entranced by what he saw, his whole body trembling from the fright it had brought into his heart, Falcon Moon grabbed the knife quickly from the warrior's hand.

This brought Bull Nose from his trance. He

looked at the knife that was now in Falcon
Moon's hand instead of his own, then looked
into Falcon Moon's eyes.

"You know that the bear is my power . . . my
medicine, so you should know that what
brought the bear to me today, as it has come at
other times when I was faced with danger, is because you, someone I trusted and lent my knowledge to, have betrayed me, your chief, in the
worst way," Falcon Moon said. Blood no longer
seeped from his wound, a wound that now was
scarcely there. The bear's magic had touched
him and made him well.

"I . . . ," Bull Nose stammered, his eyes still
wide from having witnessed something so mystical, even though he knew these types of things
did occur among his people.

He had just never been blessed with such
medicine himself, and he now understood why.
Only those with a pure heart had such powerful
medicine. Only those who were meant to lead
were given such powers greater than someone of
a mere mind and body possessed.

Bull Nose swallowed hard, looked over his
shoulder, and saw that the bear was no longer
there, then turned and made a lunge for Falcon
Moon. "Your medicine, your magic, is gone!" he
cried as he tried to grab the knife from Falcon
Moon.

But Falcon Moon was too fast. He reached a
hand out and grabbed Bull Nose by the throat.

"Did you truly believe that just because my medicine is no longer visible, I have none of the strengths or powers left that it brought to me?" Falcon Moon said between clenched teeth. "Look at my chest. Do you see a wound there any longer? Do you believe now in the strength and magic of your chief? You were so wrong, Bull Nose, to go back on your pledge to follow me with a pure heart and mind. Because of your lack of morals, you lose everything that could have been yours. You have shamed your parents, your people, your chief, not only once, but many times over now. What did you think you would gain by stealing my woman? Did you truly believe you would achieve victory against your chief in that way? Shame on you, Bull Nose, to hide behind the skirts of a woman in order to avenge what you felt your chief did to you. You chose my woman as your act of vengeance? What could you have been thinking?"

"You put this woman before me, the one who was to follow you into chieftainship," Bull Nose growled. He purposely didn't look at his chief's chest, having heard that Falcon Moon did have such mystical powers, although he had never personally witnessed the magic before now.

The situation made Bull Nose know the foolishness of having returned, after being banished, to try to achieve vengeance against his chief, for although this need ate away at Bull Nose's gut, he understood that he should have gone far away from this place, this mountain, this chief. He knew now that his time on this earth was short-lived.

He expected to die unless he could make Falcon Moon believe that he was not touched whatsoever by the magic that he had seen today.

He growled like an animal as he yanked himself free of Falcon Moon's grip. He doubled up a fist and slammed it into Falcon Moon's belly, the suddenness of it causing Falcon Moon to drop his knife.

Bull Nose bent quickly to retrieve the knife so that he could finish what he had started.

But Falcon Moon was too quick for him. Falcon Moon lifted a knee into Bull Nose's gut just as the younger warrior bent over. His hand only grazed the knife before the impact of Falcon Moon's knee caused Bull Nose to cry out in pain as he was thrown back on the ground with a thud.

Wylena covered her mouth with a hand as she watched Falcon Moon leap onto Bull Nose and hold him prone on the ground with his wrists above his head. The two warriors glared into each other's eyes, and then it was Bull Nose's turn to best his chief again.

He raised his head quickly from the ground and slammed his forehead into Falcon Moon's. Wylena cried out and felt faint at the loud cracking sound the impact made.

While Falcon Moon was momentarily stunned by the impact, Bull Nose took the opportunity to roll away from him. He reached for the knife again, but Wylena hurried over and slammed a foot onto it.

With the knowledge that he had to win this battle or die, Bull Nose gave Wylena a hard shove, sending her away from the knife. She landed on her rear end on the ground, causing her to cry out with pain just as Bull Nose had the knife in his possession again.

Leering, he stood over Falcon Moon. When Falcon Moon realized that Bull Nose was standing over him with the knife, ready to make the death plunge, he rolled away and leaped quickly to his feet.

Bull Nose grumbled as Falcon Moon lunged at him and grabbed him around the wrist, where the knife was only inches away, in a tight grip.

"Drop the knife," Falcon Moon growled, his dark eyes battling with Bull Nose's. "If you do not drop the knife, you will die by it."

"You are wrong," Bull Nose said, succeeding at yanking his wrist free.

But just as he swung the knife around and was ready to thrust it into Falcon Moon's chest, Falcon Moon reached out his leg and tripped him.

Falling clumsily, Bull Nose landed awkwardly on the ground. The knife was there and he fell onto it.

Seeing what had happened, and how Bull Nose was groveling on the ground, Wylena hurried to Falcon Moon and clung to him.

"It is finished," Falcon Moon said, an arm sweeping around Wylena's waist. "In the end he did prove to be a fighter. He did prove that he had courage enough to fight for what he wanted. But that courage was spent in the wrong way by using it on his chief. Ah, but he could have been such a powerful, useful warrior to our people, were he not blinded by wanting more than what he was allowed to have."

"Chief," Bull Nose whimpered as he lay face-down on the ground, the knife holding him in place. "Falcon Moon. I . . . am . . . sorry. Please . . . forgive . . . me before I die."

Bull Nose choked, then slowly turned his head so that he could look into Falcon Moon's eyes. "I want . . . to walk . . . with my chin held high in the Happy Place of our Apache ancestors," he stammered, each word becoming more faint than the last. "I want to be at the Happy Place when my parents arrive there. That is the only way we can be a family again. I cannot go there unless . . . unless . . . you forgive me."

A man of such goodness, Falcon Moon suddenly saw Bull Nose as the child he had watched grow into early adulthood, and he could not just stand there and allow this warrior to die without any mercy paid to him.

Although Bull Nose would have laughed as Falcon Moon died, had Bull Nose finally bested his chief, Falcon Moon was a better man than that.

He knelt beside Bull Nose. He slowly turned him over and saw this warrior's life's blood on the ground beneath him, and in his mind's eye he relived some special moments that he had shared with Bull Nose when the warrior was young, vital, and eager to be what he now would never be.

Falcon Moon's eyes misted with tears as he gazed into Bull Nose's. "You could have been a man of such greatness," he said, his voice drawn with emotion. "Why were you so impatient for that? I would have made certain that you had all of the knowledge you would need to lead our people when I could no longer lead them. But as it was, you wanted more too quickly and it just could never be, Bull Nose. For you to even consider killing your chief, and having actually almost done so, is something I shall never understand. What could have led you into such feelings toward me? Did I ever do you wrong? If so, this is the time to tell me so that I will know, always, how this could have come about, that you would die so young, and in such shame."

"I . . . do . . . love you," Bull Nose said, tears spilling from his eyes. "But my need to have more than was given me was stronger than my love for you."

With that, Bull Nose gasped and his eyes suddenly locked in a death stare.

Falcon Moon sighed heavily, reached down, and closed Bull Nose's eyes, then lifted him from the ground and began walking slowly, carrying Bull Nose to where Falcon Moon had tethered his steed's reins.

Wylena followed close beside him, amazed at this man she adored, how he was placing Bull Nose's body on the back of his horse.

She did not question him as to why he was giving this evil warrior such special attention when earlier he had banished him from his people. Now he was being returned? And with such kindness and forgiveness?

Knowing Falcon Moon so well now, and aware of his goodness, she understood that what he was doing was not for Bull Nose at all.

It was for Bull Nose's parents. They would have a final good-bye with their son and would see to him having a proper burial. Yes, she knew now the depths of Falcon Moon's goodness, and she loved him even more for it.

He reached a hand out for her. She went to him. For a long moment he hugged her and she returned the hug. Then he lifted her on the horse so that she would ride before him toward his village with the young, dead warrior on the horse behind them.

No words were said while they rode in the direction of the stronghold, but Wylena's eyes were drawn suddenly to the left and she marveled in silence over a bear that was ambling along nonthreateningly on all fours beneath the trees. Even when the bear turned its dark eyes toward them,

Wylena saw how it was content enough to go on its way; it looked forward again and was soon lost from her sight.

She recalled how earlier she had witnessed something so mystical that she would never forget how stunned she had been at seeing a bear in the middle of the swirl of a foggy shroud. She marveled at the man she was going to marry, who had such powers that no white man would ever believe her were she to tell him. She would certainly not tell her priest brother, for he would possibly see what had happened as something brought on by the devil!

But she could not help but gaze at Falcon Moon's chest where he had been wounded. She knew that was something she would always marvel over. She could not help but wonder just what else she might witness as the wife of a powerful, mystical Apache chief!

Chapter 25

As from the darkening gloom a silver dove
Upsoars, and darts into the eastern light,
On pinions that nought moves but pure delight,
So fled thy soul into the realms above,
Regions of peace and everlasting love
—John Keats

Everyone at the village stopped and stared as Falcon Moon came into the stronghold with, not only Wylena on his white stallion, but also Bull Nose, who lay dead across the back of the muscled steed. No one said anything when Falcon Moon rode onward and then stopped at Bull Nose's family's lodge.

Just as he dismounted and helped Wylena from the horse, Bull Nose's mother came from her tepee, her husband beside her. They both took unsteady steps backward when they saw Bull Nose.

Falcon Moon understood their instant distress and went to them. He swept his arms lovingly around them both and softly explained to them what had happened as the rest of the village people came slowly and stood in a semicircle, watching and listening.

Wylena stepped back away from them as she waited for Falcon Moon to finish this sad chore of telling the parents of a fallen son how it had happened. Wylena saw the instant shame and grief in the fallen warrior's mother's eyes. The father remained stoic and revealed no emotion at all as he walked past Falcon Moon and untied the ropes holding his son on his chief's horse. Then he took Bull Nose from the steed and carried him past his wife and into their lodge, where he remained with him.

"Soaring Moon, your son spoke of his regrets before he took his last breath," Falcon Moon said, reaching his hands to her face, framing it with them. "He truly did speak to me with apologies from his heart before he died. None of us will ever know what drove him to behave as he did, when if he had remained as he was before his change, he would have proven to be a great leader. He had all the qualities of a leader until something inside him snapped and he became someone foreign even to himself. But you can bury him now and know that I received his apology with an open heart, and because I did, his spirit can join our ancestors who have gone to the Happy Place before him. They will no longer shun him for the wrong path he took. One day you will see for yourself that he is not doomed because of how he behaved, but instead is truly at peace with himself."

"If only he could have apologized sooner and become that son I knew before something entered his heart that made him, for a while, forget who he was," Soaring Moon said, her voice breaking with emotion as tears streamed from her eyes. "But thank you for putting my heart at peace with your words about my son. I will be able to bury him now and then resume my life without him with a peaceful heart."

"And know that you could not have been a better mother than you were to Bull Nose, nor could his father have been a better father," Falcon Moon softly reassured her. "Go now and sit with your husband and son. I will postpone my wedding celebration long enough for you to mourn for one day and night before you have your burial rites."

"You are so kind," Soaring Moon said, flinging herself into his arms. "Thank you, my chief. Oh, thank you from the bottom of my heart."

As she walked into her tepee, everyone who had come to share this moment with her turned away and slowly returned to the chores they'd been busy with before Falcon Moon brought the fallen warrior into their midst.

Falcon Moon went to Wylena. He turned toward his grandmother's lodge, then smiled back at Wylena. "I must go and reassure her that I am all right, for my grandmother is someone who sees visions and she perhaps saw in a vision that I was injured," he said thickly. "I wish to reassure her personally. Will you come with me? It would be good for you and my grandmother to get to know each other better, since you already share me."

"I would love to go with you," Wylena murmured, already keeping step with him as he headed toward his grandmother's tepee, which sat somewhat back from the others. She gave him a sidewise glance, finding it hard to believe that he took his powers so matter-of-factly, for he had been wounded terribly by Bull Nose, yet there were no signs of the wound anywhere on his chest.

When they reached the small tepee, Falcon Moon swept the entrance flap aside. "Go on inside," he said softly. "Grandmother already knows to expect us. You see, Wylena, she is aware of many things before they actually happen."

He saw how Wylena hesitated at entering the tepee, then leaned closer into her face. "Are you becoming uneasy over knowing these mystical things about me and my grandmother?" he asked, searching her eyes. "You will be a part of it, you know, once we are married. Will you be comfortable with it? Or will your Christian up-bringing condemn it in your eyes?"

"I love you, so rest assured that I will never question you about anything that I feel should be left unsaid," Wylena murmured. "What I have witnessed is intriguing and I will leave it at that. Please feel comfortable with me at all times and always know that nothing you do, or say, could ever make me love you less."

He swept her into his arms and held her for a moment, then ushered her on inside the tepee, where his grandmother was sitting close to the lodge fire to absorb whatever warmth it would lend her. Falling Water looked up and squinted while trying to see through the hazy covering that had come over them not long ago. She knew that one day soon she would be totally blind and accepted that as a part of her aging. She was a woman of mysticism and magic, but nothing she had done had helped to restore her vision.

"I am so glad that you are safely home," Falling Water said, reaching a hand to Falcon Moon's face as he bent low to kiss her cheek. "My grandson, I am aware of everything that transpired between you and Bull Nose. I summoned the bear to come to you and save you. I saw it in my mind's eye as though I was there myself, helping you."

Wylena was becoming more enraptured by the minute over these two people, who were capable of so many things. She felt blessed that she was a witness to these things, and looked forward to a future of learning more about why Falcon Moon and his grandmother were blessed in such a wonderful manner.

"Grandmother, Bull Nose lost his way and I do not know why, but he has found his way home again and his parents are at peace now," Falcon Moon said as he and Wylena sat down closely together on the opposite side of the fire from his grandmother.

"Grandmother, as you know so well, to we Apache the worst crime a man can be guilty of is betraying his chief and his people," Falcon Moon said. "For that, Bull Nose has paid the highest price. First he suffered the embarrassment and shame of being banished. Then he came back to shame himself even more by what he did to my woman, and then to me. But now it is over. He will shame no one ever again, not even himself, for he is gone from this earth, forever."

"Yes, it is done. Now let us speak of other things," Falling Water said, slowly smiling as she gazed from Falcon Moon to Wylena and back again at Falcon Moon. "My grandson, I know that you have postponed your marriage celebration for as long as it takes for Bull Nose's parents to mourn and bury him, but then it will be you and your woman's time to smile and be happy. Grandson, I bless your marriage to this woman and I will participate in the celebration, but only for a while. I tire so easily. But I do want to give you both my blessings, not only now, but during the celebration."

Falling Water reached a hand out and beckoned toward Wylena. "Come to me, my child," she murmured. "Let me see your face fully with my fingers."

Wylena swallowed hard and questioned Falcon Moon with her eyes. When he smiled and nodded at her, she rose slowly to her feet, went around the fire, and stopped beside Falling Water.

Kneeling down close enough for Falling Water to feel her face, Wylena leaned closer. She felt the roughness of Falling Water's aged hands—the roughness told her that during her more youthful years she had worked with the other women of the village, planting and harvesting crops, as the warriors busied themselves with the hunt and keeping their people safe.

Wylena knew that sometime in the future her hands would be as rough, because she would do everything required of her as an Apache chief's wife to make him proud of her. She looked forward to planting the crops, since she had done that while she lived with her parents in Illinois. She had enjoyed the harvesting the most because she knew that a winter lay ahead of her family when they would have food from their food cellar even during the coldest of days.

As Falling Water's fingers crept along the gentle lines of Wylena's face, she smiled. "You are not Apache, yet you are as beautiful were you so," she murmured. "You will make beautiful babies with my grandson. I hope for at least one before I take my last breath."

"We will make that so," Falcon Moon said as he came and sat on the other side of his grandmother.

Wylena smiled past Falling Water just as the older woman eased her hand from her face and rested it then on her lap.

"I am anxious to be a mother," Wylena murmured. Then her smile faded. "Falcon Moon, since we have one more day to wait before the celebration begins, can we go and visit my brother Joshua? I want to explain the four days of celebration to him, and I hope to talk him into coming to enjoy at least a part of the celebration."

"Yes, we shall travel down the mountain tomorrow and meet with Joshua." Falcon Moon nodded.

He knew that he had given her what she wanted, so he wondered why his response did not bring more joy into her eyes. It did not take long for him to figure that out. It was her other brother who troubled her. That brother had been elusive, but Falcon Moon knew that he could not hide forever. It would be up to whoever found him first as to how he would be treated. He could not help but hope that the Apache did not find him because he did not want to be the one to set down the sentence of death to her brother. To do so might be to place a barrier between himself and his woman, and he could not allow that!

Wylena smiled softly. "Thank you for agreeing to go with me tomorrow," she murmured. "I left my brother much too hastily the other day. I wish to hug him and reassure him that I will be all right, that marrying you will assure my safety and happiness."

Falling Water listened and heard caution in both her grandson's and his woman's voices, and could not help but wonder why.

She would have to search for answers in a vision.

Chapter 26

After a restful night of sleep, Wylena clung to Falcon Moon as she sat behind him on his horse while traveling through the narrow spaces that led down the mountainside. Although she was skilled with horses, she would not just yet try riding down the mountainside alone on a horse.

Perhaps in time. But not now.

The mere thought of being alone on a horse so close to these steep drop-offs sent her into a silent panic. As it was, it was good to be with Falcon Moon alone like this, with one large problem now behind them.

If only she could prove that Jeb was not who so many said he was, then her life would be perfect. Until he was proven not guilty, he would always be with her in her heart, and her concern for him took away some of the wonder she felt about the new direction her life was taking. She would soon be the wife of a handsome, powerful Apache chief!

"Are you all right?" Falcon Moon asked, glancing at her over his shoulder. He looked straight ahead again, watching his horse's every move as they went farther down the steep slope. "You are so quiet. Are you afraid of riding this close to the edge of the pass we are now traveling on? Or is it something else that has brought such silence to you?"

Wylena laughed nervously. "Well, I must admit, I don't care much for having to ride this close to a steep drop-off, but that is not the worst of my concerns," she said. "It is my brother Jeb that I am so worried about. When will he be able to prove his innocence? How? I am so afraid that before he is able to, someone will see him and kill him. Were he to die, a part of me would die, too, for as children, before my brothers escaped the insanity of our father, we were so close. We depended on one another to get through each day. We protected one another from as much harm as possible. It was as though we were triplets instead of just the two of them being twins."

"It is good that you had brothers you could be close to like that," Falcon Moon said. They finally reached the bottom of the mountain, and continued onward on his horse as he sank his heels into its flanks to urge it into a gallop. "My mother gave birth to me and then my sister, but after that, she could have no more children. Each time she tried she could not go the full time without losing the child. Finally she just stopped trying. We were a happy family until my parents were ambushed one day while away from the village, just enjoying being together on their separate horses."

"I am so sorry. Who is responsible for their deaths?" Wylena asked softly.

"It has been five moons now since their deaths," Falcon Moon said. "And who did it? We have never discovered the one who sent bullets into both of their bodies. All bullets look the same when they come from the barrel of a gun, whether a white person, red, or Mexican sent it into their backs."

"Their backs?" Wylena gasped. "Someone shot them like that?"

"They were slain in the most cowardly of ways," Falcon Moon said, his voice tight with a renewed anger at thinking again about how his parents were taken from him. "My father was a proud chief, whose heart was good toward all people, no matter the color of their skin. He was not a man who ruled by warring. He chose peaceful means to keep his people as safe as he could. He even had a peaceful relationship with General Zamora. That is why I found it so hard to believe that the general could steal my sister away and take her to his fortress and treat her so inhumanely. It seems he forgot the friendship pact between himself and my father. I, too, have now forgotten it. If he so much as draws near my mountain now, he will not live to reach even halfway to the summit."

"You are so kind not to have attacked his fortress after learning about your sister," Wylena said, realizing that just talking about the general and where he had taken her and Bright Star brought goose bumps along the flesh of her arms and legs.

"He has crossed the line now, as far as any measure of friendship between him and myself goes, by having done that to my beloved sister, as well as you, even though at the time I saw you there, you were nothing to me yet," Falcon Moon growled. "I was successful at removing my sister safely from his compound, but his actions toward her have erased any semblance of peace we had between us. Had I not had my people to protect, I would have taken many warriors to the fortress and attacked. But as it is, I must do everything within my power to keep them from all harm. They are safe now on our mountain. I must see that it remains so."

"It is frightening to know the thin line that now separates you from the general as far as warring goes, for I just cannot believe he will not try and avenge you. You took not only one prisoner from his compound, from right beneath his nose, but two. He surely feels foolish in the eyes of his soldiers. Do you not believe he will find a way to avenge how he has been made to appear to his soldiers? Don't you think they now see him as weak and not the strong leader they thought that he was?"

"Only time will tell whether or not he will come up the mountain pass to try and find my stronghold," Falcon Moon said. "But should he try, he will get only so far. I now have many more sentries posted, not only high up, close to the stronghold, but also far below. No one will get anywhere near where my people enjoy their safe haven near the clouds, where Ussen has his home. Do you not feel Ussen's presence everywhere you go at my village? Or is it your God's presence that you feel?"

"Perhaps I feel both, because when I am at your stronghold with your people, I feel safe," she murmured.

Then she thought quickly back to what had happened to her at the hands of Bull Nose. "I was made to feel differently only when Bull Nose came and took me hostage," she quickly added.

"Only my people would know how to elude the sentries, because my people know where they are posted," Falcon Moon said, feeling torn over how to feel about Bull Nose now.

He had deserved no less than death, yet it was sad to have seen such a young Apache warrior wasted, whereas he might have been so much to his people.

"I am so sorry that Bull Nose disappointed you in such a way," Wylena said, trying hard not to recall how he had come so close to raping her.

She would one day forget, but now it was too fresh on her mind not to cause her embarrassment.

She suddenly remembered how the bear had appeared to them so mystically yesterday. "The bear," she murmured. "I shall never forget how the bear appeared in what seemed a shroud of misty clouds yesterday. Do . . . these . . . things happen often to you?"

"The bear is a mystical being in itself," Falcon Moon said. "All bears are my friends. I talk to bears and they listen. They understand and help. They do not talk back."

He smiled. "If you meet a bear and he stands on his hind feet and holds his hands up, he is trying to tell you that he is your friend. All bears are my friends, as are they my people's."

Suddenly they both grew quiet when they caught sight up ahead of a man who seemed wounded. He sat limply in his saddle, his head hanging low, as the horse rode on its way.

Wylena looked more closely at the man and her heart skipped a beat when she wondered if he might be Jeb. The man's skin was white. He wore the same sort of clothes that Jeb always wore—all black.

Even from this distance Wylena could see the lightning design sewn onto the boots, the same as Jeb's boots!

He was also similar to Jeb in weight, height, and the long, dark hair that hung to his shirt collar.

Falcon Moon yanked on his reins to slow his horse down but continued to follow the man to see where he might go. Now that Falcon Moon got a better look at the man, he saw blood on the side of his shirt. Surely he had been shot and was trying to make his way back home.

But not knowing if this man was friend or foe, Falcon Moon still only followed. He wondered if Wylena realized that this man on the horse was headed straight for the mission.

Suddenly a snake came out of the brush directly in the path of Falcon Moon's steed, causing his horse to snort fearfully and rear somewhat, yet not high enough to throw Wylena or Falcon Moon from its back. Undisturbed by the threat of the horse's hooves, the snake went on its way and was soon lost to sight in another thick stand of brush.

Falcon Moon snapped his reins and went onward, but he had lost all sight of the horseman.

The wounded man on the horse must have heard Falcon Moon's horse and been given enough warning to hurry on his way, and was now hiding somewhere.

Falcon Moon slowed his steed down to a slow lope as he looked everywhere for signs of the other horse and the injured man in the saddle. But, as though the man had waved a magic wand, he was completely gone from sight!

"Where could he have gone?" Wylena asked, stunned at how quickly the man had disappeared.

And then she became aware of something else. Through a break in the trees not very far away was her brother's mission, the tall steeple again like a beacon.

"I see your brother's steeple through the trees up ahead," Falcon Moon said.

He was glad that they were almost at the mission, for he had not liked having his woman brought into the face of what could have been a dangerous episode if he had caught up with the injured man.

An injured man was as bad as an injured animal. It defended itself even more valiantly; it fought to the death with much courage and bravery.

Wylena held on to Falcon Moon as he rode free of the trees that sat not far from her brother's mission. Her pulse raced, for if that injured man was not Jeb, and he was at the mission, she hoped that one of her brothers would hear the approach of Falcon Moon's horse so Jeb would have time to go into hiding.

It was so difficult for her to accept that her brother had to hide from all humanity. He had come to live with Joshua to help him in the garden, and do anything else that would lighten Joshua's load. But now Jeb could not even be seen outside the mission, much less be able to fell trees for firewood, or plant or harvest from the garden.

Now all Jeb could do was hide while his brother did the chores required to keep them in food and firewood, and Wylena had seen that it was taking its toll on Joshua. He had looked so weary, his shoulders bent the last time she saw him, which was on the wagon that was pointed toward Illinois. Now her brothers were back at the mission and only time would tell what would eventually happen to Jeb.

Falcon Moon rode up close to the door of the mission and drew a tight rein. He dismounted, secured the reins on a post, then helped Wylena from the steed. They stopped long enough to look slowly around them, both aware that there were no sounds anywhere, nor did Joshua come to the door to greet them.

"It seems too quiet," Wylena said, feeling as though something was wrong there, for Joshua still hadn't come to the door. He had to have heard the horse, so why wasn't he there to see who had arrived?

She looked toward the barn, wondering how many horses she would find there. Would she find Jeb's? Or would it be gone? The horse she had seen with the injured man had looked identical to Jeb's!

Her heart sank the more she thought about the injured man possibly being Jeb.

The injured man needed medical attention

soon, for she had seen how he sat slumped in his saddle. She had also seen the blood! She said a silent prayer that it wasn't Jeb and that he was safely hidden in his underground hideout. Perhaps Joshua was in his chapel, so busy praying to his Lord that he had not heard the approach of Falcon Moon's steed.

"Let's go inside," she blurted out, anxious now to see how right or wrong she was about all of this.

She saw how Falcon Moon stopped long enough to take his rifle from the gun boot at the side of his horse, for she knew that he was too cautious of a man to go inside without taking a weapon with him. She glanced up into his eyes as he gazed into hers. Then she turned and walked on to the house.

Falcon Moon stepped quickly in front of her and opened the door himself, very slowly and very cautiously.

Once the door was open, and she saw there was still no movement in the room, Wylena felt a strong fear inside her heart that something was terribly wrong. She trembled but stepped farther into the room, her eyes moving warily around her. Falcon Moon stepped up to her side just as she saw her brother's black robe draped across the back of a chair.

She knew Joshua well and he would never leave his robe hanging carelessly on a chair. Once he removed it, he would hang it where the wrinkles could fall out of it for the next day's wearing.

Wylena could not imagine why the robe was there and began to fear for her brother Joshua's life.

As for Jeb, she had no idea what to expect as far as he was concerned. If something had happened to Joshua, would Jeb have come to his rescue, or would he have stayed hidden, looking out only for himself? Her mind flashed back to the man on the horse, the blood on his shirt, and how his head was hanging. Had that been Jeb? If so, where was he? And what would he do as Wylena and Falcon Moon searched the mission for Joshua?

Wylena stared at a back room that she had been told was used for storage. She had never been there long enough for her to have needed to go into the storage room. She eyed it for a moment, then shrugged and hurried on to her brother's study, for surely if he wasn't there, she would find him in the chapel. When she opened the door to the study, her heart dropped, for Joshua was not there.

She left that room and headed for the chapel. She would shout out his name, but if he was deep into his prayers, she would not want to disturb him.

Suddenly she stopped. Fear was like a hot poker in the pit of her stomach, for she truly believed that things were wrong at this mission. She was afraid to check the chapel, for she did not believe she would find her brother there. But she gave Falcon Moon a half smile, wanting to reassure him that everything was all right. Then she hurried to the chapel and opened the door.

There were the lovely stained-glass windows, which the sun came through, splashing all sorts of colors along the pews where her brother usually knelt for his prayers. Again her heart felt as though it were dropping slowly to her toes when she didn't find any signs of her brother there.

She turned to Falcon Moon. "I just know that something terrible has happened to Joshua," she said, her voice breaking. "He isn't here!"

Remembering the storage room that she had not yet entered, she ran past Falcon Moon. She stopped, though, before opening it. Something within her told her that what she would find was not good. Tears filled her eyes as she grabbed the doorknob and slowly opened the door. When she saw what was there, she shoved the door all of the way open and screamed.

There was just enough light filtering through a small window at the top of the room to reveal that the room's contents did not belong there.

There was a ghastly stack of scalps, some with fresh blood on them.

Almost fainting from the sight, and the stench, Wylena stepped back and grabbed one of Falcon Moon's hands, hoping to receive strength from him at a time when everything seemed to be falling apart all around her.

How could any of this be real?

Could her very own priest brother be the scalp hunter, while all along everyone looked to Jeb as the one responsible for taking the scalps?

"It can't be," she sobbed as she looked up at Falcon Moon through her tears of sorrow. "It just can't be Joshua. He is so godly . . . so . . ."

She had thought the wounded man might be Jeb, but now she could not help but believe it might have been Joshua. He could have slung his robe across the chair just prior to leaving to take more scalps, but got wounded in the process.

Falcon Moon slid an arm around her waist and took her from the room. He led her to a chair and eased her down onto it. She hung her face in her hands and cried.

"Then where is Jeb?" she suddenly cried out, now fearing for the life of the brother everyone had thought was evil through and through.

Had he discovered Joshua bringing scalps to the mission to hide them?

She looked over at the tapestry. She was afraid now what she might find down below in the hideout. Had Joshua felt he had no choice but to kill his twin brother?

She looked up at Falcon Moon standing protectively over her, the rifle ready should he need it. "Why, oh, why would Joshua do these things?" she cried. "Only a tormented man could do this, and Joshua always behaved like a man of peace. And why scalp if not to sell them? You saw how many there were. Oh, surely there are even more somewhere else in the mission."

"He planned to sell them later," Falcon Moon said thickly.

Suddenly they both heard someone groaning.

They both looked at the same time at a room they had not yet searched. It was the room that had been assigned as her bedroom!

She rushed to her feet and with Falcon Moon at her side, the rifle aimed straight ahead of him, followed the continued moans until they came to the closed door of Wylena's bedroom. Wylena glanced up at Falcon Moon, swallowed hard, then placed her hand on the doorknob. After opening it only a fraction, she saw one of her brothers sitting in a chair, naked down to his breeches. He was tied to the chair, and his mouth was gagged. It looked like he was only now awakening after having been knocked unconscious.

Her brother's eyes opened and he tried to speak through the gag. He also worked hard at trying to free himself of the ropes that held him in place. Wylena was suddenly confused as to which brother this was. Everything about them was identical!

Of course she was used to seeing Joshua in his robe, yet beneath that robe he wore breeches like the ones this brother wore . . . exactly like the ones Jeb always wore.

Seeing the pleading eyes above the gag, and realizing that she had been just standing there staring, puzzled over who she was actually looking at, Wylena rushed to him and untied the gag.

"Wylena, oh, Lord, Wylena, Jeb has gone mad," this brother said in a rush of words.

When he realized that she was confused about his identity, he spoke again, this time more quickly.

"Wylena, this is no time to be confused about which brother is sitting here waiting for you to untie the ropes," Joshua rushed out. "Wylena, you have to know that I would never do anything like what I have been forced to see. It's Jeb, Wylena. Jeb is most certainly the scalp hunter. He has brought the scalps he recently took from some unfortunate souls here, because he was wounded while taking them to his usual hideout. He left again. I don't know where he went. I imagine to his hideout to get the rest of his scalps. He knocked me unconscious, Wylena. Our very own brother!"

Still confused, and not yet ready to untie him in case he was the guilty party, Wylena only stood there, her eyes locked with whichever brother this was.

She was wrong to have suspected Joshua. Or had he always been the devil in disguise, hiding behind the Lord's clothes in order to get around unharmed by anyone? Perhaps the man they'd seen had been wounded while tying her brother in the chair, and was now on his way to the closest fort to turn Joshua in.

Then something came to her that made her feel a trace of hope inside her heart. There was one true way to tell her brothers apart. She rushed around to stand behind the chair, and she was able to see enough of this brother's back to see the scars. She sobbed with relief when she saw the scars that proved to her that this man was Joshua.

Her heart sank, though, to know now that the other brother was the scalp hunter, for that was what Joshua had said, and Joshua would never condemn his brother unless it was a fact. Then the man she and Falcon Moon had seen was Jeb. He was on his way to his true hideout to get the rest of his scalps!

"Oh, Joshua, I am so sorry," Wylena cried. "Falcon Moon, this is my brother Joshua. The scars that were inflicted there by our father so long ago prove it! Please come and cut the ropes away with your knife. Please free my brother!"

After Joshua was freed, he stood shakily and grabbed Wylena into his arms. "I can understand your confusion," he said thickly. "Just imagine mine when I caught Jeb bringing scalps into the mission. And a part of me died when I saw the wound on his side. I had much to accept too quickly."

"For now, you must return to the stronghold with me and Falcon Moon," Wylena said, gripping her brother's arms. "Joshua, there isn't anything we can do for Jeb now, but we can keep you safe from harm by taking you with us."

"I will send many men out to search for your brother," Falcon Moon said, sliding his knife back inside the leather sheath at his right side. "I do not believe he has long to live on this earth after seeing how badly he was wounded. But I will see to it that he or his body is found so that you can give your brother a final resting place."

Wylena stepped away from her brother and hugged Falcon Moon. "Thank you," she murmured. "Oh, thank you."

"I don't think I should leave," Joshua said. He left the room to grab the robe he had been forced to discard at the orders of his brother.

"You must," Wylena said, going to him. After he had donned his robe, she gave him a determined look. "Jeb isn't himself at all. When, or if, he returns, you might be in mortal danger. He is a deranged man. Who is to say what he will do, and to whom, the next minute?"

Joshua hung his head, then raised it and looked slowly around him, as though he was memorizing all that was dear to him. "Yes, I will go," he agreed. "But I will return to my mission, where I will await anyone who might want to share the Lord's presence with me."

After two horses were taken from the barn, Wylena deciding she was going to be brave enough to ride up the narrow pass on a horse alone, they headed away from the mission.

"Joshua, we were coming today to tell you something wonderful," Wylena said, trying to find something good to speak about after having been faced with such evil. "We were coming to tell you about our upcoming marriage. Joshua, there will be four days of celebration and then I will be the proud wife of Falcon Moon. We had wanted you to come and be a part of the celebration. Can you stay with us long enough to share this with us? Can you even think about anything else now but Jeb and what we know about him? Joshua, please say that you can."

"I shall stay, and I shall pray for Jeb, too," Joshua said with tears shining in his eyes. "I cannot imagine where he went so wrong, and why, when it was I who was the recipient of so many whippings from our father."

"People don't always have to have a reason to be bad—they are just born that way," Falcon Moon said, nodding toward the pass that led upward to his stronghold. "I shall follow behind. You two go before me. Just go slowly and make certain your horses are far enough from the steep drop-off. I have traveled this pass many times. It is safe enough."

Wylena gave Joshua a wary glance. She knew that he had never enjoyed being on horses, but he had learned the skills anyway, because he knew that he must, or face another beating for having shown such cowardice to their father.

It seemed to Wylena that at least in that, her father had done the right thing . . . made certain that all three of his children could ride skillfully enough on horses, for at this moment horses were taking two of his children to safety!

Chapter 27

Near the stronghold, with just a little more of the zigzagging trail left to travel, Wylena was more at ease than she had been while they rode close to the steep drop-off. But she was still close enough to be able to look down from the dizzying height and see a trail below that wound from the timber along the river to the foot of the mountain. She gasped and her insides tightened when she saw some movement far, far below.

She breathlessly watched a long line of men on horseback—from this distance they resembled a string of ants—as they rode across the open country, then disappeared at the foot of the mountain.

"Mexican soldiers," she whispered. "General Zamora!"

She was directly behind her brother, who was now riding on his steed between her and Falcon Moon so that he could feel safer until they reached the stronghold.

"Falcon Moon," Wylena cried, getting his quick attention. "Did you see them? Did you see the soldiers down below?"

"No, did you see soldiers?" he asked, and drew his horse to a sudden halt. He wheeled his steed around, and managed to get close to Wylena.

"Down there." She pointed. "I saw them enter the base of the mountain."

She looked at Falcon Moon, her eyes wavering. "Falcon Moon, there were so many," she gulped. "And I know they were Mexicans. General Zamora is coming up the mountain to find your stronghold."

Falcon Moon gazed down below and saw nothing but a beautiful eagle flying next to the mountain, and then two more soared against the loveliness of the blue sky.

"Like I said, they are no longer where we can see them, but I know they are coming up the mountain," Wylena said. "What are you going to do?"

"I am prepared for them," Falcon Moon said drily. "There are many warriors posted where they can watch for intruders on our mountain. The word will be passed along quickly enough for me to prepare the rest of my warriors, so that they will be positioned at various places, far below, away from my village. No one will get anywhere near my—our—people."

Suddenly the ground beneath them tremored. Rocks scattered and tumbled down in all directions. Yet none came close to where Wylena and her loved ones sat.

"Can it be the beginning of an earthquake?" Wylena gasped, a sudden fear in her eyes as another tremor shook the ground beneath her horse's hooves.

Falcon Moon's insides tightened, for although he did not want to tell Wylena, he did believe this might be the first signs of an earthquake. He suddenly remembered his grandmother's premonition of an earthquake, one that would destroy everyone in its path.

She had gone as far as to say that all of their people would die in it and then would return again, whole, and with a new start in life away from the threat of whites and Mexicans, who would not live through the quake.

Falcon Moon did not believe that his people would all die, although most of his grandmother's premonitions did come true. But she was older now and too often what she said would come to pass did not. It was the aging of her mind that made her make such mistakes.

"We must hurry to the stronghold where we will be safer from the quake," he said. "I believe we will have one, but I do not see it destroying my people—only those down below, who are evil."

Falcon Moon moved into the lead position again and rode more quickly up the mountain pass.

When the land flattened out even more, he led Wylena and her brother past a tall canyon, then into another, where only a short distance away they could see tepees nestled beside a softly flowing river with a waterfall at its very end.

Just as they entered the village, the earthquake's worst jolt yet came with a force that caused the earth to open in small, winding cracks. Some tepees collapsed. Some caught fire as the lodge fires were scattered around inside the dwellings, the embers falling against the buckskin coverings. People ran screaming and crying from their lodges.

Mothers carried children.

Fathers gathered their families around them, holding them as best they could against any subsequent ravages of the earthquake.

Wylena had already dismounted and stood with her brother as they watched Falcon Moon go through his village, giving comfort and love. The earth shook some more, this time more violently, causing large rocks to tumble down the canyon on both ends of the village. Wylena saw Falcon Moon rush to his grandmother's tepee and gently lead her from it. He brought her to Wylena. "Watch over her while I go to my sister," he said, stopping only long enough to give his grandmother, and then Wylena, soft kisses of comfort.

Then it was suddenly over.

The earth went quiet. Only soft sobs could be heard throughout the village. Wylena heaved a deep sigh of relief.

She looked over at her brother, whose eyes no longer expressed a sense of peace.

"My mission," he said as he gazed into Wylena's eyes. "And Jeb?"

"We are fortunate that the quake was not worse," Falling Water said. "In my vision I saw everything destroyed. Our people all died. Yet they came back alive. But today no one died. My vision was wrong. Ussen has blessed us and watched over us. All will be well now."

Bright Star came running over to them. She embraced her grandmother.

"Please take me back to my home," Falling Water said, her voice trembling from weakness. "I need my bed."

Bright Star eased a gentle arm around her grandmother's waist, and Wylena did the same. They walked her to her tepee, which had not suffered any damage. She was gently helped to her bed of blankets as Joshua came and placed a log in the fire pit.

Falcon Moon hurried into the tepee and saw that everything was all right.

He then turned to Wylena. "No one was injured and only a few homes were destroyed," he said, a keen relief evident in his voice. "Ussen watched over us. He made things right for us."

"My mission," Joshua said, drawing Falcon Moon's quick attention. "I want to go and see if all is well there."

Wylena noticed he avoided saying Jeb's name, but she knew that he wanted to go down from this mountain mainly to see if he could find his brother, and see if he survived the earthquake— and his wound.

Wylena wanted to know the welfare of her other brother, too, but also knew that he was a dangerous man, even to his own family. He had proven such when he tied up Joshua and left him alone in the mission.

"I will check on my sentries who were posted along the pass as I take you down the mountain to your home, Father Joshua," Falcon Moon said. "I will instruct them where they should go now."

Wylena thought of her wedding ceremony, which would have begun tomorrow, after Bull Nose's burial was behind them all, but now wondered if there would be more delays because of what had happened today.

She prayed that no sentries had died where they were posted along the mountainside, for then there would be days and days of burial rites to see to.

She was mainly concerned about the sentries because she had learned to love Falcon Moon's people and did not want anyone to suffer a loss such as this from the earthquake.

After everyone had been seen to and the warriors were given their special duties, Falcon Moon led Wylena and her brother down the mountainside again, stopping here and there to check on his other warriors, finding none of them injured.

As they traveled slowly onward, the pass became smaller and the drop-off more dangerous. When they were halfway down the mountain, Wylena kept an eye on Joshua. He seemed practiced now in how to protect himself against falling down the steep precipice. But she believed that his anxiousness to return home might make him forget the dangers of this narrow pass. She knew that although Jeb had proven to be the devil incarnate, it was not in Joshua's nature not to worry about his twin's welfare.

She could not be that forgiving. She would never forget the sight of Joshua tied to the chair, or the bloody scalps!

Finally almost to the bottom of the mountain, Wylena gasped and looked up at Falcon Moon, who had already seen what she just saw.

Just below them, where the pass flattened out to straight stretches of land, the Mexican soldiers lay dead.

Wylena stopped beside Joshua. Falcon Moon grabbed his rifle from its gun boot and rode down to where the dead lay on the ground. He went from man to man on his horse, checking for any survivors, for it seemed that the worst of the earthquake had been at the foot of the mountain, and the land that stretched out away from it. Everywhere Wylena looked, she saw wide, open craters in the ground. Smoke spiraled strangely from some of those openings.

It made her gag when she saw how some of the dead soldiers lay halfway down a crater, their fingers raw from having tried to dig into the ground to save themselves from falling and being swallowed whole by the earth. But most of the soldiers' deaths seemed to have come from the fall from the mountainside before they fell into the holes in the ground. They had lived just long enough to keep themselves from fully sliding into the open craters.

Wylena rode through the dead, until all of a sudden she saw General Zamora stretched out on the ground, half-buried by rocks. His face was almost unidentifiable—it had been hit so many times by the falling debris—but she knew it was he by the uniform that he wore.

Then she became aware of a warrior approaching on a horse. Falcon Moon rode out to meet him. Wylena and Joshua soon followed and stopped beside Falcon Moon when he reached the warrior.

Wylena heard the warrior, who she assumed was from another band of Apache, talking to Falcon Moon.

"The Mexican fortress has burned to the ground and there are no survivors," Falcon Moon told Wylena after the other man finished speaking. "But General Zamora was not among the dead. He might have escaped with his life.

"But since they were on their way up my mountain to find my stronghold, I think Ussen had different plans for them. He made the mountain shake violently enough to kill the general and all the soldiers who rode with him."

Falcon Moon said to Night Shadow, "This is my woman. Her name is Wylena. This is her brother Joshua. Wylena, this is Chief Night Shadow of the Owl Band of Apache. They have established their stronghold on another mountain that can be seen in the distance from the heights of ours."

"It is nice to know you," Wylena said, extending a hand out for him.

When he took it, she noticed his grip was almost the same as Falcon Moon's, one that showed that he was a man of strength and power. He was handsome, but in a much different way from Falcon Moon. He did not have the same soft friendliness in his expression when he smiled, and his face was not as sculpted. But she was discovering that she rarely found an Apache male, or female, who was not pleasant to look at.

Night Shadow dropped his hand from hers and looked over at Joshua. "I know Joshua," he said, smiling at the priest. "I have sat with him at his house of God, and have seen the ways of his prayers. I told him about our Ussen. He accepted our way of worshipping without trying to force his on me."

Night Shadow's smile faded. "Father Joshua, if your mission was destroyed by the quaking of the ground, send word to my stronghold and I shall send warriors to help rebuild it," he said. He looked over at Falcon Moon. "You will join me?"

"I will," Falcon Moon said, smiling from Joshua to Night Shadow.

"You are both generous chiefs and I thank you," Joshua said, yet he nervously looked in the direction of his mission. It proved to them all that he was anxious to go there and see if it still stood, or if it had been rendered into a pile of stone.

"And Chief Night Shadow, thank you for your kindness," Joshua said, looking at the chief again. He reached out and patted the warrior on his shoulder. "If my home is still standing, come soon and sit and talk with me."

Wylena watched this exchange between her brother and another Apache chief, stunned to know that not only had Falcon Moon made friends with her brother, but others had, as well. It proved why he had not wanted to leave his mission to return to Illinois—he had decided to do so because of his brother and sister, whom he obviously placed before his own desires. She loved him even more now than before, and admired him so much for his kind heart and love for humanity, no matter the color of their skin.

"We shall leave now to see if his mission stands," Falcon Moon said, nodding at Night Shadow. "Come soon to my stronghold. Come tomorrow. Come and share one or more days of the wedding celebration that will be held in my and my woman's honor. The earthquake will not delay it. Only a few of my people's lodges were destroyed by the shaking of the earth. We are still able to start the celebration on the morrow."

"I will be there," Night Shadow said, smiling broadly from Falcon Moon to Wylena, making her happy to know that she was not condemned in this chief's eyes for marrying one of their Apache people.

Although most white people were hated with a passion for interfering in the lives of these wonderful people, she was magically being accepted, as her brother Joshua had been treated kindly by them.

Night Shadow rode off in the direction of his mountain as Wylena followed her brother and Falcon Moon in the direction of the mission. It did not take long before they saw the high rise of the steeple up ahead, proving that God had saved it, as Ussen had watched over the Apache people.

"It is still there," Joshua cried, and his eyes beamed with relief and happiness. "My house of worship is still there for all who want to visit it!"

They rode onward, suddenly finding crater after crater in the ground and having to ride around them.

It seemed that the earthquake had been worse in certain places and had skipped others, as though it knew whom and what to destroy with its power.

Wylena's heart seemed to drop to her toes when she saw someone up ahead, lying halfway down in a crater, a horse standing beside it, eating grass as though nothing had happened to the one who'd ridden it.

But Wylena saw the man well enough now, and soon recognized who it was by the long, black hair and his clothes. Even the horse looked familiar to her.

It was . . . Jeb.

"No," she cried, feeling a keen sadness sweep through her as she rode on ahead of Falcon Moon and Joshua.

She drew a tight rein and dismounted quickly. She knelt beside her brother, whose eyes were open in a death stare and whose face seemed strangely twisted as he lay halfway down in the crater. Wylena saw many snakes crawling around at the bottom, around his feet, some of them rattlers, their rattles sending off ominous sounds.

She concluded that it was not the earthquake, nor the wound on her brother's side, that killed him. The snakes that had fallen into the open crater in the ground with him had caused his death.

"Lord, oh, Lord, Jeb," Wylena cried as she slowly, mercifully, closed his eyes.

She ran her fingers through his long hair, as she had done so often when they were children, for he had never seemed to care if it was blocking his vision. So often it seemed as though he hadn't cared about anything.

"My brother," she sobbed, drawing her hand away when Falcon Moon and Joshua came and knelt beside her.

Joshua reached a hand out for Jeb and touched him gently on the shoulder and began a soft prayer for his salvation. Wylena and Falcon Moon knelt on either side of him, bowing their heads in respect for the dead and the prayer being said for him.

Then Joshua stood up along with Falcon Moon and Wylena. "He was dead inside his heart, oh, so long ago," he said, his voice catching with emotion. "No matter what I did or said, I could not reach inside my brother and give him even a little measure of peace. He was tormented. It seems the devil had claimed his soul way before he came to me, perhaps in a small way to seek some salvation even though he was the one who was killing innocent people."

He glanced over at his mission. "For a while, I had some hope that Jeb would be all right," he said thickly. "I had hoped that while he was in

the house of God, he would put his anger and
hate behind him. But . . . but . . . it seemed he
was doomed no matter where he was, or who
with. Now it is up to the good Lord to see if my
brother deserves any salvation, or not."

"Joshua, let's get him buried, then resume our
lives," Wylena said, going to hug him. "We did
all that we could to help our brother. Now it is up
to the good Lord to decide what will happen to
Jeb. Our time with him is over. We now have our
own lives to live."

Joshua nodded as Falcon Moon gently took
Jeb from the crater. He placed the body over the
back of Jeb's steed, then went to Wylena. He
took her gently by an elbow and ushered her to
her horse as Joshua went to his own and
mounted it.

The three of them rode onward toward the
mission, which had not been touched whatsoever by the earthquake, whereas there were
cracks in the earth on all sides, stopping within a
few feet of the building, as though God was
there, purposely protecting it.

Wylena felt a strange sense of relief that Jeb
had finally found a sort of peace that only death
would lend him. She would not let herself remember the moment she realized that he was the
scalp hunter.

Soon her brother would be buried.

There would be no trace left of him or his evil.

And with the Mexican general now dead, as

well, Wylena did see a life of happiness and peace ahead of her.

But she knew that there would always be those who would resent the Apache being any-where, for the white people were adamant about how they desired all men and women with red skin no longer to have a place on this earth.

She knew that although Falcon Moon and Night Shadow had hidden their people on their own separate mountains, they were still in dan-ger of those who came to this land for whatever reason. She would hold her head high as the wife of a proud Apache chief and take life one day at a time. She could hardly wait to have children in the image of the man she would marry, yet would they not have much to fight against, themselves, in order to help keep the Apache race alive?

She looked over at Falcon Moon. How could anyone not see the goodness in this man? How could anyone want him erased from the face of the earth?

Falcon Moon gazed over at her and smiled as though he sensed her concerns. He gave her some semblance of peace with his silent reassurances.

She returned the smile, so in love with him she could hardly stand having to wait another four days before she would finally be able to say she was this wonderful man's wife!

She was made to forget all of this once they reached the mission and Jeb was taken from his horse. She watched Joshua go inside and get a shovel, his face gray with overwhelming grief at having lost his twin ... a man who was in his own likeness, but only on the surface.

"Let us get him buried quickly," Joshua said, glancing over at Wylena, then looking at Falcon Moon, who came quickly to him to take the shovel from him.

As Wylena stood with Joshua, her arm around his waist, Falcon Moon dug into the earth. Soon Jeb was buried and prayers had been said, and Wylena gave Joshua a hug of reassurance.

"Are you going to return to the mountain for my wedding?" she asked as she stepped away from him and gazed deeply into his eyes.

"My place is here," Joshua said, placing a gentle hand on her cheek. "Somewhere out there, there are people who have lost everything due to the earthquake. I will be here for them if they need a place to rest, especially a place to pray."

"I understand," Wylena murmured. She gave him another hug, and a kiss, then went to her horse as Falcon Moon mounted his.

They rode away together for another trek up the mountainside, but this time they rode in peace, for the three men who had caused them stress and danger were now dead. She hated putting Jeb in that category, yet he had been a man who left a path of fear wherever he traveled, who killed to have scalps to take and sell to a man who paid him well for them.

Yet Jeb had never seemed to have anything of his own. She knew that somewhere out there he had established a hideout away from the church. She could not help but think that perhaps he had had an ally in crime.

Yet she would not allow herself to think of that possibility. She had four days ahead of her that would be filled with much merriment and love!

Chapter 28

Love is a circle that doth restless move
In the same sweet eternity of love.
                                        —Robert Herrick

Autumn had arrived on Mount Torrance. Aspen and paper birch turned golden, and mountain maple and shrubs added a touch of red.

Wylena sat contentedly beside the lodge fire with her husband close by working on a new saddle; she was beading a new dress made of the whitest doeskin.

She smiled as she paused long enough to gaze at the closed entrance flap of their tepee. Outside many women were busy preparing for a celebration of love for one of the Bear Band's young women who would soon marry a warrior from the Owl Band. Wylena had helped earlier as cook pots of assorted foods were placed around the big central fire outside, while venison roasted on smaller beds of coals.

She felt a warmth of happiness as she recalled the time she had been horseback riding with Falcon Moon, and how they suddenly came upon a cliff, under which hung a large honeycomb. She and Falcon Moon had dismounted their steeds and then she had watched him spread a hide on the ground beneath the honeycomb. He shot masses of that honeycomb loose with arrows, and when it had fallen on the hide, she and Falcon Moon had squeezed the honey out into a buckskin bag.

She would never forget how sweet and good the honey was, as it would be today. Some of that same honey was awaiting them today—it would be spread on baked meal cakes made of sweet acorns.

Yes, it was going to be a wonderful day. Soon drummers would appear and the celebration of love would begin.

Still taking a break from her beading, Wylena gazed over the fire at her husband, who was intensely involved in working on a new saddle. It was hard for her to believe that so many years had passed since the four-day celebration that made Wylena Falcon Moon's bride. But the years had slid by, her happiness making her not even realize when a year turned into another.

Soon she and Falcon Moon would celebrate

having been married eight winters. They had two darling children who came from those wonderful nights they spent together on their plush pelts and blankets.

Their firstborn, Wolf Hawk, had been named after she and Falcon Moon saw a pair of ferruginous hawks soaring above their village only moments before Wylena went into labor. Seeing them had taken her breath away, for she had never seen such a bird before. Falcon Moon had told her that this bird was the largest of all hawks, with a four- to five-foot wingspan.

She had watched them that day until they flew away, into the clouds, but she would never forget their size or their color. They were of a rusty iron, or ferrous, coloring, the sun's glow on their wings making the colors bright and breathtaking.

Falcon Moon had explained to her that these hawks hatched eggs only once a year, between May and early June, and that the adults took turns hunting and guarding the nests.

The ones that they had seen were later found nesting on a high butte that overlooked the village. They were seen at times flying toward their nest with a prairie dog or a desert cottontail hanging from their sharp talons.

In awe of those birds, who had come to her so close to when she gave birth to her son, she and Falcon Moon had agreed that the name Wolf Hawk was the rightful name for that son.

The "Wolf" part of the name came from Falcon Moon having seen a pack of wolves moments before their child came into the world, with strong lungs that announced to the entire village that their chief had had his first child.

And then, two years later, a daughter was born and her name had come from Wylena's love of snow in the Illinois winters, and how the snow seemed to be dancing as the northern winds would blow it in swirls across the front lawn of her home.

Dancing Snow was now two winters of age, her brother four. Both loved the out-of-doors, and loved horses even more. They loved playing games with their friends, who were at this moment outside chasing and playing and laughing while Wylena and Falcon Moon were alone in their tepee.

Wylena smiled at Falcon Moon's astuteness at what he was doing, and thought back to how it had taken him several days to find the right shape of a tree for making his saddle.

She had learned from him that cutting a new saddle from the felled tree trunk was a slow and tedious task after the wood had been dried and shaped to fit the body of the horse for which it was intended—in this case it was a new midnight black stallion that Falcon Moon had caught while out with his friends on a hunt.

He had seen this horse with many others and it seemed to have singled him out as it came and gazed directly into Falcon Moon's eyes. It had not taken much effort for Falcon Moon to rope it and make it his own—and he had never ridden another one since.

He had let his white stallion return to the wild and he occasionally caught sight of it as it stood on a high precipice that overlooked the river and village.

Wylena brushed some fallen locks of hair back from her face. She took this opportunity to rest for a moment as she watched how intensely her husband worked on his saddle.

He had used both fire and his knife for shaping it. He was now rubbing the almost-finished product smooth with pieces of sandstone. She knew this process well, for he had made saddles for friends who did not have the same skill as he. She knew that the next step would be for him to cover his saddle with tanned hide. He would finish it off with a wide band of cowhide.

"I feel someone's eyes on me," Falcon Moon suddenly said, smiling as he looked slowly up at Wylena. "My wife, are you admiring my new saddle, or your husband?"

"Both," Wylena said, giggling like a schoolgirl who had been caught admiring a young lad who had infatuated her.

She laid her sewing aside and crawled over to Falcon Moon and looked him square in the eye. "My darling, I feel that I need a break from my sewing," she murmured teasingly. "Do you not think that you should take some time, too, from saddle making? Our children are busy playing, and I doubt they will be home for a while. Should I tie the entrance flap closed? Do you feel a sudden need for privacy, as I am feeling it?"

"My wife is ready to seduce her husband?" Falcon Moon said huskily as he brushed everything away from him. He reached out and ran his fingers through her long, black hair, which she had not yet braided this early morn. "Do you want my body?"

"I want your everything," Wylena said, sucking in a wild breath of pleasure as he reached down and ran one of his hands slowly up inside her dress, his hand warm against her soft flesh.

When he reached that part of her that already throbbed from want of him, and he slowly caressed her nub of pleasure, she threw her head back in a sweet agony and soon stretched out on her back. Her husband removed his breechclout, and his body looked ready and hot for her.

"The ties," Wylena said breathlessly as she quickly disrobed. "We must not chance the children coming in and witnessing their parents making another baby."

Falcon Moon gave her a teasing smile and went quickly to the entrance flap and secured the ties, which gave them total privacy.

He crawled back to her and he stretched out above her. He swept her into his arms and leaned over her with burning eyes.

"I love you," he said huskily, his one hand slipping away from her, sliding slowly over her body, causing her warm flesh to ripple with each new touch.

And then he found her wet and ready place again and began caressing her. He pressed his lips teasingly to her throat. When his mouth covered hers with a steamy passion, ecstasy came to Wylena with a bone-weakening intensity. She clung to his neck as they kissed and he continued pleasuring her where she now throbbed unmercifully with a hot need for him.

She was imprisoned against him, his body now ruling hers. His mouth forced her lips apart as his kiss grew more and more passionate. Then he eased his lips from hers so that he could look into her eyes at that very moment that he shoved his heat within her warm place. He saw a sudden fire burn in her eyes when her pleasure mounted with each of his thrusts inside her.

His mouth bore down again on hers, exploding with raw passion, his lips sensuous, hot, and demanding.

Yearning for him, she hungered for that moment when the familiar ecstasy that she had found in her husband's arms exploded within her, making her gasp and moan.

Hearing and feeling her pleasure, himself— his whole body afire with it—Falcon Moon moved his lips from hers and placed them against the curve of her throat. He left them there, smelling and tasting her, reveling in this ecstasy that she had brought into his life.

He thrust more intensely into her, his body tight as he tried to prolong this wondrous passion they shared, but it was too much, so he clung to her and gave those final shoves inside her that brought them both moments of intense pleasure. They clung and moaned and kissed and quivered against each other until the final throes of ecstasy had been felt, leaving them both soaring.

Wylena was the first to break the silence that had fallen between them. "It never seems less passionate and wonderful than the last time we made love," she murmured as Falcon Moon rolled slowly away from her to lie on his back. Yet his hand still stroked her softly.

He cleansed her with a freshly moistened piece of soft doeskin. After laying the material aside, he moved where he knew she found pleasure during those other times when he had loved her in such a way.

The instant his tongue touched her where she was still swollen from their lovemaking, Wylena closed her eyes and let the rapture take hold all over again.

She twined her fingers through his hair and led him further into this sort of lovemaking. Her whole body throbbed as she felt the urgency building all over again.

"My love," she whispered, still holding her

eyes closed, her whole body afire with a renewed ecstasy. "Oh, my darling . . ."

He knew when she found pleasure again by how she moaned and clutched his head, causing his tongue to press harder into her.

"Now," she cried, her whole body a massive heartbeat, it seemed, as the pleasure rocked her senses.

And then he was on top of her again; he shoved his heat deeply inside her and joined her moments of ecstasy as he quickly found his own again inside her.

This time, when she finally came down from that plateau of pleasure she always found with her husband, Wylena sat up and quickly dressed.

Falcon Moon quickly pulled on his breechclout and went back to making his saddle as Wylena untied the ties at the entranceway. She brushed her fingers through her hair to straighten it, then went back to beading her dress.

"I am so happy for Bright Star," Wylena suddenly said, smiling at Falcon Moon as he paused and gave her a secret sort of smile that always came after they made such wondrous love. "Yet I miss her so much."

"It is not the way of the Apache women to live among their own band when they have married someone from another band," Falcon Moon said. He smiled at the thought of his sister's marriage to someone he so admired, Blue Wolf from Night Shadow's Owl Band.

"Their son, Kicking Bear, is so sweet," Wylena murmured, stringing beads now to store until she was ready to make another dress, as this one was finally finished. "And she is with child again. It will keep her busy having a one-year-old to care for as well as the newborn. I'm glad that we had more space than that between our children."

"If only my grandmother could have seen her grandson's and granddaughter's children," Falcon Moon said, setting his saddle-making equipment aside and resting before the fire.

"Yes, Falling Water would have been so proud," Wylena murmured, sad that his grandmother had not lived long after the four-day celebration of their marriage.

"She is proud," Falcon Moon said. "She looks now from her home in the sky, seeing much better than when she was still a part of we earthly creatures. When she arrived at our people's Happy Place, everything that hurt within her while she was a part of this earth became well again, and that included her eyes. They are now like a newborn's eyes. She sees all colors and movements. She feels things that she had forgotten how to feel. You see, once someone has gone away, their body left behind, it is their spirit that soars and becomes brand-new again."

"I wish that could be so for Jeb," Wylena said, her voice catching with emotion. "But I'm certain he did not arrive at any Happy Place. His evil ways surely assured him a place where no one would ever want to go."

"Ussen is a forgiving God, as I am certain your God is, as well," Falcon Moon said. "So who is to say whether Jeb was forgiven of his sins and is whole again where your people go once their spirit is set free of their bodies?"

"That is a wonderful thought," Wylena murmured, but she doubted that Jeb was anywhere but where fires burned hot for eternity. He had probably found their father there, and now both were together, fighting their own demons.

She looked over at Falcon Moon. "I shall never forget how the bear appeared to us that day just before Bull Nose died," she murmured. "It was, oh, so mystical, such a beautiful thing to have witnessed."

"The Apache believe that the spirits of bad people, such as Bull Nose, cannot go directly to the Happy Place, but must instead be reincarnated," Falcon Moon softly explained. "Sometimes that person is reincarnated in the body of a bear more than once before being admitted to the Apache Happy Place. You see, if an Apache kills a bear, he might be murdering one of his relatives or friends. He may not even touch the hide of a bear, and eating the flesh is unthinkable. Our people do not eat or kill bears."

"But you wear a bear's tooth on a leather thong around your neck," Wylena said.

"I found this tooth at the entrance of my tepee

just moments before I became chief," Falcon Moon said thickly. "A friend from the Happy Place brought it to me and left it there for me, so that I would have a part of my medicine with me at all times."

"Was it your father who brought it to you, perhaps just as he died, to be certain you would have it when you became chief?" Wylena asked, her eyes wide.

Falcon Moon's eyes twinkled as he gazed intensely into hers. "You are learning, my woman," he said, smiling. "You are learning."

"Mother, Father!" a voice squealed from outside the lodge. "Come. See what we have found!"

It was Dancing Snow's voice. Her voice always made Wylena smile, for her daughter was the sweetest of the sweet, and never found ugliness in anything.

Wylena and Falcon Moon hurried from the tepee, stopping when they saw Dancing Snow holding a tiny black-footed ferret.

"She must have gotten lost from her family," Wolf Hawk said, standing beside his sister.

"May we keep her?" Dancing Snow asked, her dark eyes pleading with her mother and father. "I promise if I ever come across her mother, I shall give her back to her."

Wylena smiled with pride at her daughter's kindness. She watched Falcon Moon squat on his haunches before his daughter and give a soft caress across the tiny animal's back.

"Dancing Snow, you can keep the animal if you wish, but I doubt you shall ever find those she got lost from," he said. "I shall teach you what to feed it. For now, just enjoy it and be gentle—she is quite small, you know."

"I know, and I shall," Dancing Snow said.

Falcon Moon went back to Wylena and stood with her as the children all circled around Dancing Snow to take turns petting the small animal.

"Our daughter is like you," Falcon Moon said, his eyes dancing into Wylena's. "She is all sweetness."

Wylena laughed softly, then took his hand and went back inside their lodge with him.

"Life is good," Falcon Moon said as he stood with Wylena over the slowly burning embers of the fire. "No white pony soldiers or Mexican soldiers have come close to our mountain for some time now."

"If anyone ever learns about the gold that the Mexicans found, everything could quickly change," Wylena said solemnly.

"I did not tell you, but after the earthquake, I went with my warriors to the Mexican fortress, did away with the gold, and made certain the mountain it was being taken from was sealed up so that no man could find it again," he said. "Yes, the gold could have given us much wealth should we have kept it, but it could also bring us much bad luck. Such things only attract greedy people and with greed comes death."

"You are such a wise chief," Wylena murmured. She moved into his arms and gazed up into his eyes. "And you are mine."

He brought his lips down onto hers and gave her a kiss that left her weak. She knew that it would always be this way with Falcon Moon, for he was so special, so kind, so compassionate. She was so glad that he had stolen her away from the Mexican general, for he had introduced her to a life that she adored.

"Come outside with me again," Falcon Moon said, taking her by the hand.

She went with him and stood at the far edge of the stronghold, on a high butte where they could see far into the distance.

Falcon Moon swept his arms around Wylena's waist and drew her up next to him. "I have a deep, spiritual connection to the land," he said huskily. "This land, this mountain, is the center of my heart. I am so happy that you are here, to share it all with me."

"I would be nowhere else," she murmured. "I love you forever and ever, my Falcon Moon."

She placed a hand on his cheek. "My wonderful Falcon Moon . . . my husband," she said, so content it sometimes frightened her.

But she would take this contentment . . . this happiness . . . a day at a time and feel so blessed for it.

Letter to the Reader

Dear Readers:

I hope you enjoyed reading *Falcon Moon.* The next book in my Dreamcatcher Indian series, which I am writing exclusively for Signet, is *Raven Heart,* about the proud Miami tribe. *Raven Heart* is filled with much excitement, romance, and adventure . . . and a few surprises!

Those of you who are collecting my Indian novels and want to hear more about the entire backlist of these books, as well as my fan club, can send for my latest newsletter and an autographed bookmark.

Write to:

Cassie Edwards
6709 North Country Club Road
Mattoon, IL 61938

You can also visit my Web site and find a link to my MySpace page at www.cassieedwards.com.

Always,
Cassie Edwards

Also from
New York Times bestselling author
CASSIE EDWARDS

RUNNING FOX

Nancy Partrain's life in pioneer Michigan has
become a nightmare since her mother married
her stepfather, who has involved her in his
underhanded whiskey trading scheme.
Then Nancy meets handsome Running Fox,
chieftain of the Fox band of the Lakota tribe,
who wants to put an end to her stepfather's
corruption of his people. In each other they stir
feelings of hope, freedom...and longing. Stolen
away to eerie Ghost Island by Running Fox,
Nancy finds herself falling for her abductor.
But can she allow his tender passion to finally
heal her wounded heart?

Available wherever books are sold or
at penguin.com